PRAISE F(

"Chiavaroli delights with this homage to Louisa May Alcott's *Little Women*, featuring a time-slip narrative of two women connected across centuries."

PUBLISHERS WEEKLY on *The Orchard House*

"As a longtime fan of Louisa May Alcott's *Little Women*, I was eager to read *The Orchard House*.... [It] invited me in, served me tea, and held me enthralled with its compelling tale."

LORI BENTON, Christy Award-winning author of *The King's Mercy*

"Captivating from the first page....Steeped in timeless truths and served with skill, *The Tea Chest* is sure to be savored by all who read it."

JOCELYN GREEN, Christy Award-winning author of *Between Two Shores*

"*The Hidden Side* is a beautiful tale that captures the timeless struggles of the human heart."

JULIE CANTRELL, *New York Times* Bestselling author of *Perennials*

"First novelist Chiavaroli's historical tapestry will provide a satisfying summer read for fans of Kristy Cambron and Lisa Wingate."

LIBRARY JOURNAL on *Freedom's Ring*

"*The Edge of Mercy* is most definitely one for the keeper shelf. "

LINDSAY HARREL, author of *The Secrets of Paper and Ink*

WHERE GRACE APPEARS

HEIDI CHIAVAROLI

To Elizabeth,

I hope you enjoy!

With Hope,

Heidi Chiavaroli

Hope Creek Publishers

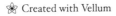 Created with Vellum

ALSO BY HEIDI CHIAVAROLI

The Orchard House

The Tea Chest

The Hidden Side

Freedom's Ring

The Edge of Mercy

The Orchard House Bed and Breakfast Series

Where Grace Appears

Where Hope Begins (Summer, 2021)

Where Love Grows (Fall, 2021)

For my sister, Krystal
I appreciate our relationship more and more as we grow older.
Love you, Sissy!

❧ I ❧

The nature of secrets is that they long to be kept and long to be told all at the same time.

At least that's the conclusion I came to as I stared at the solid wood door of my childhood home. Only a year away from my master's in clinical psychology at NYU, and the one thing threatening success...the secret lodged in my belly.

I knew all about the psychology of secrets—our need for self-preservation, why we held our confidences close to our hearts, the proven healing of mind and body that often comes with their release. And so I had followed James Pennebaker's advice and written my secret on a torn page of my journal. Then I burned it with a match over my sink, watched my words dissolve into ash, and convinced myself that it had been freed from my conscience.

I would put Pennebaker's theory to the test over the next several weeks. For yes, I had known all about the psychology of secrets from my textbooks.

And now, I would know about them firsthand.

I pushed open the door, remembering the many times I'd crossed this threshold to find Mom pulling a batch of oatmeal cookies out of the oven for the latest PTO fundraiser. Maggie would be pacing before the kitchen bar, fretting over an upcoming date, while Lizzie sprawled on the floor patting Scrabble's furry belly. Bronson would be laboring over an algebra problem at the dining room table, while Amie pasted wildflower petals onto cardstock beside him.

And Dad...Dad would be holed up in his office, of course, or out at the mission, saving the world.

"Hello?" I wrestled my suitcase through the doorway, filled with more books and notebooks than clothes and accessories. "I'm home!"

The rooms echoed back uncharacteristically silent despite the scent of freshly-baked brownies. I passed Dad's office and a pang started in my breastbone. I forced my gaze away from the partially open door, not yet ready to see what I knew was there— the hollow curve of his chair, the dust thick on his dear books. I'd crack at least one open in his honor this summer. Maybe a Bertrand Russell book, or Aristotle, maybe *Fate* by Ralph Waldo Emerson. It wouldn't be easy, but I'd pull on my big girl pants and do it, if not for Dad's sake this time, then as a sort of toast to his memory.

The roar of a compressor came from the back of the house and I left my suitcase to search out its owner. Where was everyone? While I wasn't vain enough to expect a welcome home party, I did think at least Lizzie would have ensured I didn't return home to an empty house. It had been five months since I'd seen them, after all. Five months, and in some ways, a lifetime.

"Hello?" I entered the dining room to see a familiar form standing on a small ladder, holding a nail gun to freshly-painted crown molding.

He turned, and my heart gave an unexpected lurch.

Tripp Colton was the last person I needed to see right now. I still couldn't think of that day last summer without a flush of embarrassment creeping over me. He should have never said those words. And he definitely shouldn't have kissed me like that.

He had ruined our perfectly lovely, comfortable relationship in one stormy, steamy afternoon.

We'd never be the same again.

"Josie." His voice possessed a warmth I didn't expect. Maybe there was still hope for us to reclaim what we'd once had. Maybe there was still hope for our friendship.

These past silent months had been torture but now, glimpsing a promise of goodwill, I longed to fight for the old order of things. To not lose Tripp's friendship no matter how we got to this place. No matter the regret tied to that summer day. No matter the secret singeing my chest.

He stepped off the ladder and gave me a hug, eliciting a lurch of longing. I wanted to sink into those strong arms, into the spicy aroma of cologne and wood shavings and sea. So familiar. So achingly comforting. So unlike Finn's book and leather scent.

I shook my head free of the forbidden thoughts, glanced at Tripp's khakis and polo shirt, searched for solid ground between us.

"Grandpop didn't up the dress code for his best project manager again, did he?"

Tripp smiled that delicious smile, the one that drove all the girls in high school crazy. Curly black hair matched his deep eyes, the faintest five o'clock shadow making his mysterious dark looks and white teeth all that more alluring.

Not that I'd ever been one of the crazy high school girls, of course. I'd just been Josie, his best friend.

Tripp shrugged. "The old boy has high standards, what can I say?" His smile spread wider. "I'm kidding. I was on the way to the library but had a half-hour to spare. Figured I could put this up for your mother—I caught her with power tools last week."

I groaned. Ever since Mom had taken off a piece of her thumb with a belt sander when I was twelve, we'd tried to keep her away from the power tools. It had become a running joke in the family that she stick with what suited her best—books and good home cooking. "Then consider the Martin children—and Mom's fingers —forever in your debt." We laughed, and it felt good. Like the old us, instead of the after-that-summer-day us.

I headed to the adjoining kitchen and took a glass from the corner cupboard. I pushed it against the water dispenser on the refrigerator, noting the dispenser light was out. My thoughts turned to Dad again, just as hopeless as Mom when it came to handy house fixes. Poor Dad had always been too caught up in the mentally constructive to have anything to do with the physical improvement of anything. Lucky for us, Tripp didn't mind trading handyman services for dibs on whatever came out of Mom's kitchen.

I turned from the fridge, catching sight of a neatly folded sheet and pillow on the corner of the living room sofa. I wondered who Mom had allowed to crash on our couch this week. "So, a library visit, huh? They get in a new Calvin and Hobbes or something?" Despite my best efforts, I never could get Tripp to crack much more than an occasional graphic novel.

"Ha, ha." He shook his head, picked up a smaller molding, climbed the ladder, and fit it in the corner like a perfect puzzle piece before nailing it in place. He smoothed his hand along the wood, testing it out, searching for a bump or imperfection— something to fix. Because that's what Tripp did. Fix things.

Too bad he couldn't fix what happened between us just as easily.

"I'm going to the library for your mother." He climbed down the ladder and our gazes caught. For a terrible moment, I felt the awkwardness I feared would be ours from here on out. He shifted his attention back to the molding above.

I cleared my throat, grasped for words and understanding. Mom was one of the librarians. "Why does she need you to get something for her? She's working today, isn't she?"

"Her retirement party? At three o'clock?" Tripp rolled up the hose of the nail gun.

"R-retirement?" Surely, I hadn't missed that piece of information. Yes, I'd been distracted of late, but not so distracted I'd miss such big news.

And a party? I'd received a text from Maggie last week, something about the twins' Little League tournament. Nothing mentioning retirement. Lizzie called a few days ago to play me a new song she'd written. Had she said anything?

Tripp squeezed my shoulder. "Hey, you okay? No one has to know you forgot. It hasn't even started yet. We'll head over together...if you want."

His hand landed steady on me, solid if not a bit hesitant. I so needed firm ground right now.

But no, arriving at Mom's party together would never do. I needed to create clear boundaries between us. No mixed signals, especially now.

I pulled away from his warm hand. "I didn't forget. No one told me."

Right. That was it, wasn't it? I pulled out a chair and sat heavily. "Mom's really retiring?"

"That's the word."

We'd always been tight on money, and Mom was still young—too young to think about retiring. Unless...I gasped for sudden breath, chest tight. "Is she okay?"

"She's fine, Josie. Better than fine, I think. She's just ready for a change, you know? Even talked about renting some space over on Main Street, opening up a bookstore."

I stared, mouth agape.

Tripp's face reddened. "Amie talks too much sometimes."

"Apparently," I muttered. Still, it annoyed me that Tripp knew more than I did about what went on with my own family. I mean, a bookshop? That was *huge*. And no one thought to tell me?

An unpleasant twinge of guilt came as I recalled the many phone calls and text messages—especially the ones from Mom—that I'd either ignored or acknowledged with simple "likes" or smiley-faced emojis. I had my reasons, of course. Not particularly good ones, but reasons nonetheless.

Finn *had* been a distraction. One I'd kept to myself, hadn't even shared with Maggie, never mind Mom. He'd been from Dad's world, after all. It would be too much for Mom, especially not even a year after Dad's death.

Not to mention that my obsession with Finn was such an incredibly un-Josielike thing to do. Yes, I'd always been the wild Martin. The impulsive, blunt, opinionated, passionate Martin. But I'd never lost my head around a man and I certainly never let anything get in the way of my big career plans. Not until Professor Finn Becker came along, anyway.

My face burned as I remembered the moments we shared, how the alluring power of him had been enough to swallow me up, to create oblivion in all other areas of my life.

I'd forgotten the careful outline I'd sketched out for my life. I'd forgotten respectability and reason. I'd thrown myself into the dangerous. Played with fire. It shouldn't be a surprise I'd gotten burned. Torched.

Now, I had nothing but sizzling shame in the depths of my spirit. Too bad it wasn't enough to undo all that had been done.

I sighed. None of those memories deserved a place here, on my homecoming day. Mom's retirement day. Just think...a *bookshop*. How many times had Dad sat at this very dining room table talking about this long-held dream?

Tripp waved a hand in front of my face, and I blinked to see something like disappointment marring his features.

"I'm sorry. I'm more distracted than usual, I guess."

"Planning that next book in your head?"

I averted my gaze. "I haven't written since high school, and you know it."

"That's right. Too busy strapping all those letters to the end of your name in the Big Apple to consider silly things like stories, is that it?"

His scoffing tone rubbed me the wrong way. I breathed deep, pressed my lips together, and attempted to reign in that old temper. "Because you're such a huge proponent of deep, well-told stories, I suppose? Don't worry, Colton. I could never match the likes of Captain Underpants, anyway."

"Hey, that is a brilliant series concept." He grew serious, studied me without cracking a smile, a thousand unspoken words in his gaze. "You do know I would have gobbled up anything you'd written, Jo."

I bristled at his nickname for me. It was bad enough Mom and Dad had the entire *Little Women* thing going on with our names, but sometimes I wondered if our association with the March family hadn't cursed us in some ways. Mom had been so thrilled when I wrote my first story in elementary school. *I'd Cross the Desert for Milk*. It was awful. But you wouldn't have known it by Mom's enthusiasm.

Over the years, as Amie gravitated to art and Lizzie to music, as I bucked against the urge to write, and even last year as Maggie threw away her marketing career to be a wife and mother, I wondered if we'd inadvertently formed some sort of name-fulfilling prophecy. Had knowing Mom and Dad named us after the March family led us to mirror them in some ways? Many times, in ways we didn't even want?

Over time, I'd pulled away from creative writing and moved toward philosophy and psychology. Towards Dad's dreams for me. For who was I to compete with Jo March?

I shook my head, forcing myself back to the present. Back to Tripp stating he wanted to read my stories. Back to that horrid nickname he had for me. "Don't call me 'Jo.' Besides, we both know you never had the attention span for anything more than a graphic novel."

He leaned forward. "Remember *Noah and the Seed?* That was a brilliant story."

A grin tugged at the corners of my mouth. "It had pictures.

That's why you liked it."

Amie had drawn the pictures, and we'd presented it at story time at the children's hospital a month after Lizzie's thyroid surgery. There'd been nothing better than seeing those little faces light up as they transported from the bright playroom corner of a hospital to a world I'd created with words.

Enthralled by my story and Amie's pictures, the uncertainty etched on their small faces had disappeared, replaced by a look of wonder.

I pushed the memory away. I'd decided on a different route to help people now. Dad would have been proud of all I'd accomplished so far in making a name for myself in the field of psychology at NYU.

I sniffed, not quite able to push away the full memories of those times in the hospital—with Tripp leaning against a wall enjoying the stories as much as the children.

He pulled out a chair and sat beside me. "I loved all your stories, even the ones without pictures. Still love them." His gaze held mine, and something about it brought me to the edge of longing, so much so it was devastating.

I shot to my feet, familiar panic working its way to my chest. "Why don't you head on over to the library? I have to put some things away. I'll see you there?"

He swallowed, the thick bob of his Adam's apple moving along his smooth neck. "Yeah, sure. Whatever you want."

"Thanks." This was what I wanted. It was. To be left alone.

He gathered up his tools and ladder, seemed prepared to leave in silence.

"Tripp." I caught him before he headed out the back door to his truck. "It's good to see you."

His smile, etched with a sadness I'd expected to have disappeared by now, didn't quite reach the edges of his mouth. "You too, Josie."

I didn't breathe until the sound of his truck was an echo down our quiet street.

We would clear the air between us sometime soon. But it didn't have to be the very afternoon I came home.

TRIPP STARTED UP HIS WORK TRUCK AND LEANED BACK AGAINST the headrest, his thoughts filled with his encounter with Josie. She joked he wasn't much of a reader, and that might be true, but he read one thing very well, even if she'd never admit it—her.

That sad, desperate look in her sharp gray eyes, hidden beneath that mass of wild chestnut hair, covered something she didn't want him to see. It didn't matter that it'd been five months —five long months—since they'd seen one another. He knew.

Something was wrong. Was it just being home again, realizing the loss of her father anew? She used to confide in him, but those days vanished faster than coffees on a construction site.

Seeing her was like reopening an old wound. With much pain, he realized he still held out hope for them to be together some- day. His best friend. The girl he'd loved all his life.

But she'd rejected him, tore his heart to shreds like one would an old bank statement. He'd convinced himself he was getting over her, even went on a date or two, but always found the poor girl, who sat across from him at dinner, lacking. Not with any kind of blatant physical or character flaw, but with the simple fact that she wasn't Josie, the girl who took up every inch and corner of his heart.

He put his truck in drive and sent up a quick prayer for what- ever the future brought for them. How would he even survive this retirement party? Josie'd want to catch up with her siblings no doubt. Would she even acknowledge his presence?

But he wasn't going for Josie, he was going for Hannah. The woman had been like a mother to him all these years. He couldn't miss her big day. Seeing Josie again—even if she didn't give him the time of day—was just an added benefit.

His phone rang out over his Bluetooth and he turned left on Bay View Street toward the library, the sparkling Maine coast on his right. He picked up. "Hey, Pedro. What's up?"

"You at the office, Boss Man?"

"I can be." His best foreman didn't ask for much, so when he did, Tripp tried to accommodate.

"I gotta talk to you before I lose my cool."

Pedro didn't lose his cool often. Not over receiving the wrong materials on a job-site. Not over a picky homeowner who changed their mind a hundred times over tile backsplash choices. Not even over a four-hundred-dollar table saw gone bust.

An unpleasant knowing settled in Tripp's stomach. "I'll be there in five minutes." He'd have to be late to the library. Keeping his foreman happy trumped being on time for a retirement party. Better to keep Grandpop out of it all if possible. Especially if... "This doesn't have anything to do with a certain blond-haired college kid who'd rather be surfing than building houses, does it?"

"You called it, Boss."

Tripp groaned and hung up with Pedro, his fingers tight on the wheel. He probably should have fired that kid a week ago. Probably should have sent him packing, told him to get a job at a beach club where he could have smiled pretty for tips all summer long. If only it wasn't so complicated.

If only the lazy laborer was someone other than his own brother.

2

If my hometown of Camden was the jewel of the Maine coast, as so many claimed, then its library was the jewel of the town. Perched on a hill overlooking the harbor, the historic building boasted just enough old charm to be considered unique and just enough modern-day essentials to be considered practical. I couldn't count how many times I'd sprawled on a bench overlooking the naked masts on the harbor or perched on one of the stones that made up the generous backyard amphitheater with nothing but a book and my imagination to pass the time.

While my father's throne had been his study, my mother's was the library.

But to imagine the library without my mother was almost as painful as imagining Dad's empty study chair. And a bookshop? How had I not been told of such a major decision? So much was changing, and changing fast—yet I couldn't pretend my life wasn't among them.

I turned onto Atlantic Avenue to park, but not before glimpsing the orchards in bloom behind the massive Victorian home just around the corner on historic High Street. I'd always been drawn to the place, dubbed Orchard House, with its wide wraparound front porch, its many gables that hid secret rooms and hiding places, the historical mysteries that clung to the curves of its turrets.

Too bad I couldn't say I felt the same draw to the home's solitary resident.

Still, I should visit her soon. The peppery octogenarian could be a trial, but my great-aunt Pris made it possible for me to attend NYU. Even if paying for my college *was* her attempt to make restitution for past wrongs. While I admired my great-aunt's independence, I could have done without her blunt opinions and irrational finagling in the lives of her great-nieces and nephew.

I parked my beat-up Honda Civic and crossed the street to walk the pavers, carved with bookish quotes, to the library's front entrance. The large-domed windows illuminated chandeliers and walls lined with books and people—many people—within. It looked as if the entire town had come to pay tribute to Mom.

I swallowed the lump in my throat, pushed off the notion that I should have accepted Tripp's offer to accompany him, and pulled the door open, suddenly conscious of my empty hands. I should have brought Mom a gift, or at least picked up some chocolates or a bouquet of flowers at French and Brawn Market. As usual though, my good intentions lagged behind my actions.

I stepped into the building. Small groups of people congregated throughout the large room, some sitting in chairs and at tables, others standing in clusters. The delicious scent of books mingled with that of food and various colognes and perfumes, making me dizzy. I searched for members of my family but spotted only unfamiliar heads of hair and a few of the library staff. I squeezed against a bookshelf before feeling a hard poke in my side.

I whirled to see the rubber end of a cane in my face. I was convinced Aunt Pris carried it around more for the jabbing than for balancing. The top of her coiffed white hair barely reached my shoulders, yet what she lacked in height, she made up for with her commanding presence.

"About time you showed up, girl."

"Nice to see you, Aunt Priscilla."

"Have you seen that brother of yours? I've been after him to help bring some boxes over to the house for me."

I shook my head. "Sorry, I just got into town." I turned my attention to the small toy poodle perched inside her large pocket-book. I didn't think dogs were allowed in the library, but I doubted anyone would question my great-aunt. I held my hand out to the fat, spoiled pooch, hoping for a different response than I'd received in our previous encounters. "Hey, Cragen." Aunt Pris was a big Law & Order fan. "How's things?" My attempt at conversation earned me a sharp, yippie snap. I snatched my hand back. "Same as Christmas then, huh?"

Aunt Pris eyed me. "Hmph. You done with school yet? Still, don't see how a fancy degree is going to help you make something of yourself."

I was four the first time I met Aunt Pris. Sometimes—okay, all of the time—I didn't understand how Dad and Aunt Pris were even related, no matter how distantly. Not for the first time, I wondered why Aunt Pris hadn't taken my father in after her sister died while giving birth to him. I wondered if Dad would have turned out differently—more rigid and hard instead of the soft-hearted man I knew. Perhaps I should be extra thankful for Dad's adoptive parents, who died in a house fire before I ever knew them.

Maybe deep beneath my aunt's crotchety exterior lay a generous heart to go with all that gumption. She'd certainly helped Dad out of a financial pickle more than once, even though Dad's adoption as a baby hadn't connected us with his birth mother's sister until later in his life.

I breathed deep and opened my mouth to defend my chosen study to my great-aunt. Surely helping people, digging deep into the human psyche, and promoting internal healing was of more worth than a career that would bring in bucket loads of money. Not that I had an aversion to bucket loads of money, mind you. But some things were more to be treasured, Dad always said. Despite the often fleshly temptation to think otherwise, in the end, I couldn't help but agree.

Aunt Pris raised her eyebrows. "Well, aren't you going to tell me how that degree is going to benefit you? Unless you met a rich city man, Josy-phine...that would be the most worthy news this family has heard in a long time. Especially after your sister's... choices." She jerked her head to the corner of the large room where my oldest sister corralled two young boys with a plate of cookies.

"Oh!" I turned to Aunt Pris. "Do you mind? I haven't seen her since Christmas."

Aunt Pris waved me away. "Go on, I got my quilting club over yonder there." She waved her cane at a group of silver-haired ladies who for some mystical reason, enjoyed my great-aunt's company.

"Maggie!" I called, waving and tripping over my own feet as I made my way toward her.

My sister lifted her dark head after setting the cookies down, her delicate pretty features made all the more so by the pleasant look of surprise on her face. She threw her arms around me in a tight embrace, and I sank into them, clinging tighter. For the first time since those two little blasted pink lines showed up, I felt that everything was going to be okay. Somehow, like a storybook ending, it all would be right in the end.

We parted, and I discreetly brushed the wet corners of my eyes.

Maggie dipped her head. "My Josie—crying? Are you okay?"

I sniffed, nearly swatted her hand away. "Just glad to be home."

"Well, I thought you were going to leave us forever the way you never returned my calls."

A tug at the hem of my blouse caused me to turn to see five-year-old Davey. "You remember me, Aunt Josie? You took care of us when Daddy and Mommy went mooning."

I stifled a laugh and wrapped my nephew in a hug, inhaling the scent of maple syrup and soap. It had been too long. "Of course, I remember you, you silly goose."

Maggie ruffled his hair, smiling. "It's called a honeymoon, Davey."

Indeed. For certainly the idea of my sweet, responsible sister mooning the neighbors was nearly as preposterous as Aunt Pris getting emotional over a Hallmark movie.

I turned to my second nephew, who stuffed his face with a sugar cookie. "Isaac." I wrapped him in a hug. "It's good to see you, little guy."

"You too, Aunt Josie," he said around a mouthful of cookie.

"Oh," I dug in my small purse. "I have something for you guys." I pulled out two little plastic packs of LEGOs I'd seen at a Walmart back in New York a couple weeks ago. One was a helicopter, the other an airplane.

The boys let out whoops and thank you's before collapsing to the floor to empty and assemble their loot.

My heart swelled. "How's it going with...everything?" My older sister, as prim as a China aster, had surprised everyone by getting knocked off her feet by a whirlwind romance to a man ten years her elder—a widower with twin boys, no less. To be honest, we'd all been hesitant to jump on board with the idea. Too much baggage, too much room for hurt—and all too fast. But after we'd lost Dad, what was really important rose to the surface. Josh and his parents had been such a help to us, particularly to Mom in handling the details of the will and life insurance. In truth, we couldn't help but fall in love with the high school teacher as Maggie had. The two had been married last summer just before I returned to school.

Maggie blew her hair out of her face as her gaze lingered on the boys. "It's good. Great, actually." She leaned toward me. "In fact, Josh and I talked about it just this morning and we've decided to start trying."

I stared at her as I sought to comprehend her words.

Maggie's laughter bubbled up, and she bumped my shoulder with her own. "Oh, Josie. You know, the birds and the bees?"

I stared at her, uncomprehending.

"A baby, silly. We want to have a baby."

I grasped for words. A baby. But of course. "I—that's wonderful. I'm so happy for you, Mags." I gave her another hug.

"Well, I suppose it could take some time, but I think I'm ready. I think we're ready. I can't believe how fast Davey and Isaac have stolen my heart. It's not always easy, of course. Some days are hard. *Really* hard. But when I think about growing up in a big family like we did—well, I can't imagine it any other way for my own."

"You're a *great* mother." And she was. How many times had I been on the phone with her last fall while she led the twins through bath times or uncomplainingly stopped a brotherly quarrel from escalating into a wrestling match? *She* was the one who should be popping out babies, raising them to be functional, caring human beings. My sister was made for such things. I, on the other hand, was made for runs on the beach, getting lost in a library, writing dry research papers only twenty people read in an obscure psych journal, maybe even scribbling down a secret murder-mystery once in a while.

I was not made to be a mother.

We chatted a few more minutes about the possibility of a new baby for Maggie before I couldn't take it anymore. I searched the room for Mom, guessing her petite frame to be lost somewhere in the crowd. "So, Mom retiring, huh? That was sure a surprise. And what's this about a bookshop?"

Maggie bent to wipe chocolate from Isaac's mouth. "If you

returned my calls or read my texts the last several weeks, it wouldn't be a surprise."

I winced. "I-uh..." Yes, I hadn't been great about returning calls, but I always read my texts. Vaguely, I remembered a couple of particularly lengthy texts I'd ignored the week my life collapsed around me. But hadn't I skimmed them? I wouldn't have missed such an important detail as the Martin family opening a book-shop, would I?

Then again, that week—the week my plans and future were crumpled up and torn—nothing had seemed to matter except my pain. Even my precious classes had fallen by the wayside. The dinging of my texts had filled me with hope—a hope never real-ized—for each time I'd spotted Maggie or Mom or Lizzie's names and not Finn's, I'd put the phone down, allowing the messages to drag me further into despair.

Maggie pushed a stray hair from Isaac's face, the move natural and without thought. Gracious me, she was a good mom. "Don't sweat it, Sis. I know you've been busy. I'm just glad you're here now. I was worried about you."

"I'm fine. Really." My voice practically squeaked.

She narrowed her eyes at me, but didn't push, for which I was thankful. As my closest friend, I couldn't deny that I'd taken her marriage hard. And so soon after Dad died. Maggie had gained a new family in only a day, and I'd felt my world shift, felt that every-thing I held dear was being taken from me. But being with Maggie now, I could only feel grateful. She was still here. Unlike Dad, I could still talk to her. Yes, things changed. This new dimension of my sister—the wife and mother dimension—didn't take away from who she was, it only added to the already beautiful person I was proud to know. If I ever worked up the courage to tell her my secret, which I'd have to sooner or later, I hoped she might have wisdom to offer.

After she got over her initial disappointment in me, of course.

Even now, at the thought, prickles of heat speared my pride.

Shame and embarrassment surged forth. Maggie, Mom, my entire family, even Aunt Pris...I'd let them all down. I was the driven one, the determined-to-grab-the-world-by-its-horns-and-wrangle-success-from-it one. And I'd always kept my principles in line.

I tortured myself further by thinking of Dad. A fresh wave of humiliation washed over me. I'd give anything to have him back, and at the same time I was so very glad I wouldn't have to see the look of displeasure on his face when I finally shared my news. That it involved Professor Finn Becker, a man he had extended charity and fellowship to during my growing up years, would have been the ultimate betrayal.

"Josie."

I blinked, shook my head. "Sorry."

Maggie put a hand on my arm. "We need a girls' night. Bad. And you're going to tell me what's going on in that head of yours and what happened in New York, you hear?"

I sniffed, nodded. "I'm free until September."

And maybe even past then.

My sister took out her phone, started tapping. "I'm heading up the spring fundraiser at the twins' school. Dinner at Mom's with the sibs Friday night. Twins have a t-ball tournament on Saturday. Oh, and I've got to finish up the last few Bible study lessons for the women's group. John has track meets on Mondays..." She looked up at me, guilt drawing out her features. "Could you do next Wednesday night?"

Six days away. I suppose I'd take what I could get. I'd basically ignored my sister the last couple of months, after all. I was lucky to get anything. "Sure. That sounds wonderful."

I stood on my tiptoes, searching out Mom. While I'd always been closer to Dad, I felt a sudden, childlike need for the woman who'd always bandaged and kissed our boo-boos, fed us peanut butter chocolate chip cookies, and in short, simply made everything better. While I admired Dad with a fierceness I couldn't explain, it was Mom who had always been there for us. Mom who could be counted on.

"So she's really going for it, huh? Their dream? Tripp mentioned she was thinking right downtown. You know where?"

Maggie raised an eyebrow. "You saw Tripp?"

"Just at the house for a minute." I tried to brush her off.

She nodded. The brushoff seemed to work. This time.

"There's a place for lease on Main. Right near The Smiling Cow."

"That's a great spot. I'm glad to see Mom going after her dreams, even with..." My voice trailed off. The words *Dad gone* stuck in my throat. Apparently, a year battling grief wasn't enough for me to voice the obvious. A year working through the stages. Denial, anger, bargaining, depression, acceptance.

Yet knowing the stages and studying them in classes didn't make them any easier to live through. I wondered where I fell on the spectrum. For the first time since I decided on a career in psychology, I doubted the neat little compartments we attempted to slide grief into.

"Dad's dream, you mean." Maggie shifted from one foot to the other.

"What?"

"A bookshop was Dad's dream. A book-inspired bed and breakfast was Mom's."

"You're right," I whispered, remembering now the many B&B magazines Mom had collected over the years, the large scrapbook of clippings she'd carefully tended during my elementary years.

But somewhere along the way, the scrapbook hadn't come out as much. Instead, she'd poured herself into her family, coming alongside Dad at every turn with new projects that benefited the community or helped those in need. I didn't remember the scrapbook sitting on our living room coffee table at all by the time I'd reached high school. I was ashamed to admit I hadn't thought anything about it until now—until I faced the possibility of my own dreams being crushed.

I'd always known I wouldn't think of marriage or family until I'd reached my career goals. But now, for the first time, I saw how a woman could be swallowed up by a man—how intoxicating that could be. I wondered if that's how Mom felt about Dad. True, she'd been able to finish her degree in the last months of her pregnancy with Maggie, but had she wanted more for her life? While there wasn't a doubt in my mind she'd do anything differently, I wondered if she ever wished they'd handled their money differently. If they'd saved a little more for rainy-day dreams instead of giving so much away.

"She should open her bed and breakfast," I said.

Maggie shook her head, a smile tugging at her lips. "That's good of you to say. I thought the same, but we went over the numbers. The life insurance she received from the college was just enough to pay off the last of their debts. Mom doesn't want to go back there now that she's free of the burden."

My father's varied interests had run us in the red over the years. If only he'd been as good at fundraising as he'd been at philosophy. As a part-time theology professor at the local community college, Dad was also on staff at our church as a counselor. It was no secret he volunteered more than his part-time hours demanded of him. Add in a start-up soup kitchen, a charity ball for the historical committee, free grief counseling, and even a kid's camp. All worthy, beautiful endeavors...that we didn't have money for.

Even the bookshop Dad dreamed of was intended to be a non-profit launched in Portland to empower and support vulnerable teens and young adults—those in the foster care system, those involved in court, or those out of jobs. I wondered if that's what Mom planned on doing. If so, would she be able to support such an endeavor long term, particularly in our privileged, relatively crime-free town of Camden?

I still heard Dad's voice, reciting the value of treasures in heaven over earthly treasures. And though it was hard at times for me to see past the nonexistent college fund, lack of money for guitar lessons for Lizzie, and Bronson's second-hand clothes, I never questioned my father—and deep down believed that maybe the five of us were even better off for his rather radical views. But now, with Mom alone and Dad gone, shouldn't she at least make an effort to go after her dreams—and support herself in the process?

"What if she sold the house?" I asked.

"Wow, I'm surprised you'd suggest that. Believe it or not, she actually considered it. But it would only be enough for a decent piece of Camden property, not enough to renovate or build, not to mention all the startup costs a B&B would take."

"She *could* take out a loan. It's not unheard of, after all."

"On the single income of a librarian? I'm not sure she'd get what she needs. Besides, she says she never wants to owe money again, is dead set against it. And I think she's scared a bed and breakfast wouldn't take off, that she'd get behind on the loan, and be in the same boat she and Dad have always been in."

"It would take off. We're in Camden. This is like the B&B capital of the country."

My sister put a hand on my arm. "She's excited about the idea of the bookshop, I think. It's okay. Some dreams are just not meant to be, I guess. And the bookshop—it's a good thing. A noble project for Mom, a worthy contribution to the town."

Something welled up within me, something fierce I couldn't name, couldn't voice to Maggie. I tried to push out a half-hearted, "I guess," but it wouldn't come forth.

Were some dreams not meant to come to fruition? I'd never believed that, not with my father's endearingly optimistic attitude as my champion. But maybe that belief lacked practicality and wisdom. Maybe, as I grew older, I saw the cracks in the foundation of such a belief. Looking at my life the last several months... well, maybe my sister was right.

"Hey, when'd you show up?"

I turned at the sound of my youngest sibling's voice. Blond hair braided and piled on her head, large rust-colored earrings shaped like leaves, pretty face with tastefully applied makeup, and white flowing pants. Everything about Amie spoke of both confidence and a flashback to the sixties.

I hugged her tight, relishing the feel of her in my arms. No doubt, she was the most challenging of my siblings, the one hardest to get along with, the one with a temper to match my own, the one least likely to embrace the values Mom and Dad tried to instill in us. Then again, Amie wasn't the one who'd been knocked up by her college professor.

"Look what the cat dragged in." A deep voice came from behind me. I released Amie to hug my only brother, Bronson. His dark looks and broad shoulders—not to mention his amazing mind—had to leave the college girls drooling. I hoped he used that amazing mind to be smart around them.

"I thought guys stopped growing at twenty? You keep it up and we won't be able to see anything but chin stubble and nose hairs pretty soon."

"Josie," Maggie admonished.

"Me next," piped a small voice behind me.

"Lizzie." I clutched her tightest of all. Though we were complete opposites, we went together like Cheerios and milk, water and sand. And though her sweet, quiet, sometimes anxious nature as well as her scary bout with thyroid cancer when she was fifteen left me a bit protective of her, I didn't mind the job one bit. While Maggie had always looked after Amie, I'd willingly taken up for Lizzie over the years. All of us fawned over Bronson enough that he could never feel left out—quite the opposite, in fact.

From somewhere in the corner of the large room, Marianne

Norbert, head librarian, proud member of Aunt Pris's quilting club, and the tallest woman in town at six-feet, counted down to singing *For She's a Jolly Good Fellow.* The crowd parted and there was Mom, the candles on the cake lighting her delicate features, so like Maggie's. Though the lines around her eyes and mouth ran deeper than last time I saw her, she looked happy. A bit tired, perhaps, but content, her chestnut hair pulled back in a loose ponytail, her eyes scanning the crowd in appreciation.

Maybe Maggie was right. Maybe the bookshop was a good thing, even if it wasn't her original dream. Maybe dreams took different forms, shifting and shedding and growing into something more suitable, better even.

Mom blew out the candles, then opened her eyes, her gaze landing on me. Her mouth formed my name against the applause and she rushed toward me, arms outstretched.

I sank into her embrace, willed the tears not to come. For though I was just shy of twenty-four, if there was ever a time I needed my mother...if there was ever a time I needed to be in the embrace of everything *home*, it was now.

3

Tripp didn't presume to know much outside of building things. Except for the one fact he was learning faster than he wanted—that fact being, women were trouble. Namely one woman in particular.

Tripp closed his eyes, promising when he opened them that Josie Martin would be pushed to the darkest corner of his mind and the estimate he worked on would be at the forefront. He kept them closed for another moment, seeing for the twentieth time that day Josie sitting at her kitchen table with that haunted look in her eyes.

He shook his head and dragged in a deep breath, opening his eyes to look at the drawings on his office desk. The proposed colonial on Sherman Cove would run a pretty penny. If Colton Contractors secured the job, it would keep Tripp's biggest crew busy for most of the fall.

And Grandpop happy.

Little by little, Edward Colton was releasing the reins of his beloved business to his grandson. Tripp knew it wasn't easy for him, even at the ripe age of eighty-two. But Grandpop had nothing to worry about—the business of fixing and building things, of creating something lasting, functional, and beautiful out of wood and nails, ran in Tripp's blood. Sure, it may have skipped a generation with his father, and been lost on his younger brother, but it was there, inside Tripp, sure as the sunrise over Camden Harbor each morning.

He finished listing the lumber he needed for the second floor and the last of the rooms, including finish work, then sent an email to his supplier to get a price on it all. Once he heard back, he'd add that price to the labor and subcontractor estimates.

If the job went through, maybe he'd even be able to get his hands dirty himself. Surely, the office work wouldn't suffer too much if he got out with the crew for a couple of framing days on this one.

A knock sounded at the door.

"It's open!"

Clothed in a surfing t-shirt better suited for a California beach than a construction site, his younger brother had always been more at home with a pencil and sketchpad or surfboard than a hammer and pouch of nails.

And at the moment, that was the problem.

Especially after his talk with Pedro the night before. By the time their conversation was over, Tripp had just enough time to get to Hannah's retirement party to wish her well before the library started emptying out. He'd helped Josie and her siblings clean up the place, and Josie had seemed happy enough. If only it weren't for those anxious eyes at her kitchen table earlier in the afternoon. What was troubling her?

"Hey, bro." August pushed back dirty blond hair and took a seat in one of the two chairs across from his desk, an ankle casually draped over a tanned knee. "You wanted to see me?"

Tripp shoved his calculator aside. "Yeah...you missing school yet?" Better to ease into the conversation.

"Only been out a week, not much to miss except the girls." He wiggled his eyebrows.

Tripp would have to address too much partying at college at a later date. Even he knew one lecture at a time was all any kid could handle.

He sent up a quick, desperate prayer for the course of the conversation. He'd never quite known his place with August, a brother seven years younger. Both boys had been under their grandfather's care since August was six and their parents had died in a train crash while on a business trip in France. While Grandpop supplied their every physical need, emotional ones—particularly August's—had been harder to meet. Tripp played the part of older brother as much as the part of subsidiary father, something August didn't exactly appreciate.

Now, with classes out, Tripp would also play the part of employer, something he relished as much as a nail through the thumb.

"I talked to Pedro last night. He has some concerns about the Banks renovation."

"I don't know what he said, bro, but I wouldn't listen. That guy's got an entire jackhammer up his—"

"That guy is my best foreman and your immediate supervisor. You've been on the job four days, August. None of the guys are going to take kindly to you screwing around. Just do what he asks you to do. If he tells you to clean, clean. If he tells you to move lumber, move it. And put your phone away until break time."

"I'm not some kid, okay? I don't need you to tell me when I can and can't use my phone."

Tripp's anger mounted, the fuse to his temper a short one August knew the best way to ignite. "You're right. You're not a kid anymore, so start acting like an adult." Great balls of fire, now he really sounded like an overbearing parent. But he couldn't stop. Didn't August see how his actions affected the entire business? "You don't get a pass because your family owns the company. You don't get to sit on your sorry behind and play on your phone because of your last name. If anything, your last name means you should work all the harder."

"Okay, okay, Grandpop. Chill, all right?"

Tripp gritted his teeth and fought the urge to pound his fist into the mahogany desk and stand up to deliver his wrath. Instead, he eyed his brother with the reserve one might give a chicken in the henhouse destined for that night's dinner. "No one asked you to work your summer at Colton Contractors. You could just as easily have gotten a job waiting tables and flashing those dimples for tips at any number of the restaurants around here. Maybe it's just not a good fit, August, and maybe that's okay."

His brother exhaled with much show, swung his head dramatically to the side. His long hair landed neatly over one eye. "You're right. Are you happy? Give me another chance. I'll do better, I promise."

Though his heart wasn't in it, Tripp would take whatever his little brother would give. Tripp reached toward the side table and grabbed a package of gray t-shirts embroidered with the company name. He threw it hard at August. "One more thing. Make sure you're wearing one of these every day. No more surfer-dude t-shirts and no holes in the pants. Got it?"

"Yeah, yeah. Man, you're getting more like the old man every day."

Tripp hated to admit it, he *really* hated to admit it, but August was right. Still, the business couldn't be run on rainbows and unicorns. Someone had to get junk done. And yeah, that person was him. So while he'd rather be out in the field, what got done in this office made what happened in the field possible.

"Wait. I saw Josie outside Dr. Sutka's office today. She's back, right? Is that what's got your panties in a bunch?"

"August..." Tripp swallowed the rest of the warning, tried to ignore the familiar, humiliating pain that threatened to rip him in two wherever Josie was concerned. Everyone had thought they'd end up together, including him. What had gone wrong?

August had seen her at the doctor's? Probably just a checkup, surely nothing serious. Josie was the picture of perfect health, running marathons up and down the Maine coast. He'd been at every grueling finish line to cheer her on.

Maybe it hadn't been enough, though. Maybe she wanted more than cheering. Maybe he'd buy some new running sneakers this weekend, see if she wanted to take a few laps with him. Surely, he could handle a few miles pounding pavement if it gave him an excuse to spend time with her, to figure out what was going on with those sad gray eyes....

August walked around the desk and put a hand on Tripp's shoulder. "Man, I know it sucks, but you gotta get back out there. You're not too ugly for an old man, after all. There's gotta be a girl desperate enough to take you up on a date."

Tripp broke loose with a grin, backhanded his brother's abs, causing him to curl over in mock agony. August didn't lose his playful smirk. "And hey, if you can't win her with your looks, flash her your wallet. We all know Grandpop's millions are going to you."

Tripp grabbed August in a headlock. "I'm not so old I can't take you out in five seconds, flat. Don't you ever forget it." He released him, messed up his hair to get in one more good jab.

"Yeah, yeah." August pushed his hair out of his eyes, glanced at the drawings on the desk. "Hey, what are those?"

Tripp felt his muscles relax after the roughhousing. He always did like the brother role best. "Drawings for the Smythe family. A new construction on Sherman Cove. Colonial."

August leaned closer, studied the interior layout. "Aly Smythe, right? Her mom teaches painting on the weekends." He looked at the drawing another minute, pointed at the second-floor rooms. "That bathroom's as big as a dance hall. If they scaled it down a bit and moved that closet here"—he pointed—"she'd be able to have an extra room, probably with a great view. Maybe an art room with a small balcony."

Tripp squinted at the drawings, imagined August's suggestion. "You know, I think you're right. I'll mention that to them when I deliver the estimate. Not bad, Little Colton."

"I'm not just around here for my stunning good looks, you know."

Tripp delivered another light punch to his side. "And clearly not for your humility either. Go on, get out of here. Maybe I'll catch you for the game later? Sox are taking on the Blue Jays."

"Maybe. All depends how my date with Mackenzie goes."

"Mackenzie Brown?"

"Yup."

The girl lived a street over from Grandpop's estate. Pretty, though hard to tell with so much makeup. Her usually revealing, too-tight clothes didn't leave much to the imagination. She didn't strike Tripp as the kind of girl August would be—should be—drawn to. But lately he wondered how well he really knew his brother at all. Then again, maybe he wasn't being fair to the girl. Maybe August saw something in her Tripp didn't.

His brother opened the door.

"August, just be careful and don't—"

"Yeah, yeah. Don't do anything you wouldn't do. But then I wouldn't have any fun, would I?" He chuckled as he walked down the hall, whistling.

Tripp groaned. That boy needed Jesus or a father or a sweet girl who would set him straight. Preferably all three.

Tripp leaned back in his chair, stared blankly at the blueprints in front of him. He'd always thought Josie Martin would be his future and Amie Martin would be August's. They would hang out together, maybe have their own families one day. Real families, with parents and aunts and uncles and cousins—something the Colton boys never had.

But lately it seemed all those dreams were as good as the rotten boards in his latest demolition project—torn down and thrown in the back dumpster, never to be repurposed or used again.

He stood, shoved his chair back against the desk with more force than necessary. He wasn't fond of playing the lovesick puppy, and truth be told, it was growing old. Maybe he *should* take a lesson from August's book and date more. Ashley Robinson had been flirting with him for some time. A pretty elementary school teacher on the worship team at church. They'd talked a few times at town events. Maybe he should ask her out, get over this crazy Josie hump.

But when he thought of sitting across from Ashley on the balcony of The Waterfront Restaurant, or buying her ice cream at the Camden Cone, all he could think about was a woman with long chestnut hair who ran like the wind, who had convinced him to dress up for Halloween as Romeo their junior year of high school, who would probe his thoughts on life and purpose and faith and humanity with the tenacity of a lawyer cross-examining a witness in a high stakes trial but listen to his responses with the compassion of Mother Theresa. A woman who could make him laugh with her wittiness and take his breath away with her beauty.

The Martin family had filled so many gaps in his life—in August's too. Their poor neighbors, the most unlikely of benefactors, had poured themselves out in love to the two little rich boys. It was only natural Tripp fell for his best friend. But that horrible summer day when he'd admitted his feelings, Josie had rejected him. Accused him of wanting her for what he'd never had—a ready-made family. Said he only thought of her as a logical step to adulthood, to becoming a man.

Was any part of what she'd said true? He'd wrestled with that question last year and still didn't have a solid answer. He only knew his heart. He only knew who he wanted to be with forever.

He thought of August seeing her at the doctor's, thought of that desperate look from yesterday. It wasn't his place to question anymore, maybe it never had been. But it didn't mean he couldn't swing by the Martin house later. He used to stop by for a game of chess with Josie without a second thought. Besides, there was more trim to put up, and he'd never stopped to question his motives for a visit before.

Why should Josie's presence change that?

❧ 4 ❧

Dad had drilled into me the importance of fulfilling my "God-given potential," and I never questioned that the plans I had for my life would steer me in the right direction of said potential.

Until now.

The tiny blob on the screen changed everything.

I had failed. The evidence was plain before me, making me feel all sorts of emotions I couldn't even begin to wade through. Defeat. Shame. Remorse. And something so small I hardly recognized it...surely not *amazement*?

I'd put off calling my doctor while at school, telling myself I'd figure things out once I'd gotten home. It took every last ounce of willpower for me to drive myself to the office today.

Now, as the midwife moved the wand over my small, hard belly and studied the portable screen, reality hit.

The quick flash of a heartbeat showed strong and sure. There was an *actual* tiny human growing inside of me. Unreal.

"When was your last period, Josie?"

"Um, mid-January sometime, I think."

She made a small sound of acknowledgement, but it held a

hint of disapproval. Or was I being overly paranoid? She didn't know me from Adam, but had she already formed her opinions about me?

My face burned at the realization of what I'd done to be in here, answering her questions. I'd always planned to wait for marriage and children until after I'd obtained a dependable career. If only I'd remembered those good intentions in Finn's presence.

From a psychological standpoint, I could make excuses for my poor decisions this past year. The grief following Dad's death, Maggie leaving us for her new family, trying to embrace school and New York and my future, trying to make Dad proud from heaven...then meeting up again with Professor Becker as a graduate student instead of a wide-eyed freshman. He'd heard of my father's passing and expressed his condolences, apologized for not making it to the funeral. I thanked him for the kind card and the generous donation he'd made to the college in Dad's memory. Told him I'd missed his presence at Thanksgiving last year.

When he asked me out for a drink to share a few untold stories in honor of my father, I accepted, even as I felt out of my element. Like a naïve freshman once again—one of two-hundred held spellbound by Finn's dynamic presence in the classroom.

We toasted to Dad, and Finn spoke about how they'd met in a class they'd taken together some eighteen years ago. Dad had gone back to school for some psychology classes to better prepare him for his role as a counselor at the church. He and Finn had shared a battle of wits over the logical existence for God—Dad owning there was plenty of evidence to support such an existence, Finn claiming there was none.

Despite their opposing opinions, they enjoyed the challenge of their debates. When about to leave for Thanksgiving recess, Dad had asked Finn what his plans were. Finn admitted he'd had none. Ever the giver, Dad had invited him to our home for the holiday and although Finn wanted to object, he hadn't.

Never marrying or having his own family, Finn had shown up

for many a Thanksgiving. Not last year, though. Our first without Dad. Mom had extended the invitation, but Finn had declined.

"You know," Finn said, his eyes reflecting warmth from the lights above the high top table we shared. "Your dad and I may have disagreed about a lot, but I don't know if I ever told him how much I appreciated those Thanksgiving invitations. I wish I had."

I'd smiled, put my hand on his. "I think he knew."

By the time we parted for the night, my heart swam with anticipation, the warmth of the wine pleasant in my veins. I couldn't wait to attend Finn's class the next day.

But no one was more surprised than me when he asked me out again that weekend, this time without citing my father's memory as a reason to get together.

Things had escalated fast. Too fast.

Fifteen years my senior, Professor Finn Becker was sophisticated, handsome, and ambitious. He filled an emotional void within me, made me forget about home and Dad and Tripp—even my family with whom I now connected to grief and dead dreams. For the first time, I allowed my levelheadedness to get swallowed up in obsession.

Mystical and massive, pulling at me like the swell of an enchanting crystalline sea, Finn's boundless energy and surety, coupled with the intellectual world he lived in, enchanted me until I gave him all I had.

Finn didn't believe in marriage. He said it was a man-made restriction that ruined the beauty and potential of true love. While I'm not sure I'd call what we had love, it was something powerful enough to cause me to lose my senses.

Looking back, I'm ashamed to admit his words sounded intelligent, enlightened. Why couldn't I pursue my career alongside a man that inspired and encouraged me? Maybe that's why my parents' love had seemed lacking—their marriage had been weighted down with burden and sacrificial responsibility, most of which fell on Mom. Finn believed in equality and teamwork, in two free spirits who made the choice of caring for one another with each new sunrise.

I blinked at the small spark of my baby's heartbeat on the screen, Finn's words coming at me.

"*I'll go with you to the appointment, Josie. It will be quick and over and we can put this all behind us, continue living our lives, completely and totally wrapped up in one another.*"

And then later, when I'd rebuffed his suggestion.

"*It's me or it, Josie.*"

Finn had refused to take responsibility.

The screen went blank as the midwife took the wand off my belly. "Everything looks good." She dug out a cardboard wheel from her white coat pocket and spun it slowly. "You're about fourteen weeks along, which will make your due date October 19th. We'll need to schedule you for a more detailed ultrasound in a few weeks."

My heart picked up speed. This was all happening so fast. Ready or not, October was less than six months away.

The midwife pocketed the wheel, her eyes softening for the first time since our visit. "I don't know your situation, Josie, but if you need me to refer you anywhere, please let me know."

Anywhere? Like an adoption agency? A therapist? An abortion clinic?

That last thought caused my knees to shake, and I moved my head back and forth, hard. I'd already wrestled with this. Despite my beliefs, despite my upbringing, I couldn't deny that simply getting rid of the entire problem had tempted me. No one would have to know how far I'd fallen. I wouldn't have to disappoint my family. I could keep my heart whole and Finn in my life. I could go on to do those great things I'd always planned.

But in the end, none of that mattered. I hadn't entertained the thought for more than a minute. Quite simply, I wouldn't be able to live with such a decision.

Adoption, though...perhaps that would be my baby's best chance. Not once had Dad voiced regret over being given to a loving family as a babe. All had benefited. Perhaps this would be my own child's path.

I swallowed, refusing to ask the midwife to elaborate. I didn't want to know what she suggested, wasn't even sure I wanted to come back to this room ever again.

As I pulled my shirt over my stomach, I thought of the hard road ahead of me, of Mom's face, of Lizzie's, Bronson's, and Amie's disappointment when I finally revealed my secret. Aunt Pris would likely die of a coronary on the spot. And yet, as surprising as the news would be, I knew my family...they would stand by me despite myself. Maybe, despite my failures, there was still a chance to attain the dearest wish of my heart—to earn the praise of those I loved.

I'd talk to Maggie first. She knew me best. She knew my flaws, my passionate nature, my temper and bold blunders. She'd defied Aunt Pris's objections by marrying into an already-made family. I needed someone on my side and I couldn't think of anyone better.

I opened the door to the exam room and threw my shoulders back. I would face this. Take the bull by the horns and decide how this baby fit into my plans. Keep it and by some miracle become a mother, or give it away and bless another couple.

Either way, I would wrangle something good out of my mistake.

I pounded on the door of the downstairs bathroom, my bladder desperate for release. "Bronson, is that you in there? You better not be smelling it up, either. Come on, get a move on. I have to pee!"

Though I'd gone before my walk, I'd found myself racing home for the bathroom—just one of the changes taking over my body. Amie was in the upstairs shower. Chances of Aunt Pris offering a pre-dinner stand-up comedy act were better than getting into *that* bathroom.

I pounded again, desperate. "I swear, Bronson, if you're taking your pretty little time in there just to—"

The door opened. A head of white hair matching that of the fur in her arms caused me to step back. "Aunt Pris."

Cragen yapped, his fierce mouth quivering.

"Truly, girl. Must one yell about bodily functions loud enough for the neighbors to hear?"

This coming from the woman who brought her dog into the bathroom as religiously as one might use toilet paper. "Sorry, Aunt Pris." I rushed past so relieved I didn't even mind that Mom had invited her for dinner.

When I was finished, I went upstairs to change into jean shorts, noting their new tightness at my waist. The day hung warm, my room in the attic stuffy. I opened the window and slid the fan inside, turning it on high.

I glanced around the room, my simple twin bed pushed against one side, my tiny desk where hundreds of stories had been born on the other. So very small, but all mine. Mom had been my champion, knowing how I longed for my own space to simply be —at that time, to write.

"You truly are my little Jo," she'd said.

I looked in the full-length mirror, pulled my shirt tight around my waist. It wouldn't be long before all would know. Then any illusions about me being Mom's *little Jo* would be righted, for Jo March would have never allowed herself to fall into such an unfixable mess.

I turned from the mirror and left the room to go downstairs, but a box at the top of the railing, set apart slightly from others, caught my eye. It was labeled in black permanent marker. *B&B.*

Interest piqued, I dragged it into my room where the fan now blew cool. I shut the door, took scissors from my desk, and cut open the packing tape, while squelching a hint of guilt at how Mom had taped this box not expecting anyone to open it soon, if ever.

On the top lay a *Yankee Magazine*, a prominent article on the front featuring the Five Best Cozy B&B's in New England. Beneath that, a *Bed & Breakfast* magazine highlighting gourmet seafood breakfasts. Below that a stack of *Better Homes & Gardens* magazines. I took each one out, noted the dog-eared pages, the careful notes on the sides. Photos of gorgeous inns around the world, tasteful dining rooms, wide porches, beautiful gardens, and romantic rooms. Article upon article featuring the best places to stay in the country. Another dozen on how to start a bed and breakfast. One on the Royal Family opening an inn in Scotland.

Another featuring eleven Southern B&B's perfect for mother-daughter getaways.

I pulled the magazines out, knowing I should get downstairs to help with dinner, yet mesmerized by this private glimpse inside my mother's dreams. At the bottom lay a familiar white three-ring binder—Mom's scrapbook, the one I remembered from my childhood. It lay bare and unmarked on the front, almost as if she wasn't bold enough to title the dreams within. Or maybe, like me, my mother wanted to keep her secrets.

I opened it, a stale, musty smell meeting my nostrils. I inhaled the scent of old dreams tucked away and gazed at the collage of carefully arranged photos. Sweeping gardens and verandas. Large windows with oceanfront views. Breakfasts fit for a queen. The following pages each featured different rooms. The first was titled the Alcott room. No surprise there. Pictures of Louisa and her siblings, original artwork of *Little Women*, a photograph of the Alcott Orchard House and of Louisa's half-moon desk where she'd written her famous book.

The next room was the Dickinson room, containing Emily's poems and photos of the poet's bedroom. Then the Frost room, the Emerson room, the Thoreau room, the Hawthorne room. Each with just as much detail, just as much passion as the one before.

The sound of steps echoed on the stairs and I shoved the binder beneath my bed, worked to pile the magazines back in the box. Silly. It wasn't as if I were snooping. Not really. The box was there for anyone to see. Though breaking the packing tape *had* been a bit presumptuous.

"Josie! Dinnertime!"

The deep baritone outside my door caught me further off-guard, plucking at the high and low strings of my heart even as relief caused my body to relax. Not Mom but rather the person who, up until last summer, I'd told *most* of my secrets.

"Come in!" I'd not thought Tripp's presence in my room would be anything but normal. But when he opened the door and stood there, part GQ magazine, part sexy construction worker, my stomach did a flip. I couldn't make the mistake of pretending things could ever go back to the way they were between us. Tripp had ensured that last summer. And I'd ensured it by the mess I'd gotten myself into with Finn Becker.

⚜

"YOUR MOM ASKED ME TO GET YOU. I DON'T KNOW WHAT'S she's cooked, but it sure smells good." Tripp tried not to let the sight of Josie sitting cross-legged on her area rug get to him. How many times had he barreled up here, caught her munching on an apple while tapping a pen against a notebook, staring out the window at a world she would never fully share with him?

He looked around, tried to distract himself. "You want an AC unit up here? I have a couple lying around the shop."

She shook her head. "No thanks."

No surprise there. She always did like her open windows, no matter how hot it got. "Suit yourself."

She stood, tugged at the bottom of her shirt. "Let's go. I'm famished."

Tripp turned, but not before catching the box of magazines. "Josie Martin, is this *graphic* literature you're hiding in your room?"

She rolled her eyes. "It's not porn, Captain Underpants."

"But it's not exactly F. Scott Fitzgerald or Steinbeck, is it?" The corner of his mouth twitched as he stooped and grabbed up a copy of *Bed and Breakfast* magazine, flipping through the pages.

She grabbed it from his hands. "They're Mom's. She packed them away and I was just having a last look."

"Ah, her old dream, right? A bed and breakfast. I'd almost forgotten."

"I think we all had." Josie placed the magazine he'd held onto the top of the pile and closed the box, folding one edge under the other in a clockwise manner. "This was her dream, Tripp. To run an inn. But now...a bookshop. She's settling."

She met his gaze and a bubble formed in his throat. As close as they were, he felt light years away from her. He wanted to reach out a hand, smooth a finger down her round cheek, but knew such an action would cost him dearly. He should be grateful Josie even spoke to him. He refused to ruin that.

She bit her lip, stared at the box on the ground. "Do you think that's bad? The settling, I mean."

He ordered his feet still so he wouldn't take that one step forward to close the gap. "What do you think, Josie-girl?"

"I think she should go after her dream. She's not under any grand illusions about the hard work of running a B&B. She worked as a chambermaid and assistant chef at Bar Harbor Inn for seven years before she met Dad. She's got a gift for hospitality."

"What's stopping her, then?"

She shook her head, flashed him a mischievous grin. "So how about those Red Sox?"

He put a hand on her bare arm. "Oh no you don't. What's stopping her?"

"Forget it, Tripp. It's not your problem. We better get downstairs."

By her avoidance, he could surmise that the thing stopping Hannah Martin was of the monetary kind. Josie always clammed up when it came to her family's financial burdens—likely because she knew he'd offer help, something all of the Martins doggedly refused.

He let it go.

"You up for a walk after dinner?" He turned toward the door, tried to keep his tone casual.

"I don't know ..."

"Please, Josie. I'll behave myself, I promise."

She breathed deep and let it out. She looked strained. Beat. As if the world had done her in. He remembered her trip to the doctor's and a short burst of fear jabbed his insides. "Hey, is everything okay?"

"Yeah, of course." But her answer was too quick.

"August saw you at the doctor's." He felt the tips of his ears redden. "He was driving by."

She groaned. "You're all too nosy for your own good. One thing I'll miss about the city this summer is no one cares about anyone else's business."

He let the comment roll off him, pretending it didn't hurt. "So...you good?"

"It was just a checkup, Colton. Ever hear of those?"

He released a breath, long and slow. "Good. So what do you say? Walk after dinner, then?"

"Only if Amie breaks out Pictionary."

He chuckled as he followed her downstairs. If Josie disliked graphic novels, she *loathed* graphic games. Lucky for him, Amie could always be counted on to break out Pictionary.

❧

I INHALED THE COMFORTING SCENTS OF SAUSAGE AND TOMATO sauce, yeasty homemade garlic bread, and Mom's honey-mustard salad dressing. All my favorites.

Davey and Isaac crawled to their places on all fours under the table, Josh directing them not to bump their heads or take the tablecloth with them and Maggie pulling out their chairs.

"Coming through!" Amie yelled, a nine-by-thirteen pan of lasagna cradled in her potholder-clad hands. Lizzie followed with salad.

"Watch it!" Bronson balanced three baskets of garlic bread, nearly tripped over Cragen's pudgy body on his way to the table. Aunt Pris gathered the furry fellow to her, but the stooping caused her curled gray head to tickle Davey's face. He squeezed himself against the wall and scrunched up his nose. I hid a giggle. Mom set another lasagna down, then scurried to light the candles on the table, set against a magnificent display of heliotrope and tea roses.

It truly was a beautiful sight. Each setting with a woven placement, wineglasses filled with sparkling cider, and enough utensils to supply an army. Mom always said the beauty of a table was worth the dishwashing at the end. Tonight, with the table edged on every side with a face I loved, I had to agree.

Bronson sat in Dad's old chair, and my heart ached anew as I remembered Dad's jolly laughter, his boisterous call to sit down quick so we could give thanks to the Lord before the food ran away with itself.

Voices hummed, and I took it all in, memorizing the features of those around the table. I caught Maggie's gaze and she waved from her spot at the end of the table, her other hand in Josh's, one twin on either side of them. Aunt Pris sat beside Mom, and Tripp took his customary place beside me. I didn't begrudge his presence. All of us here, as it was so often growing up...it just seemed right.

"I might need to add another table at this rate," Mom said, her eyes light and happy. "Although we might reach the bathroom if I do that." She turned to Bronson. "Would you mind saying grace, honey?"

We bowed our heads, and when Tripp reached for my hand, I allowed it, even as I tried to focus on Bronson's words instead of comparing the hard calluses of Tripp's hands to that of Finn's soft ones.

When my brother finished, glasses clinked, voices mixed. From down the table, Davey protested a piece of onion on his plate. Amie told Lizzie about the prom dress she'd just bought, and how she planned to wear flip-flops instead of high-heeled shoes that night.

"Aren't you hungry?" Mom peered around Aunt Pris to speak to me.

I looked at my plate, where globs of ricotta with parsley lay alongside the feta cheese I'd taken out of my salad. I'd read an article in a pregnancy magazine at the doctor's about the potentially harmful effects of soft cheeses. There was so much I didn't know. How would I get through it all?

"Just taking it all in." I shoveled in a bite of pasta. "It's good to be home."

Mom smiled. "It's good for you to *be* home. How'd your finals go?"

"I'll find out Monday. Hopefully well." Certainly not the best I'd ever taken, but my grades had remained high throughout the semester. I trusted they'd float me through any low marks.

"And what are your plans after you obtain this mighty degree?" Aunt Pris asked.

"I plan to practice under an established therapist. Learn the ropes, gain experience. I might work toward my PhD in time. My undergrad degree in philosophy could open up some doors as well." Even as the words left my mouth, I wondered how I could accomplish all these things with a baby. Would I keep my child? If so, would he or she live in daycare? How would I afford that?

"So you'll be dealing with nutcases all day, is that it?" Aunt Pris lifted her cider to her mouth, leaving smudges of lipstick on the rim.

From my side, Tripp elbowed me lightly, as if to say he understood my thoughts and yes, best to keep them in my head.

I felt a furry body brush my ankles, and I grit back a comeback, reminding myself that this woman made it possible for me to attend NYU. No matter that she nearly ruined my life a couple years before that with her meddling. Nearly ruined my chances for college by allowing mindless gossip to run rampant through the town at the hands of her quilting club. How Aunt Priscilla had thought questioning my virtue in public after a simple, completely explainable incident was blown out of proportion was beyond me. It'd been nearly impossible to obtain a good recommendation after the gossip club was done with me. Thank God for Dad stepping in to save the day.

I pushed aside a flash of grief at the thought of my father and sucked in a steadying breath. "Most of what I want to deal with is just everyday people like you and me wading through problems. Relationship issues, marital problems, things in their childhood they never worked past."

Oh, this was rich. Who was I fooling that *I* could help anyone?

I was about to excuse myself when Tripp, God bless his intuitive soul, broke in. "I saw my buddy over at your place on my way to work this morning, Aunt Pris. Gary Shube. Excellent realtor, let me tell you. You're not thinking of selling the place, are you?"

Only Tripp could turn the conversation in such an innocently winsome way. I eyed him, wondering if his comment was truly as inoffensive as it appeared.

"What I do with my property is my business, young man." She wiped her mouth with her napkin, placed it carefully on the side of her plate, a trail of lipstick peeking at the edges. "Really, you might think your grandfather would have taught you some manners."

"Aww, give a fellow some slack, Aunt Pris. I was just happy to see that two of my favorite people knew one another."

Aunt Pris's face reddened. "Now you're mocking me."

Tripp held up his right hand, fingers crossed. "Scout's honor. This table would be quite a bore without you here, and that's the truth. Isn't that right, Josie?"

"That's right." A snarl started at my feet. "Though I could do without your little sidekick," I muttered so only Tripp could hear.

Aunt Pris straightened. "If you must know, I'm selling off the orchard. I can't look at that land another year. It's overgrown, a breeding ground for who knows what type of insects. It's a shame

I've kept it this long. I'm getting on in years and could use more assistance around the house. Selling the orchard is a perfect way to gain some cash."

"Oh, Aunt Pris...the orchard. That was such a big part of your childhood, wasn't it?" Mom placed her fork down.

Aunt Pris pushed around a spinach leaf in her salad, an uncharacteristic action without purpose. "I suppose it was, yes. But its purpose is no longer. I'd rather it be put to good use."

"Are you selling the barn as well?" Tripp asked. The barn had been used for washing and packaging the apples back when Aunt Pris was a girl.

She shook her head. "No, that belongs with the house. They can build a separate barn on the orchard property if they want to."

"Will the person who buys it run the orchard?" Lizzie shifted in her seat, concern on her face.

"They could, but I suppose that's up to them." Aunt Pris gave up on the spinach leaf and put her fork down. Her voice had lost its usual spunk, and a pull of pity started in my belly.

Tripp reached for the spatula to dish up another piece of lasagna. I'd forgotten how that boy could eat. "Unless someone's actively looking for an apple orchard, chances are a developer will buy it. That's enough land for at least eight house lots. Prime historic Camden land. Make sure you're asking enough for it, Aunt Pris. Grandpops could talk it over with you if you'd like."

"Thank you, young man. I might just take you up on that offer." She turned to me. "I knew I always liked that boy. Why'd you say no to his proposal again?"

I stood, smacking my knee into the table leg, but my pain was likely unnoticeable beneath my embarrassment. "It's time for Pictionary, isn't it?"

❧ 6 ❧

"Aunt Pris hasn't lost any of her pluck, has she?" Tripp turned right on Bay View Street, and I followed. We'd end up at Curtis Island Overlook as we had a million times before. Though we hadn't been there since *that* day. I wondered how it'd feel to be back there with him.

We'd played one round of Pictionary—me partnering with Davey and trying to make out his crude scribbles of Mr. Potato Head and a pirate. We'd lost, and though I'd been hesitant to take Tripp up on his offer of a walk, especially after Aunt Pris's comment, I found that some quiet was preferable to another round of picture-game torture.

"She certainly hasn't." I opened my mouth to apologize for my aunt's last comment, but then snapped it shut. Best to move on. "I'd forgotten how loud family gatherings can be. It's wonderful, but I guess I've gotten used to the quiet."

"You always did like your alone time."

I smiled. Maybe Aunt Pris was right. Maybe I'd been crazy to turn down Tripp's proposal. No one knew me better, understood me more. Although who I was now was a far cry from who I'd been last summer.

I crossed my arms over my chest. "I can't believe Aunt Pris is really selling the orchard. That seems drastic for her."

The road simmered from the business of the day, no cars in sight, just the gentle sound of a seagull in the distance.

"It does." He kicked a pebble off the road as we crossed. "I suppose I shouldn't have said anything, but I thought your mother had a right to know. You're all Aunt Pris's only family, right?"

I nodded as we entered the path. Less than a half mile from my home, the Overlook was an out-of-the-way nook in the woods off Bay View Street, and it offered the best view of the island and its picture-perfect Maine lighthouse. "Dad didn't even know of Aunt Pris until after his adoptive parents died. He was in his thirties by then. I guess Aunt Pris didn't feel led to take him in after her sister died, and she never had any children of her own—I would have pitied the poor dears if she had." I shrugged. "Or maybe it would have softened her up some."

"She has a heart under all that Yankee puff and independence. You don't make it easy for her."

"*I* don't make it easy for her? Have you forgotten the mess she got me into just a few years ago?"

Tripp's brow furrowed. "Believe me when I tell you I'll never forget. And it was wrong, of course. But I think we're doing more harm than good by not letting it go."

We. As if Aunt Pris had wronged Tripp as much as she had me. I dragged in a cleansing breath, the pain of the town gossip still fresh in some ways. Never in all my life, when I fell asleep in the school library with Alan Ash by my side while finishing up a special edition of the school newspaper, could I have predicted the far-reaching effects. While Alan bragged of the night and did nothing to quell the school gossip, neither did my great-aunt and her quilting club.

Aunt Pris, ever the genteel lady of impeccable upbringing, found herself mortified to have her niece in such a predicament.

She, of course, took the only path available to her: all but disown me and my "wild" ways to her quilting club friends, who happened to include a committee member for a memorial scholarship for which I had applied. I'd been a shoe-in for that scholarship.

But I hadn't received it, and by the time Dad had marched into a quilting club meeting and defended my honor, setting Aunt Pris and her club members straight on the surety of my virtues, it had been too late.

I may not have received the scholarship anyway. But in my mind, it was one step back. No New York college, but rather a local community college for at least four years.

When Aunt Pris offered to foot the bill for NYU and graduate school years later, I couldn't help but be grateful. I tried hard not to harbor a grudge over our past differences. Tried hard not to let it bother me how she had been so quick to believe town gossip over her niece. I tried. But I didn't always succeed.

Now, I spoke carefully to Tripp. "I feel I have forgiven her. Forgetting is another matter." And yet what did it matter? In some ways, I had now proven such gossip true. And my virtues? They were no longer worth defending.

I bit my lip, hating what would come out of my mouth next but knowing it was the honest truth. "I think me and Aunt Pris might be more alike than I want to admit." I could be crusty and hard-edged too. Set in my ways, determined to succeed and be right. But did I want to cling to those values so much that I grew old and alone, without allowing people to get too close?

Not for the first time, I wondered about my grandmother, Aunt Pris's sister. Did I share any qualities with her? The only person alive who would be able to tell me was my great-aunt, and I'd never known her to speak of anything having to do with Dad's mom, Hazel.

We reached the end of the path, and Tripp sat on the bench. A light haze hung over the lighthouse and the island, but the salty scent of the sea soothed the edges of my ruffled feathers. I used to start my morning runs here. I'd sit down on the dirt, the earthy scent mixed with the briny smell of the sea, and stretch my limbs. My head would clear, my simple plans for the day would come together.

I'd been so anxious to escape to better things back then—the hustle and grind and excitement of the big city, the race to grab hold of a respectable career, to change the world, and maybe make some money in the process. To solve the human mind, as if it were a clever riddle or a two-thousand-piece jigsaw puzzle. And yes, to put all those letters after my name.

"Maybe just try with her a little more, you know? Show her some grace and maybe she'll give you some in return."

I didn't like his self-righteous tone, but preferred not to tackle it head on. I swept my hand regally toward him. "Whatever you say, oh wise and wonderful Captain of Underpants."

I half expected him to grab my wrist, pull me on his lap, and tickle my ribs. But that was something he used to do, a carefree act from our carefree days. Instead, he just stared at me, growing serious.

I didn't like it. Much safer to interact with jokes and banter.

"Okay, I'll try. I promise." I stepped away, tucked my arms around myself, and looked out toward Curtis Island, the lighthouse white and picturesque at the point of the island, the keeper's house beside it. Tripp and I had kayaked around Curtis Island countless times as teens. I could still remember him playing chicken with the schooners, making the boaters raise their fists while we rowed madly out of danger, him laughing and me screeching the entire time. "You think she doesn't want to sell the orchard? I don't really see how we can help. Unless..." Slow as clumpy porridge, an idea began to form. Us helping Aunt Pris. Her helping us. But no, it was crazy. She'd never agree. Mom would never agree. "What if...?"

I sat beside Tripp on the bench, my thoughts racing, trying to keep up with the implications of such a hare-brained scheme.

"What if *what*?" Tripp slid farther over on the bench as if too scared to get close, too scared he'd frighten me away.

I shook my head. "Never mind. It's ridiculous. Too much good food and Pictionary."

"Tell me, Josie." He now moved closer, not showing any hesitation as he had a moment earlier. It wouldn't have been the first time I read him wrong.

He pulled my hand onto his lap and it felt so natural, so good and right. It was big and warm and strong and capable, and if I wasn't careful I could fall right into its pull, let it lead my heart to places it didn't belong—places I knew, from experience, only caused pain. Even if I'd never truly been in love with Finn, he'd left a gaping hole within me. It wouldn't be fair to allow Tripp to fill it now, when it was convenient.

I slid my hand from his. "It's probably the craziest idea I've ever come up with."

"Crazier than hanging two-thousand candy canes in one night?"

I smiled at his reference to our all-night Christmas Eve endeavor the summer of my junior year. I'd wanted to give a little magic to the town children, so I'd bulk ordered the special treats online and we'd sneaked around frost-covered yards to hang candy canes on trees and fence posts and porch rails of as many homes of young children in Camden as we could. Tripp had been a trooper that night. Though the idea was mine, I'd become tired and cranky sooner than I'd anticipated. As always, he'd been the one to push us through.

I'd always been one for brilliant, heartfelt ideas. The passion to see them through was sometimes the problem.

Was this idea brewing in my head just another thing I'd grow cold on? I looked at the man beside me, noticed how his shoulders and arms looked broader than they had at Christmas. He'd been working out, and he looked good. Did he go on many dates? Was he seeing someone special?

The thought threw a wrench of unwanted jealousy into my stomach. I was horrid. I turned down Tripp's offer of marriage, but still wanted him to pine away for me forever. How absurd.

"Come on, Josie. You have to tell me now."

Tripp at least would be truthful. He'd tell me if my idea had any merit.

"What if we—my family—moved in with Aunt Pris?"

Tripp blinked. "Did I miss the invitation?"

I stood, shook my head. "It's crazy, forget I said anything."

He caught my hand, pulled me back down on the bench. "No, I want to hear it. Your crazy ideas are sometimes your best."

I dragged in a deep breath, sat straighter to summon the courage to spill my thoughts. The faint scent of honeysuckle teased my nostrils, propelling me forward. "What if I asked Aunt Pris if we could turn that gorgeous home of hers into a bed and breakfast?"

He didn't speak, and I thought to cast the idea aside, but something within me grabbed onto the notion all the more now that I'd spoken it aloud. "We could move in, help her with the day-to-day things she wanted to hire someone for. She wouldn't have to sell her orchard. Mom would get her B&B."

Tripp shook his head, and my heart deflated. Of course it was stupid. As usual, I had gotten lost in the moment, carried away with myself.

"Living under one roof with the old girl? I don't know, Josie. I'm not sure either Aunt Pris or your Mom would agree. And what about the house? *Your house.* Can you picture your Mom just up and leaving it after all those years there with your Dad?"

"Mom already asked Aunt Pris to live with us once after she fell a couple winters ago, remember? So although it'd be hard, Mom's open to helping her out. And she has already talked about selling the house with Maggie when they were trying to brainstorm how to make a B&B feasible. If Mom sold the house, she'd have plenty of startup money."

"Aunt Pris's place would make a great inn." Tripp spoke with a slow pause between each of his words. "But it would need a lot of work, some updating. Individual bathrooms to the upstairs rooms, a remodeled kitchen...I suppose those would be the major things. But what about her bookshop? Your mom seemed excited."

"That was Dad's dream, not hers. And though its sweet of her to honor his memory, I think it's time for her to do what's on her heart. She's always telling us God gives us gifts and dreams for a reason. Why is it right for her to ignore hers?"

Tripp nodded, stared at the ground at our feet. I could practically see his thoughts racing, maybe faster than mine. "Maybe it doesn't have to be either or."

"A B&B *and* a bookshop? Now you're making me tired."

"A bookshop as *part* of the B&B. A gift shop kind of thing."

I gripped his forearm. "Tripp Colton, you're brilliant. Mom always wanted a book-inspired bed and breakfast, so a bookshop makes sense."

I could feel myself flying away with the idea, but didn't want to bother reining myself in. "I could help her with it, of course. I know what kind of books people like, what they're more likely to buy on vacation. She had these amazing ideas for rooms in that scrapbook of hers. We could even have small sections in the bookshop that corresponded with each guest room. Maybe recipe books, too. Mom has some great ones. I could help her put together—"

"Whoa, whoa, whoa. Not that I'm not loving the idea of you hanging around to put all this together, but don't you have a degree to earn? A life, you know, in New York?"

Something in me deflated. A life. Right. A degree. Plans to succeed, to make a difference.

But Tripp didn't know my secret. The tiny baby growing in my belly changed everything. Did I really plan to go back to school in September only to have a baby in October? And yet if I decided to give the child over for adoption, the time out of school could be minimal. But was that what I wanted to do?

I groaned, rubbed a hand over my face. "The idea doesn't hinge on my presence. Mom could do this. She could."

"There's a lot the idea hinges on. It's a good one, Josie, it is. And your heart is good for it, but what if your mom isn't comfortable with it? What if Aunt Pris doesn't want her home turned into a B&B? What if she doesn't want people coming and going as they please on her property? That's a big change for a stubborn woman."

"You're right. That's a huge ask, especially for her."

"You have an enormous heart. Nothing wrong with that." He caught my gaze and my heart tripped over itself. I felt his unasked question, and it speared something deep within me.

Why wasn't it big enough for me?

For so long, I couldn't think of Tripp as more than my best friend. But this time apart, my time with Finn even, had me reevaluating every decision from last summer onward. I'd been so sure I didn't need a man or marriage until after I established a steady career. And I was right, wasn't I? I didn't need a man. Especially one that turned out like Finn Becker. There were lots of brave, smart, single mothers out there, and if I didn't give my baby away, that's what I would be. Brave. Smart. Alone.

It was okay.

I watched a sailboat make its way lazily around Curtis Island, the white of its mast caught in the haze of the sea. "I need to talk with Aunt Pris before I do anything else. Or maybe Mom, just to make sure this is still something she wants—that she would be open to running it on Aunt Pris's property."

"I agree."

I turned to him. "Will you come with me? When I talk to Aunt Pris?"

"Josie, I don't—"

"She likes you. She'll respect what you say."

"Enough to turn her house over to your mother and all your siblings, to allow contractors to reinvent her home?"

"So you don't think I should even ask her?"

He pressed his lips together, making the creases on his cheeks deepen. "I didn't say that. I think she's a lonely lady, maybe a lady with some regrets. And there's no denying she holds a soft spot in that cranky heart for you and your siblings, even if she has a funny way of showing it sometimes. Who knows, she just might surprise you by agreeing to this. She's probably already willed the estate to your family. Maybe she'll want to be a part of this next chapter before she's gone."

"See, Tripp? This is why I need you to come with me. You'll help her see reason. You have a way with words when you want to."

He raised an eyebrow at me. "Despite my choice in literature, you mean?"

I grinned. "That's right, Captain."

"Fine," he ground out. "I'll go."

I placed a hand on his arm. "Thank you."

His gaze dropped to my hand, and I stared at my fingers on his bare arm a moment. "I've missed you, Josie. I've missed *this*. Us."

"Me too," I whispered.

I took my hand from his arm, and we sat in silence for a few moments before I couldn't stand the wall between us anymore. "Why'd you do it, Tripp? Why'd you have to go and ask me to marry you like that? Out of the blue, practically?"

He spread his legs out, leaned his elbows on his thighs, hands folded in front of him. "Remember when I kissed you that day?"

My face heated at the memory. It'd been a month after Dad's funeral. I'd gone for a long run and ended up here, on this very bench, to have a good cry. Tripp found me, simply sat on the bench and put an arm around me, allowed his shirt to dry my tears.

It was the first time anyone had seen me cry over Dad, and it felt good to release it all, felt good to feel my best friend's strong arms around me. I'd smelled of sweat and salt from my run, but Tripp didn't seem to care. He let me wipe my tears on his button-down, collared shirt. Then, he'd kissed me. And I let him. And while it was as wonderful as it was weird, when we'd parted I'd told him to never do that again.

"Yes, of course," I said now, my face heating at the memory.

"You didn't understand what that kiss meant for me. You didn't take it seriously."

I swallowed. "I was hurting. You were comforting. We got carried away in the moment."

"It was more than that for me. I wanted you to know I wasn't going anywhere. I wanted you to know how serious I was about loving you for the rest of my life."

"Tripp, stop. Please."

"You asked." He leaned back against the hard bench. "I know you, Josie. You were going to brush that kiss off, but I couldn't. I knew you'd be gone to graduate school for months at a time. I knew you were grieving your Dad hard, then Maggie getting married. I knew you were restless, anxious to escape. I was scared you'd do something you'd regret. I was scared to lose you. So I threw it all on the table and asked you to marry me. It wasn't a surprise, not to me. We had to have it out, one way or the other. I've always loved you, Josie Martin."

My bottom lip trembled. "But you ruined us. I lost my father and Maggie *and* you all in one summer." And I did go off to New York, did things I regretted. I closed my eyes in defeat.

"There was no part of you that could ever love me?"

His innocent question threatened to break me in two. "I do love you. You're my best friend."

He shook his head, hard. "No, that's not what I mean, and you know it. I mean like a woman loves a man, Josie. Could you ever love me like that?"

"I can't believe we're back to this again."

He stood, flung up a hand in frustration. "Did we ever get past it? You just left, wouldn't return my texts or calls."

"I'm sorry," I whispered. "I didn't know what to say to you. Tripp, it wasn't you. It was the idea of marriage in general. I had too many plans, too many great things to accomplish first." Even as I spoke the words, I felt their untruths. For when I'd come to Finn, told him about his unborn child, I'd vowed to make things right. To accept a proposal of marriage even, if it came. I thought a baby would change Finn's views, that he'd eventually see reason and put things straight.

But he never had.

"I'm not the same person I was last summer." I lifted my head. "But I don't want to lose your friendship. I never wanted to lose your friendship."

He hung his head for a moment, then lifted it to give me a sad grin. "As painful as it is, I'd rather have you my friend than not at all." He held his hand out to me, and I took it so he could help me stand.

"Thank you." I squeezed his hand. "Because I've missed you."

He smiled but it didn't quite meet his eyes.

I wiggled his fingers. "Who else but me can pick on your terrible choices in literature?"

He shook his head. "Touché." We started back down the path toward the street. "So when do you want to go talk to your aunt?"

"I have to talk to Mom first. Tonight maybe. Can I let you know how it goes?"

"Sure."

"Thanks, Tripp."

I stepped over a root, following Tripp's boat shoes through the path, grateful for his company, grateful for his presence in my life.

Even if I wanted our relationship to go in a romantic direction, even if he didn't totally hate me for sleeping with another man and having his baby—which I was quite sure he would—I'd forever be questioning my motives. Tripp was the safe choice, the secure choice—a man too good to be a last resort. And I was too wretched a person to think, or hope, that he would ever give me a second chance after finding out the truth.

Whether or not I should have agreed to his proposal last summer was neither here nor there. None of it mattered any longer. Tripp deserved so much better.

So much more than Josie Martin had to offer.

7

Professor Finn Becker was a logical man. And tears were just not logical.

At least not now, as he lay in his king-size bed alongside a beautiful young blonde. Emily. Apparently she wasn't the answer to stopping the tears that made a nightly appearance in the middle of his dreams.

He pushed the bed sheets off his legs, their weight suddenly unbearable. He sat up, listened to Emily's deep breaths. They'd drank enough wine before—and during—their arduous physical activities to ensure they'd both sleep well.

At least that's what Finn had thought.

He stood, tugged on a pair of gym shorts. This wasn't him. Sleeping with students. This wasn't what he'd set out to do, who he'd set out to become. And the tears? Those *definitely* weren't him.

He exited his bedroom, closing the door softly so Emily would sleep. In the kitchen, he pushed the button on his Keurig. Might as well get something accomplished while he was awake.

He opened his laptop and sat at his office chair. A pile of

papers from his summer class needed grading—far better use of his time than weeping like a little girl in his bed.

He ran a hand over his face, the week-old growth unfamiliar. He'd thought he needed a change. A little less clean-cut college professor and a little more cutting-edge adventurer.

Without warning, an image of Josie popped into his head. She had a habit of running the back of her fingers along his smooth face, and for just a split second, he missed her with a tenacity that pulled at his gut. In some mysterious way, he knew she was connected to the middle-of-the-night tears that had begun waking him almost a month earlier.

A gorgeous distraction like Emily should have been enough to kick such wayward emotions to the curb. But apparently his psyche was more bothered by how he'd left things with Josie than he'd realized.

And then there was the voice. Saints alive, he was actually starting to *hear* voices. Him, the psychology professor. He was cracking up.

To be fair, it wasn't a voice out of nowhere. As familiar as it was unwelcoming, they were words he'd memorized as a child but had long since set aside.

Even if you should suffer for what is right, you are blessed.
Perfect love drives out fear...

No use pushing it aside any longer—the problem was his conscience. He felt guilty for abandoning Josie. Amos's daughter. No doubt, his inner self was taking on Amos's own convictions and faith, drawing on the faith Finn himself had been raised in, in order to make him feel guilt. Truly, the human mind was so intricate, it would go to great lengths to fool him, going so far as to use words from an ancient book he himself had deemed unreliable. An ancient book fraught with racism and sexism—a cause for division instead of unity. Religion was, as Freud himself put it, an attempt to control the uncontrollable world in which one was placed by means of make-believe ideals. But it would always fail, because the Bible hung on a culture of a different time. It didn't take into account the progression of humanity.

What then was this feeling within him? If at the root of the human psyche was self-preservation and self-interest, how would feeling guilty about Josie help him?

The Keurig fizzed and sputtered, and he went back to the kitchen, replacing the scent of guilt with that of strong coffee. Josie was a grown woman, an adult. They'd been responsible in using protection. She was the one who insisted she didn't want an abortion. What choice did she leave him? In all his thirty-nine years, his plans had never included being a father. Never had he wanted to be tied down that much. All Josie had to do was make an appointment. He would have gone with her, held her hand. Then it would have been over, done with, and they could have gone on with their lives.

It wasn't like he didn't care for her. She was a breath of fresh air, the most fascinating, intelligent woman he'd ever known. When he'd first met her, sitting down to Thanksgiving at the Martin's table, she was just a topsy-turvy teenager with a whirlwind of ideas and theories. Then a few years later, in his freshman Intro to Psych class, he'd been drawn to her. But it wasn't until he read her paper on how cultural norms influence social cognition that his intrigue grew into something more. He'd known she was brilliant—being Amos's daughter, how could she not be? But the brave honesty and clarity of her words... Well, he rarely saw such skill even at the graduate level.

That had been back at the community college in Maine. Before he was offered a tenure-track position in the Psychology Department at NYU. He'd accepted without looking back, and certainly hadn't given Josie Martin another thought.

Until she showed up in one of his graduate classes in New York five years later. More beautiful, and if possible, more brilliant than the last time he saw her. Only she was grieving Amos's death hard, and though he'd lost touch with his older friend the last several years, he thought it only honorable to fill in gaps where he could.

Honorable. Yeah.

And who was he kidding about having a friendship with Amos? They were more debate partners than friends. At his lowest of times, Finn admitted how Amos probably saw him—not as a friend, but as a charity case.

Still, he couldn't shake his admiration for the man. So incredibly open, so incredibly smart, Amos held a certain genuine pull that everyone longed to be around. Including Finn.

He groaned. What would Amos say about the mess he'd gotten his daughter into?

Finn honestly hadn't expected the fast fall. Josie was not who he pictured himself with, not like his cast of previous girlfriends. She had depth. Heart, spirit. And she wasn't easily swayed in seeing his view of things.

She didn't drink and party to excess, didn't stand for flighty, attention-grabbing friends. She'd choose time with a book over time at a bar or frat party any day. She was a virgin and they'd taken things slow. He genuinely cared for her, was beyond patient. In truth, he would have waited a lot longer than she'd made him.

Finn took a long swig of his coffee, the burn in his throat satisfying. Maybe that's what bothered him. Maybe deep down some of those childhood convictions still leeched the life out of him. Though twenty-three and intelligent, Josie had been endearingly innocent as well. She'd trusted him, looked up to him not only as a teacher, but as her father's colleague. And he'd used both positions to their full advantage to get what he wanted.

Not knowingly, of course. He did care for her. Loved her even. In truth, he still did.

He sat in his chair again, gazing at the lights of the Manhattan skyline twinkling so bright they obliterated the stars. The gentle fan of the AC came through the vents, cooling the apartment. He picked up his phone, hit the message icon, and pulled up Josie's name.

Just wanted to check in and see how you're doing, he typed. His thumb hovered over the send arrow, but before he worked up the courage, he threw the phone down in disgust. What was he thinking? Texting Josie while another woman lay in his bed? And what was he thinking reaching out to her anyway? He was free.

He'd made it quite clear he wanted no part in raising a baby. No child support. No visitation. Not that he expected her to ask. So why would he give her ideas through one simple text?

He looked at his laptop's screensaver—an image of him skydiving the summer before in New Zealand. He closed his eyes and relived the intense rush of it all. The wind blasting his face, yet hovering like a pillow below him. The feeling of soaring, conquering the world. The sudden, satisfying snap of the chute and gentle float to the ground.

And then wanting to do it all over again.

Two years ago, he'd joined the United States Parachute Association, intending to become an instructor during his summers off. It was a worthy thing to do—help people conquer their fears, experience the world, test their limits. He'd logged one-hundred of the five-hundred required jumps last summer, and then he'd returned to school and met Josie. He'd spent his spring break with her, forgetting his desire to become an instructor—or even to jump again.

He'd lost some of himself to Josie. It was good they'd broken it off, after all. Maybe his conscious was simply crying out for a little pampering. A little time to do what *he* wanted to do, to remember who he was without emotional encumbrances.

He picked up the phone again, erased his message to Josie, and typed Sven's name. Sven, a buddy and skydiving instructor who'd convinced Finn to jump in the first place.

Summer's young and I'm looking to log some jumps. What's your schedule look like?

He sent the text, put the phone down, and opened up his email to download his students' papers. Taking action. That's what he needed. Remembering what it meant to be Finn Becker. While Josie'd been a fun temporary distraction, she'd only left him a weaker, unfulfilled person. Better off to sever the ties sharp and quick. No contact.

With the help of a new goal and a few dozen jumps, by the end of the summer Josie Martin would be nothing but a faint memory.

8

The clink of dishes and swish of water mixed with Mom's quiet humming ushered me into our home. A single light over the kitchen shone down on my mother, hands deep in the sink.

"Everyone bail for cleanup?" I scooped up a dishtowel and picked up a salad bowl from the drying rack. The dishwasher ran beside us, no doubt already full with the first round of dishes from our dinner.

A wistful smile passed over Mom's face. "I don't mind. I'm just grateful to have had you all here tonight."

I wiped the inside of the bowl, careful to get every last water droplet. "It is nice to be home. I appreciate it more this year than usual."

"Is that so?"

"Yeah," I whispered. I placed the bowl down and propped a hip against the counter, turning to my Mom. "I have kind of a crazy idea I want to run by you."

"That mind never stops working, does it? So like your father."

"You miss him, don't you?"

She swallowed, placed a plate on the drying rack. "Of course I do."

"Mom, what if I told you I thought you shouldn't open a bookshop?"

She turned from the dishes, her mouth parted. "What?"

"I think you should open your bed and breakfast instead."

Her forehead softened. "Oh, honey. I'm afraid that ship has sailed."

"But it's what you've wanted. And Maggie told me you guys were trying to figure out how to make it work."

"And we came up with nothing. I'm ready to turn to a new dream." But her tone lacked surety.

"I thought of an idea you and Maggie may have overlooked."

"Is that so? I'm all ears, then."

"What if we used the Orchard House for your bed and breakfast?"

She laughed. "Aunt Pris's home? This may be your wildest idea yet, my girl."

"No, I'm serious. She said she's having trouble keeping up with the home. What if we moved in with her and ran a joint business?"

"We, huh?"

My face heated. "It wouldn't hurt to ask, would it? If you could part with this house, that is."

"It's not a matter of parting with this house, it's logistics. Not to mention one of those logistics being your aunt."

"But if she agreed, what would you say?"

Her gaze caught mine, and she shook her head. "If Aunt Pris agreed to such a venture, of course I'd consider it. But my dear girl, she'd never agree. She likes her independence too much. She probably likes her home even more."

"But if she agreed, you'd consider it?"

She closed her eyes.

"Mom, I know you're settling with the bookshop. You should have your dream. I want to help you get it."

The edges of her lashes shimmered. "You have such a sweet heart, Josie, and I appreciate your intentions. I really do. But Aunt Pris would never agree and I fear it's presumptuous to ask."

"But if she did go for it, would you be willing to move in with her and make it work?"

"That's a lot to consider—Bronson, Lizzie, Amie...I'd be asking a lot of them to leave this house."

I laid my hand on her arm. "What about you, Mom? I'm not asking about anyone else. They're not going to live here forever. This is about you. Would *you* be willing to move in with her and sell this house?"

She inhaled a quivering breath. "I suppose if the opportunity arose...if I had a chance to run an inn..."

I threw my arms around her. "Okay, then."

"Josie, you're scaring me. Your ideas are well-intentioned, but I simply cannot go to your aunt and ask her such a thing."

I grinned. "Oh, I know you can't. But lucky for us, I have no qualms about doing so."

❧

I TURNED INTO AUNT PRIS'S DRIVEWAY, TRIPP IN THE passenger's seat beside me, and pushed the gas pedal harder up the slight incline of the pavement. A massive weeping beech tree partially blocked the left side of the wraparound porch, its graceful limbs reaching out to the house as if beckoning, begging for secrets.

And there had to be secrets. In a house that old, how could there not be?

The sprawling home was built in 1791, the very year Camden was incorporated as part of Massachusetts. Aunt Pris's four times-great grandfather, Joseph Cranshaw, was a shipbuilder from Boston who started anew in the northern wilderness after losing his young wife and son to yellow fever. He built the home in honor of his departed wife and began an apple orchard, seeking peace and a new kind of living in the planting and growing and harvesting of fruit trees. After harvest, he would sail the fruit to Boston, where it sold well enough to keep him afloat until the next year.

In 1800, he married the daughter of Captain William McGlathry. The War of 1812 pulled Joseph back into the ship-building industry and he worked for his father-in-law building and repairing vessels all while making his fortune.

By the time Maine became a state in 1820 through the Missouri Compromise, Joseph and May had six children, and he continued adding to the home. His second-born son eventually took over the orchard and as generations passed, both the orchard and the shipbuilding thrived. By the time Aunt Pris was a girl, though, the business of the sea had long been forgotten. The orchard, though, was another matter altogether.

Aunt Pris's husband had taken over the orchard after they married, but by then most of the family money had been lost in the stock market crash, and her new groom had trouble keeping away from the bottle. From the little bit I'd heard, my great-aunt's marriage had not been pleasant. No children, no joy, and little love. Still, Aunt Pris continued the running of the orchard, keeping things afloat during her marriage. After her husband passed, she ran it another twenty years herself before allowing the weeds and ivy to climb over the beautiful apple trees, as if her family's dreams had died alongside her youth. Yet, she'd been able to support herself with the saved earnings of her hard work. Until now, it seemed, when she considered selling the orchard.

Now, as I drove up to the cleanly-landscaped house with Tripp, I studied the orchard that stretched as far as the eye could see to our right and to the back of the house. It showed off brilliant blooms despite the ragged look of the weeds and dried grass beneath. I wondered if it pained Aunt Pris to look at the overgrown mess of it all. I wondered if in some way, she felt she had let her family down, too.

Maybe Aunt Pris and I really *did* have a lot in common.

"I never understood how one woman could live alone in such a huge place." Tripp surveyed the sprawling home.

I parked my car in front of the brown barn, the place where the apples used to be cleaned and packed. "Hopefully she's ready for some company."

Tripp opened the door of my Honda on a sigh. "I really can't believe I let you talk me into this."

"I really can't believe you didn't let me drive your truck. I would have felt so much more respectable driving up in a Colton Contractors F-150 than this beat-up old thing."

"Uh-uh. There's no way you're turning this all on me. Last time I let you drive my truck I ended up with a V-shaped bumper. Besides, I like your little sedan." He wiggled his nose at me in a tease. "It's homey."

I bit back a smile and opened my door. I couldn't argue. Tripp coming to see Aunt Pris with me meant more than a few rides in his truck. Despite my show of bravado in front of Mom, I didn't know if I'd have the guts to approach Aunt Pris with my proposition without him by my side.

We walked beneath the side veranda and up the stairs to the door. I pressed the doorbell, sending Cragen yapping from within. "Oh good, he's chipper as ever," I muttered.

"Come in!" Aunt Pris's voice came from behind the screen door and I opened it, the scents of lavender and old books a pleasure to my senses. A grand winding staircase leading up to the bedrooms served as the focal point of the entryway. A long dining table and fireplace in the room beyond gave way to generous windows. I imagined the table Mom could lay out for guests in such a beautiful environment, but quickly reined in my thoughts. No use getting ahead of myself.

"Who's there?"

I followed Aunt Pris's voice to the sitting area, where she sat on her Queen Anne sofa with all the poise of Queen Anne herself. Cragen perched on her lap, his nose twitching in the air, his growls low as I entered the room.

"It's just me, Aunt Pris." I stopped short at the sight of quilting club member Esther Glendale in the seat beside Aunt Pris, a cup of tea in her hands. "Oh, I'm so sorry. I didn't know you had company. We can come back another time."

Esther waved a weathered brown hand through the air. "Young lady, I'm practically a fixture in this house. Company!" She laughed a bubbly sound that filled the room. "And I see you brought me some eye candy, so don't be bashful now you two."

Ever gracious, Tripp leaned over to give first Aunt Pris, then Esther, a kiss on the cheek, his face reddening. "It's good to see you both as well."

Aunt Pris stroked Cragen's wiry fur. "And for what do I owe this pleasure? And so soon after seeing you at dinner last night?"

My gaze skittered from Aunt Pris to Esther, and my heart beat wild within my chest. I should have known my great-aunt wouldn't be one for small talk. What was I thinking, coming into her home and asking that she hand it over to my family? None of it made sense. I'd heard that women who are pregnant shouldn't make any major life decisions, that pregnancy hormones affected their ability to think. Perhaps I was living proof. And why hadn't Tripp stopped me? Couldn't he see the hole I was about to dig for myself?

"We'll come back another time, really, Aunt Pris. I had a rather weighty matter to discuss with you, and I don't want to bore Esther with the details."

Esther slapped the arm of her chair with her hand. "Sugar, I'd love to be bored with details. Sure beats sitting around here, talking about the benefits of flushable wipes."

I laughed, Esther being one of the few quilting members I genuinely adored.

Aunt Pris rolled her eyes. "Esther is my oldest friend, Josephine. Whatever you can say in front of me, you can say in front of her."

I swallowed, nodded, and lowered myself onto the nearest upholstered chair, its frame draped in a quilt with pale blue stars. More than likely, Esther would forget our conversation by nightfall. She suffered from a severe case of Sundowners Syndrome and probably only had another hour or two left before she started swiping Aunt Pris's silverware and asking for her mother. Surely, her daughter would come and get her before that happened.

Proud founding members of the Camden Quilting Club, Esther and Aunt Pris grew up together right on the orchard—Esther as the daughter of a couple that worked the orchards, and Aunt Pris as the owner's daughter. I considered it one of Aunt Pris's admirable qualities that I never saw her treat Esther as anything but an equal, despite growing up being waited on by not only Esther and her family, but by many other people of color.

For every bone of rigid seriousness within Aunt Pris's body, there was a fun-loving and creative one in Esther's. Their friendship—though filled with too much gossip and crazy quilts for my liking—proved resilient over the years. Maybe even beautiful.

"Mr. Colton, please sit." Aunt Pris gestured to the chair beside mine. She lifted the teapot and poured a cup, handed it to him along with a saucer. Though not one for tea, he didn't refuse.

I accepted my own cup from Aunt Pris's well-stocked tea table.

"Well, girl? What's this matter of weight you wish to discuss?"

I shifted in my seat. No turning back now. "I was thinking about what you said last night. You know, selling the orchard so you could have cash on hand for help around here?"

Esther made a sound of part approval, part pity, which urged parserHEIDI CHIAVAROLI

me onward despite the slight shaking of my teacup and the drib-
bling of liquid onto its saucer.

"I wondered if there was a way we could work together—
you and my family—in some sort of mutually beneficial
agreement."

"Please, girl, don't mince words. And if you came here wanting
something, you best convince me that degree of yours is worth
the pretty penny I'm paying for it."

Her words almost sent me out the door. Only the thought of
Mom's scrapbook, packed away for eternity, dead and buried in
the attic, kept me from leaving.

I glanced at Tripp, and he nodded.

I opened my mouth, pushed my words into the air. "Well, it's
always been Mom's dream to own a bed and breakfast. Only she
doesn't have—"

"A bookstore, you mean, don't you?"

I shook my head. "Dad wanted a bookstore. Mom wanted a
B&B."

"A B and what?"

Esther tapped Aunt Pris's arm. "A bed and breakfast, Pris. You
know, the quaint little inns they have all over the place around
here? Guests stay over, have breakfast, then leave?"

"A hotel, then?"

I shifted in my seat. "Sort of, but more upscale. More
personal. Homey." I tried to ignore Tripp's grin at the word he'd
used a short time earlier to describe my beat-up old car. "I don't
know what sort of long-term plans you have for this place, but it
would make an amazing bed and breakfast. With some updates,
people would clamber to stay here, and with Mom's cooking it'd
be the talk of Camden."

Aunt Pris stared at me. I don't think I ever saw her go so long
without a word. Finally, she opened her mouth. "You want me, an
old lady, to go into business with your mother?"

"Sort of. If we moved in, we could help you out and you

72

wouldn't need to sell your orchard. We'd clean and cook and turn this place into a money-making venture again."

"We?"

I blinked, confused, just glad I'd gotten my proposition out. "We, what?"

"You said 'we.'" Aunt Pris said.

"She did," Esther affirmed.

"Well, we'd probably have to move in and sell our house to make it work. But you have plenty of room and—"

Aunt Pris shook her head. "Let me get this straight. You want me to open up my home to your entire family...and to strangers?"

"Yes. I guess that is what I'm suggesting."

"Why do I feel, girl, that you coming here asking me all of this is like the prodigal son coming to his father asking for his inheritance early? Is that what you're doing, you impertinent girl? You aren't willing to wait for me to kick the bucket to get this house, is that it?"

Heat bloomed at my neck. This was a horrible idea. I should have put it out of my head the minute it entered.

Tripp cleared his throat, leaned forward. "If I could just add my two cents."

I could have kissed him.

"Please do, young man. I'm not sure I can quite wrap my head around this...proposition."

"Josie herself really doesn't have anything to gain from any of this." He held out his hands, his endearing, authentic nature filling the room. "She's going back to college in the fall—"

"Maybe." I didn't think before I spoke, as usual. But nothing was definite at this point.

"Maybe?" Tripp cocked his head at me.

I shrugged. "Lord willing. Please, Tripp, go on."

He eyed me another moment before turning to Aunt Pris, who looked amused by our exchange. "We're only thinking of helping Hannah fulfill a long-held dream and helping you in the process. Wouldn't you rather have family around than a hired nurse?"

"That is none of your business. Truly, I don't even know why Josephine brought you along...unless you're planning on making yourself part of the family soon?"

I shot to my feet, mortified. "Aunt Pris, no!"

Esther cackled. "Oh, pity! He would make a nice addition, wouldn't he Priscilla?"

The two ladies exchanged a smile before Aunt Pris sipped her tea and pet Cragen's back in slow, steady strokes.

"I'm still confused. It was my understanding your mother wanted to open a bookshop, not a hotel."

"A bed and breakfast. A book-themed bed and breakfast, actually. A bookshop would be a lovely addition, perhaps if it was a part of the B&B."

Esther tapped Aunt Pris's arm while bouncing in her seat. "She could put it in that old barn of yours, Priscilla. How fun! And we could make quilts for all the rooms!"

I beamed at Esther.

Tripp nodded. "The barn would make a beautiful bookshop, actually. Plenty of room with a lot of potential. Those amazing beams could really draw attention."

"Now, just wait a minute. And that goes for you too, Esther." Cragen jumped off Aunt Pris's lap to settle on the floor. "I am not agreeing to any such thing. Just because I'm old doesn't mean I don't have my mind. This is my home and as of right now, it's staying just the way it is."

"I understand, Aunt Pris. And I know it's a bit much to spring on you all at once."

"You're darn tootin', it is." She sipped her tea, then placed her cup back on its saucer. "You said your mother would be doing all the cooking?"

"I'm sure we'd help, but yes."

"And what does she have to say to all of this?"

I ran my tongue over my teeth. "I mentioned the idea to her. While she seemed taken with it, she also seemed certain you wouldn't agree."

"Hmph." Aunt Pris inhaled deep, looked out the window toward the overgrown orchards. "I presume you have some sort of business plan? Cost projections, startup costs, marketing analysis?"

My mouth went dry. For all the oddity that was Aunt Pris, she was still as sharp as one of her quilting needles. "Well, no, not yet—"

She held up a hand. "You dare waltz in here asking for me to hand over my home to you without a plan? You really do have some nerve, girl."

Again, I fought the urge to run from the room, to race down High Street towards the harbor, let the saltiness of the sea wind sweep away my embarrassment. Oh, to run again. I should have kept my nose out of all of this. I'd just been trying to help, trying to make something good come from this abandoned piece of property, trying to aid my family. But what did any of it matter? I was a fool. I had enough problems of my own without meddling in the affairs of my great-aunt and my mother.

"Aunt Pris." Tripp placed his teacup on the table beside him. "If we did all those things—if I made up an estimate for the work to be done, if we came up with some numbers and a marketing strategy...is this something you'd be interested in? If not, we understand, and we won't waste any more of your time."

I pressed my lips together, stared at the swirls of the area rug atop the old hardwood floor. "I thought this might be a chance for us to work together toward something good. Something that benefits the town and our family. All of us. I didn't mean any disrespect by asking, Aunt Pris. Please know that. If you want me to forget the idea, consider it done."

I felt her gaze heavy on me. "It took a lot of gumption for you to come here." Did she speak in disgust or admiration?

Tripp reached for my hand and squeezed it, the gesture comforting.

"Oh, Priscilla," Esther murmured. "We could all use a bit of excitement around here, couldn't we? One last hoorah before we answer Jesus's call? The Bible commands us to entertain strangers, after all. And Hannah's cooking...I can't think of a better way to spend our last years on earth but by fellowshipping around her heavenly food."

"Now you're a part of this, I suppose?" Aunt Pris raised an eyebrow at Esther.

"I'm practically a fixture, remember?" She glowed, her brown face lighting up the room.

"I'm not agreeing to anything, you hear me?"

I nodded, even as I felt a spur of hope hitch within my spirit.

"You speak to your mother and make sure she's privy to our conversation. You set up a business plan and get me those numbers. You prove to me I won't regret this endeavor and then —and only then—will I *consider* your proposition."

I wanted to clap my hands and prance around the room. Instead, I summoned every last ounce of decorum and graciously thanked my aunt before we took our exit.

When Tripp and I sat in my Honda, I looked at the barn and the surrounding orchards with new enthusiasm. I placed my hand on Tripp's, and squeezed. "Thank you isn't enough for what you did in there."

"Don't thank me yet. That woman's given us a whole lot of work to do."

Us.

"Tripp, I don't expect you to take any time on this. It's all on me and my family."

"And you were going to hire the competition to remodel this place? No way, Martin. I've had my eye on this property forever."

I laughed. "I can't believe she's considering this. She's not stringing us along, is she? She's really interested?"

Tripp nodded. "Maybe we're not the only ones who want to be a part of something bigger than ourselves."

I pulled my hand from Tripp's and rested it on my stomach. I didn't know what the following weeks and months would bring. Already they were nothing like I'd pictured or planned. But maybe that was okay.

I pulled out of the drive, a light and foreign feeling in my chest. This could actually be *fun*. And I loved Esther's idea of a barn bookshop. "I think it's time to call an emergency Martin family meeting."

9

"Come on, Sis, it's Saturday night. I'm supposed to be heading out." Bronson tapped his foot on the hardwood floor of our living room, every inch of his six-foot frame ready to bolt.

"And I have a date I need to get ready for." Amie slumped on the couch beside Lizzie.

"I know, I know. And I appreciate you making room in your busy schedules, but this is important. And it really can't wait."

Mom walked in, placed napkins and a plate of brownies on the coffee table. "To quell the troops." She sat in her chair, hands held palms up. "I'm not sure I can stand the suspense though."

I smiled at her, but couldn't tell if she guessed my news had to do with our conversation the night before. "Just waiting on Mags."

"Well, it can't be an engagement announcement, because Tripp isn't here." Lizzie tapped her chin, and I threw a pillow at her.

"No one—especially me—is getting engaged."

"You two *have* been spending a lot of time with one another." Amie's bottom lip jutted out as she crossed her arms over her chest. She'd always had a girlish crush on Tripp, but I assumed she'd be over any childhood jealousies by now. She had her own life, her own dreams.

"Tripp has nothing to do with this...almost nothing, anyway."

The side door opened and Maggie rushed in, wisps of hair escaping her ponytail. "Sorry! Had a mishap with the Chicken Mozambique. Mom, I thought that was supposed to be a quick dish?"

"She makes everything in the kitchen look easy," Lizzie said.

Maggie dropped to the floor beside Bronson and glanced at her phone. "Josh and I promised the boys a movie night, but they have to be in bed by eight-thirty if we're going to get them up in a halfway decent state for church tomorrow, so spill your guts, Sis. Clock's ticking."

"Thanks, guys." Maybe best to dive right in. "So, I went to visit Aunt Pris today with an idea."

Mom's head snapped up, but she kept quiet.

"Was it how to keep Cragen from licking your ankles at dinner, because I've had it with that beast." Amie wrinkled her nose.

"I'll tackle that next time." I inhaled a deep breath. "It was actually about Mom's bed and breakfast."

Maggie groaned. "Josie Martin, I hope to high heaven you did not ask Aunt Pris for money. Please tell me you didn't."

"I didn't ask her for a penny."

"Thank the Lord." Maggie clutched her knees to her chest.

"I offered her something." My family grew silent, eyes fastened on me. "For us to move in with her."

The room exploded.

"What?"

"You have no right!"

"What were you thinking?"

A shrill whistle pierced the room, cutting through the commotion. Maggie. She'd perfected it since becoming a mother of two energetic young boys. "Let's just let Josie finish, okay? Maybe we misunderstood."

"Well, of course you can be calm." Bronson flung a hand in the air toward me. "She's not signing *you* up for anything."

"Or herself," Amie sputtered. "She'll be going back to New York to pretend we don't exist again in a few months."

Amie's words caught me before I could think to press onward in my explanation. While I had kept in sporadic touch with Mom, Maggie, and Lizzie, I'd all but ignored Amie. I loved her of course. She was my sister. But when it came down to it, we had little in common. Now though, I saw how my silence had hurt her.

I vowed to make it up to her somehow. We had all summer to find something to bond over.

"That wasn't the best way to start." I stood and paced the room. "I was thinking about how Mom used to want to run a B&B, and how this bookshop feels like settling."

Mom opened her mouth, then clamped her teeth over her bottom lip.

"I thought about Aunt Pris having that big ol' house to herself and selling the orchard because she needs help. What if *we* were her help? And what if she let us transform that beautiful home into a family-run B&B? A book-inspired B&B, complete with a barn bookshop?"

The room was silent. Too silent. I wished for Tripp, for his encouraging, reasonable words. "That big house isn't good for just one old lady, and Aunt Pris is beginning to feel it. It's been in the family for generations. Maybe it's time for it to tell a new story, open its arms to new people and create a place of rest and peace for guests—guests who love books. Dad would love the idea, I know he would. But it's Mom's passion and skill that would make it thrive." I turned to my mother and swallowed, the absurdity of the idea once again threatening to envelop me. "Mom, Aunt Pris *is* actually considering the idea."

Mom worked her tongue around in her mouth. "When we talked about the possibility last night, I never thought Aunt Pris would entertain the notion. What exactly did she say?"

"She gave me a hard time, of course. But Esther was there, and she thought it a grand idea, which I think buttered up Aunt a bit. In the end, she told me to talk to you, to come up with a plan and some numbers. Tripp said he'd help out with that."

"She's seriously thinking about it?" Bronson raked a hand through his hair.

"She is. Maybe she's tired of being alone. Maybe she wants to feel a part of something. Maybe she wants that house to be a part of others' stories, too."

Amie scooted to the edge of the couch. "But we'd have to live there? With—with that horrible dog? And what about this home? Our home."

"If we want to pay for everything out-of-pocket with no loans and run it ourselves, without staff, I don't see any other way but to live there." I looked at Maggie, since we'd already briefly spoke of this at Mom's retirement party. "And sell the house."

Bronson stood. "This is crazy. We can't sell this house. What if everything backfires? What if we can't take living with Aunt Pris? Then what? We lose everything."

Amie's bottom lip trembled. "This is *Dad's* house."

Mom hid a sniffle, reached out to put a hand on Amie's knee.

The room grew silent, and for the hundredth time that day, I wondered if I wasn't making a grievous mistake. I thought of Dad's study, that hollow empty chair. His hours studying, planning great things for the world.

I lowered myself to a chair. "I miss Dad, too. But he's not in this house. Our memories are, and we'll always have them. I *love* this house. I'd be sad to leave it, too. But Dad spoke to us often of the value of heavenly treasures, not earthly ones." On a whim, I decided to take a page from Esther's book. "Entertaining strangers, opening our home to them, could be a mission of sorts."

"Opening our home...for a fee. Don't pretend this is like one of Dad's profitless but full-of-good-heart adventures, Josie," Bronson said. "In fact, it's probably better if it's not. We'll all be on the streets begging for food if we don't make some sort of money."

I smiled at his reasoning. "Mom's put all she's had into us for most of her life. Maybe it's time for us to put some of ourselves into her."

"Us?" Amie gestured wildly. "How can there be an 'us' when you're going to run off to school again in a few months and leave us with Aunt Pris? We're the ones who'll be stuck with this mess. And I am *not* cleaning up after strangers."

"I don't want to drag anyone into the business unless you want to take part in it. I guess I hoped you would. I was getting kind of excited about it myself. In fact, I'm considering transferring my last year of classes online so I could be here if this all goes through."

That put the room in a frenzy again. Sooner or later, they'd know my reasons were twofold, but for now, this explanation would do.

"Josie, really?" Lizzie looked at me with such hope my eyes watered.

I blinked. "I lost myself this past year, I think. I missed Dad so much. And I realize now that I cut you all off, too. I'm sorry for that. It was wrong, and I want to fix it if you'll let me. If Mom and Aunt Pris agree, I'll do whatever I can in my power to make this bed and breakfast a success."

I may have failed by getting into Finn's bed, but I would prove myself still capable of success, one way or the other.

This was surely the right path for this season of my life. Staying home, staying with my family, helping Mom make her dream a reality. Somewhere in the last couple of days, it had become my dream, too.

And yet amid the excitement and hope, a tiny voice whispered accusations. I was just scared to go back to New York. To run into my professors, or Finn, with a swollen belly, to feel his rejection all over again. To feel anew the firm hold he'd had on me. To face being a single mother—or giving up my baby—alone.

My chest tightened and black spots danced before my eyes. Shallow breaths signaled the beginnings of a panic attack such as I'd had when Finn put that horrible choice in front of me: him or our baby.

"I think it's an honorable plan." Maggie's words served as a beacon of light within my blackness. "And I would be willing to help how I can. I'm good with numbers. I could make a website, do some online marketing. Maybe once things get running I could handle reservations."

I breathed deep, forced my thoughts away from my dilemma and onto the task before me. Slow words came from my mouth. "Once we're making a profit, we could pay ourselves."

"I won't be anyone's chambermaid, but I can be your honorary handyman between classes. I wouldn't mind trying to clean up those orchards a bit." Bronson leaned back in his chair and sighed. "I'd miss this house, but maybe Josie's right. There's more to Dad than this house, and more to our childhood than these walls. Doing this together, as a family—that would be honoring Dad, I think."

Lizzie leaned forward, her thin arms wrapped around a red throw pillow. "I've always thought Aunt Pris's home would look beautiful with more flowers. That porch could handle some big planters. Herbs and vegetables in the gardens that Mom could cook with."

Amie held out her hands, shook her head. "Wait, wait, wait. What about living with Aunt Pris? And what about you, Mom? You've been awful quiet while we all decide your life for you."

Amie was right.

We all turned to Mom, perched on her chair. She stared at the untouched plate of brownies, then finally looked at each of us. "I have to admit, when your father passed last year, I felt a part of me die. He was my life—him and all of you—for the last thirty years. And there's nothing else more worthy I have ever done— could ever do." She pressed her lips together, seemed to want to choose her words with care. "You all know how books have formed and shaped my life. But people have, too. And I'm ready for a new adventure. I thought that was in a bookshop, but this... resurrecting an old dream of a B&B, would be amazing. I never thought Aunt Pris would give it a serious thought. That she is means something.

"Yes, living with her would be a challenge, but has the Martin family ever been one to back down from a challenge? Especially one of loving the unlovable. She's family. For as long as we've known her, she has always been there when we needed her. Maybe it's time we were there for her."

Mom sat straighter, planted her feet on the ground. "But I refuse to go forward with this unless each one of you agrees to it. This is your home, too, and there's no going back if we sell it. And yet I don't see any other way around it if we go this route. I'm not going into debt again, and I don't need two houses. And yet this is *my* dream. You have your own lives to live, and more than anything, I want you to live them. I never, ever want to hold you back."

"Oh, Mom." Lizzie got off the couch to sit on the edge of Mom's chair and drape her arms around her. "I want you to have your dream. And it sounds exciting. Let's go for it."

Maggie nodded. "I'm in if the rest of you are."

Bronson leaned forward. "You deserve this, Mom. If Aunt Pris agrees, I think it has potential to be a thriving business. With your food and hospitality, how can it not?"

We all looked to Amie, whose bottom lip protruded as if she

were still four years old, pouting in the corner over not getting to stay up late to ring in the New Year. Centimeter by centimeter, it wilted. "I suppose that house *does* have some romantic qualities. And if Aunt Pris really is going to let us fix it up nice, it could be tasteful. But I am *not* cleaning guest rooms, Josie, you hear me?"

I grinned. "Loud and clear."

Maggie clapped her hands "That's it, then?"

"For now." I stood and paced the room. "We still need Aunt Pris to officially agree. That means plans for the house and plans for the business. Numbers. Mom, you and I should probably start on this ASAP. If all goes well, I think we could have it open by Christmas."

A faint smile played on Mom's lips. "The Orchard House Bed and Breakfast."

My heart sung. "It's perfect, Mom." So perfect. "It's like it was meant to be, right? Dad's ancestors no doubt weren't thinking about Louisa May Alcott when they named Aunt Pris's home all those years ago, but it suites our purposes perfectly, not to mention the *Little Women* theme we already have going on around here *and* the book experience we want to cultivate."

She blinked back tears and I gestured for everyone to huddle around her. I put my hand over Mom's, sensing a newfound closeness to her. What would this adventure bring?

Lizzie slipped her hand over mine, then Maggie, then Bronson, followed last by Amie.

"Your father would usually say a prayer at a time like this." Mom blinked shining eyes, and though I'd been the leader thus far and usually not short on words, God and I had been somewhat estranged since Dad passed. He'd seemed so far away it was impossible to find Him.

"I'll pray," Lizzie said, surprising me.

I closed my eyes, listened to the sweet, lulling sound of her voice, beseeching the Almighty to guide us in His path for the plans started this day.

"And Lord," Lizzie continued. "If there's any way for you to tell Dad we love him and we miss him, could you do that?"

She ended the prayer and we sounded out a chorus of "Amens."

Mom let out an unexpected squeal as she gripped my hands. "I'm so excited."

I grinned. "Me, too."

Maggie hugged me. "I think it's going to be fabulous. Hey, I have to go but keep me updated and let me know what you need. Meanwhile I can work on designing a sample brochure to show Aunt Pris." It looked like Maggie's business degree and experience with a marketing firm before marrying Josh would come in handy.

"Awesome. Thanks, Mags."

Bronson pointed a finger at me. "No putting the house up for sale until Aunt Pris signs off on this entire idea, you hear? And I want to see a stellar business plan before that happens."

I wrinkled my nose at him, then patted his cheek. "Someone's gotten quite bossy this last year."

He pulled out of my reach. "Only out of necessity, Sis."

I nodded, realized how much had fallen to my brother these past months with not only Dad gone, but me and Maggie gone as well. While Lizzie was older than Bronson, her quiet, introverted nature wasn't exactly a take-charge sort. The task must have fallen to Bronson.

"I'm sorry I haven't been around more." The truth of the words hit me with force. "I'm changing that. I want to be here, be involved. I want to pull my weight."

He squeezed my shoulder, tickling my neck. "Good to hear, Jo."

I swatted him. "Just because I'm embracing this Alcott theme does not mean you can call me that."

He shrugged and grinned, the gesture making him ten times more handsome. "So Tripp's putting together an estimate? If he's going over to Aunt Pris's to check things out, I wouldn't mind tagging along."

"I'll let him know."

Amie hugged Mom, but gave me a small smile which I counted as victory. "And I'll be happy to be in charge of the toiletries for the rooms. I'm thinking all-natural, locally-sourced products. Nothing cheap."

"You got it." I waved goodbye to her as she left the room.

I turned to Mom and Lizzie. "You up for a planning session, or do you both have hot dates and movie plans too?"

"The only hot date I have is one with Mount Battie tomorrow morning." Lizzie took a brownie from the plate. "I have to get out early or I'll melt onto the side of the mountain."

Mom laughed. "Josie, my wild one, you never cease to surprise me. I can't even fathom what you said to get Aunt Pris to consider this."

"I think Tripp and Esther deserve more credit than I do."

She raised her eyebrows. "Tripp went with you?"

A blooming heat started at my neck, as I moved to sit cross-legged on the floor. "He was definitely helpful. But now we need a solid plan if we're going to seal this deal."

I glanced at Mom, her skin glowing, her eyes bright with excitement. I felt at the edge of a grand adventure, and though it was the farthest quest I could have dreamed up for myself only months earlier, I couldn't imagine anything better.

✣ 10 ✣

Tripp didn't bother questioning the lightness in his step as he jogged up the stairs of Colton Contractors late Monday morning. He knew what caused the hope in his chest, even if he also knew better than to let it take root.

"Hey, Eileen." He greeted his secretary, a woman with curly platinum hair who had worked with Grandpop since Tripp was in diapers.

"Oh hi, Tripp. Just took a call from the Smythes. They want to go ahead with the job. They're dropping the contract off later today."

"Awesome. Did you tell Grandpop?"

"Was just about to, but I'll leave it to you if you want to do the honors." She gestured to the large office to her left. "He's in."

"Thanks."

Tripp knocked on the open door of his grandfather's office.

"Come."

White head bent over blueprints, Tripp felt a surge of gratitude for the older man. Where would he and August be without the love and care of their grandfather? And now, getting to be a part of the running of Colton Contractors...Tripp couldn't dream up anything better.

He closed the door behind him, focusing on the task at hand. "Eileen just told me the Smythes are dropping off the contract later today."

Grandpop grunted. "Good." He leaned back in his chair, his weathered face all business despite the soft gray eyes that lived under bushy gray brows. "We might want to consider hiring a couple more guys. Fall's looking busy."

Tripp nodded. "As long as they can pull their own weight. I'd rather pay for experience than pay minimum wage for cheap labor."

Another grunt. On occasion, he butted heads with the old man on this topic. Grandpop thought one good experienced foreman working with a ragtag group of laborers sufficient. Tripp championed paying for experience that would save hours on a job. Finding the experience wasn't always a task for the faint of heart, though.

"Put out the word and let me know what you find. How's August doing?"

"We had a heart-to-heart on Friday. I think he took it well. We'll see."

"I didn't see him around the house much this weekend. Or at church."

Growing up, Grandpop had been strict about church attendance. Sometimes too strict. But while Tripp enjoyed the weekly services and found it a valuable time to ground himself in the big picture of life, Grandpop's strict, sometimes legalistic ways, grated on August.

"He went camping with some buddies Saturday night, I think. He came in late last night."

"As long as you keep an eye on him."

Tripp ran a hand over his face. No wonder he felt part father to August. Grandpop didn't leave him much choice. Tripp considered reminding the older man that August was nineteen, capable of holding down a job or camping with some friends, but then he recalled August's form sprawled on his bed that morning a half-hour before he was to show up to work.

Tripp had done his brother a courtesy in throwing a pillow at him. August only grumbled something about having a rough night. Tripp left the house, trusting his brother to make the right decision. Again.

He could only hope he had.

He sighed. Time for a change of subject. "I'm putting together an estimate for the Martins. Meeting up with them and Kene at Aunt Pris's later today."

The older man cocked his head. "Really? Priscilla is actually doing work on that old house? What are they looking to do?"

Tripp explained the potential collaboration between the Martins and Aunt Pris.

A slow smile spread over Grandpop's face. "Priscilla must be all in a tizzy."

"She surely is. No doubt she'll have some strong opinions about any work done to make the place into a functional B&B."

"She's never been a lady to keep quiet about her thoughts." Grandpop's fond smile made Tripp wonder at the history he and Aunt Pris shared. They'd both been married to other people, but they'd lived in the same town all their lives, attended the same school. Did Grandpop know Josie's great-aunt better than Tripp realized?

"So the Martins plan to sell their home to supply the starting costs for their new venture?"

"If all goes through and Aunt Pris agrees, yes."

"That's quite a commitment." Grandpop leaned back in his seat, tenting his hands. "That family has meant a lot to you and August over the years. In many ways, Hannah's the closest thing to a mother you two have known. And those girls...they've done my heart good many a time, that's for certain."

"Yes, sir. I'd agree."

Grandpop ran a hand over his face, stared at his desk. "I still remember Hannah and your father performing in *The Christmas Carol* back in high school. I could have sworn those two kids were going to get hitched."

Tripp shifted in his seat. Josie's mother and his father? He supposed he should be grateful such an arrangement hadn't happened.

"Help them out on this one, Tripp, okay? The company can pay for the supplies. I'd offer labor too, but I know Hannah wouldn't accept. Work the numbers. Don't make it obvious, but make it generous."

Tripp grinned. He swore the old man lost more and more of his crustiness with each day he aged. "Grandpop, sometimes you remind me a lot of good ol' Saint Nick."

The older man grunted again. "Not a word to them, understand?"

Tripp stood. "Yes, sir. I like the way you work."

Grandpop chuckled along with Tripp as he headed out of the office. At this rate, Josie would have every reason to stay in Camden and see her endeavor through. By fall, perhaps New York would be nothing to her but a distant memory.

THREE HOURS LATER, TRIPP RUBBED HIS FOREHEAD, HIS HOPE from earlier fast dwindling as he stood in Aunt Pris's kitchen with Josie, Hannah, Bronson, Aunt Pris, and Kene, Tripp's in-house architect. He stared at the outdated room, the minimal counter space, and near-ancient appliances, trying to come to terms with the enormity of the project before him...not to mention Aunt Pris's seeming inability to budge on the work needing to be done.

"So you plan on tearing my kitchen apart?" Aunt Pris

demanded after Kene suggested making room for commercial-grade appliances.

Tripp held a hand out. "We need a bit more space and better utilization if Hannah's going to be cooking for potentially a dozen guests each morning."

"Plus us," Bronson said. "I hope we're not going to get the shaft on food."

Tripp hadn't realized Josie's brother would be here as well. While he liked hanging out with the guy, it was another person's ideas floating in the mix—something Kene and Aunt Pris didn't need right now.

Aunt Pris pointed her cane at Bronson. "Well, I should hope not. It's one of the perks of this entire deal."

Josie drummed her fingers on the counter. "We can't underestimate the importance of the kitchen. We need to set The Orchard House B&B off from the myriad of other establishments in the area. Of course, the book-theme might do it for a particular crowd, but for others"—she looked pointedly at Tripp—"we're going to need something more to clinch the deal."

Hannah nodded. "We decided that 'something' should be the included breakfast. We're thinking way more than muffins and a buffet. I want to do a gourmet-style five-course meal, complete with a choice between two dishes for the main entree. It will be tasteful and fancy and make our guests feel pampered." She turned to Aunt Pris. "What do you think of that idea?"

"A five-course breakfast? Sounds ostentatious and completely unnecessary. But if you're offering it to me each morning, I'd say it's perfect."

A few giggles broke out, lightening the mood.

"I will need more counter space for such an endeavor. And reliable appliances." Hannah almost winced as she said the words.

Tripp pointed to the wall separating the kitchen from the breakfast nook. "If we take out this wall, that will open up a world of space. We could curve the counters around partway to make a small bar area and give Hannah more counter space."

"But I don't see why we're focusing so much on the kitchen. Will it be for the guests?" Aunt Pris's mouth formed a thin line.

"What do you want, Aunt Pris?" Hannah took a step closer to the older woman. "Some B&B's have an open kitchen, but there's no reason we can't keep some separation. The back of the house here, including the kitchen, can serve as our living quarters, much as you have it set up now. There's plenty of space on the third floor for our bedrooms and with the separate set of staircases, it will be ideal for privacy, keeping the second floor with the main entryway and more formal living areas for the guests. You of course, would keep your bedroom in the back corner on the first floor. The butler's pantry already separates the dining room and kitchen, so that can serve as a natural barrier. We could have Tripp install a door as well."

Aunt Pris nodded. "Yes, I suppose that will do."

"I'm going to draw out several options," Kene said. "You all can decide what you like, mix-and-match ideas where it suits you."

They followed Tripp out of the kitchen and up the grand staircase to the second floor.

"The idea with the guest rooms is to remodel so they each have their own bathroom without compromising too much space. We'd love to work in gas fireplaces, jetted tubs, some cozy sitting areas within the bigger rooms." Confidence saturated Hannah's voice, the first he'd heard since Amos died.

They went through each room, tossing around ideas about the best way to maximize space but keep the luxurious feel of the rooms. Tripp pointed to the corner room. "You can squeeze another small room in here if you put the bathroom across the hall. We could run the plumbing down to the kitchen. Or you could make it an adjoining room of sorts, or do away with the idea altogether and create a master room that will have much more space than the others."

Kene walked into the adjoining room they spoke of. "What do you think of a balcony off this room? It would set it apart. We could put a claw foot tub as well as a separate shower. Really give a generous space for a sitting room. That's if we don't go with the other room and the bathroom across the hall idea."

Hannah glanced at Aunt Pris who looked almost shell-shocked. She placed a hand on the older woman's arm. "We're not deciding anything yet. This is just so we have an idea and rough estimate for what we'd be getting into, okay?"

The woman clenched her cane tight. Tripp had never seen her so out of her element. "Yes, of course."

"What about the bookshop in the barn?" Josie asked. "Are we heading there next?"

He tried to catch her attention to give her a warning look, but she already bounced down the stairs, talking to Kene about what section of the barn he thought they should build the bookshop. He could only pray Aunt Pris wouldn't kick them all out of her house before then.

Once outside, Bronson slid open the massive door to the barn and they stepped inside. The old equipment for harvesting the apples took up most of the room, but the potential for space was apparent.

Kene nodded his approval. "There's plenty of room for a decent size shop here. In fact, you're left over with extra space. It could be perfect for holding events down the line if you'd like. People would pay good money for a barnlike reception area that was done well. Long, rustic tables, beautiful beams, the decoration options are endless. Weddings, corporate parties, and the like. Camden clientele would eat it up. Hannah could cater them if she felt up to it."

Josie grabbed her mother's arm. "He's right! That could be fantastic."

"We're getting too ahead of ourselves," Bronson said.

"But it could really help create revenue, and draw attention to the business."

He loved Josie and her passionate ideas. He even loved how she tended to fly away with them from time to time. But the deer-in-the-headlights look on Aunt Pris's face set off alarm bells clanging in his head.

"You know, planning is hard. Sometimes, too many hands in the pot can make it difficult to get a vision. To tackle one thing at a time." Tripp looked at Josie then Bronson, jerking his head toward the door.

Josie raised her eyebrows high. No doubt he'd be the brunt of her anger later. But if Aunt Pris called the entire thing off, then where would they all be?

Josie jutted her chin out. "Fine, then. I can tell when I'm not wanted."

Bronson sighed. "No use getting upset, Josie. Tripp's right. This is Mom and Aunt Pris's endeavor. You sparked it, and that's great. But maybe we should leave them to it for now."

Hannah squeezed Josie's arm, and she gave her mother a small smile, but Tripp didn't miss the hurt behind it. Oh boy.

Josie and Bronson left the barn, and Tripp turned back to Hannah and Aunt Pris. "The barn isn't going anywhere. I say we focus on the kitchen and the second-floor guestrooms for now. This is about what you both want and making this pleasant—and feasible—for both of you. Aunt Pris, tell me what concerns you have and we can see how we can alleviate them, and then Hannah, we'll do the same for you. Maybe we all go sit down inside?"

Aunt Pris nodded, once again in control of herself it seemed. Tripp led them back inside, opening doors for the smaller crew. Once at the dining room table, he leaned back and listened to the older woman's concerns, half his heart thinking how he might make up the snub to Josie.

᠗

AN HOUR LATER, TRIPP APPROACHED THE PORCH RAIL, WHERE Josie looked out at Aunt Pris's overgrown orchards in bloom. Her dark hair lifted in the slight wind, her figure illuminated by the falling sun, the fly-away look to her clothes somewhat tame this evening. With effort, he overcame the insatiable urge to come up behind her, push that soft hair to the side, lower his mouth to the skin of her delicate neck. To hold her, to make her love him somehow, someway.

But he'd made that mistake before, and it wouldn't do.

He wondered how a man went about *not* loving a woman with the intensity he loved Josie. He'd thought absence could have been the answer, but indeed, it only proved the cliché correct, for if anything, his heart had grown fonder of Josie this past year—that newfound frightened look in her eyes sending him on a quest to make everything better.

"You're still here." He leaned on the rail beside her and studied the white apple blossoms, like tufts of cotton on the trees as far as the eye could see.

"Yeah, I thought I'd wait around. Hope *that* was okay."

"I didn't mean anything by it, Josie. Your aunt was getting overwhelmed. I was worried about her drawing a line through the entire plan."

She stared at her clasped hands, nails unpolished as always. "How'd it go?"

"Good. Very good, I think. Once Kene draws up the plans, we'll have something that will give Aunt Pris enough privacy, but enable your Mom to run a thriving business. And"—he wiggled his eyebrows—"I thought of a few surprises for your bookshop."

"*My* bookshop, now is it?"

"Your mom mentioned you'd be in charge of setting it up, ordering product. She's super excited, Josie. You're making her dream come true."

That earned him a small smile. "She deserves it after...everything. And yet, it's kind of sad, you know? While I can say this honors Dad, I'm not sure it'd be actually happening if he were still alive."

"How come?"

She shrugged. "He'd probably turn it into a house for the homeless or something along those lines. Maybe that's a more worthy thing to do."

"That would be worthy, can't argue with that. But that's not what Aunt Pris agreed to, and that wasn't your mother's dream, was it?"

"How can we tell, Tripp? How can we tell what's most worthy in the grand scheme of things?"

He couldn't resist tapping her nose. "Such deep thoughts for you tonight, Josie-girl."

"Well you're the one actually listening in church. Don't you have any answers for me?"

He grew somber. "I wonder if I haven't learned more from my time in your home than I have in church."

She gave a soft snort. "At least one of us did."

Her bitter tone caused something to come undone within him. Something he very much wanted to fix. He gathered a breath, hoped for the right words in the face of her vulnerability. "I think all our attempts of worth are futile if not done with the right heart. Is it worthy to feed and shelter the homeless? Sure. Is it worthy to pamper paying guests? I suppose it could be. Most of all, I think it's about loving others in whatever we're doing. God'll show us the path He wants us on. And if I know Hannah, she'll make room for the needy in whatever she's doing."

Josie grinned. "I think the couch has been empty only two nights since I've been home."

"The Hornwells?"

She nodded. "They're old enough to be out of foster care, but that doesn't mean they don't still need help."

Liam and Rose Hornwell had been in foster care since their mother died a few years ago. The Martin family had become acquainted with them when Lizzie stayed in the hospital to have her thyroid removed to stop the spread of cancer. At the time, Rose had been battling Hodgkin's Lymphoma and had lost all her hair. Tripp could still remember his horror at Josie shaving her head bald and donating the hair to Locks of Love in a show of support for both Rose and Lizzie, who fortunately, had never had chemotherapy or lost her hair. Both girls had been cancer free for more than ten years.

"I'm guessing there'll always be a couch for them at Aunt Pris's," Tripp said.

"Who knows? Maybe an entire bedroom."

He poked her in the arm. "See? That's loving others no matter where we're planted."

"You're so *good*. It's really hard to like you, you know."

"I'm not good. In fact, if you only knew some of the unholy thoughts I'm having about you right now, you'd think me downright wicked."

She punched him, but he enjoyed the blush that rose to her cheeks. "You are incorrigible."

They grew silent before she spoke again. "I'm not feeling like loving God with all my heart lately, and I don't know how to fix it." Her bottom lip quivered, and this time, he didn't hesitate to wrap his arms around her. When she sank into them, he felt like the richest man in the world. He leaned his chin on her head, inhaling the scent of coconut shampoo, and ran the back of his fingers down one smooth arm.

"I know you miss your father, and I can stand here all night and tell you that him having a heart attack isn't God's fault, but when it comes down to it, the Lord could have stopped it, and He didn't."

Her warm breaths fanned the front of his shirt. "Why didn't He?"

He circled a thumb over her shoulder. "I don't know, Josie. I'm so sorry. But He didn't leave you alone. You have so many who love you. Your mother, your siblings, Aunt Pris. Me. Don't give up on *your* dreams, okay?"

She pulled back. "Lately, I can't tell if becoming a psychologist was my dream or Dad's. I've been so confused."

"That's why you're thinking of not going back to New York in the fall?"

"Partly," she whispered.

He lifted a finger to her chin. "What happened in New York? You can tell me anything. You know that, don't you? I used to be your best friend and I'm going to love you no matter what. I want to help."

She pulled away from him, her mouth in a forced smile. "Handyman Tripp, always willing to step in and fix things."

"Is that bad? I mean, what do you want from me? You don't want me for a husband, but when I offer my friendship, you shun that too. It's like I can't win with you."

She lifted that stubborn chin, set her jaw. "Some things you can't fix. Some problems we need to figure out on our own."

"And sometimes help is as simple as opening ourselves up and letting another person in."

She closed her eyes, her chest rising and falling with a single deep breath. "I can't, Tripp. You don't deserve the mess I've made." She sniffed once, swiped the back of her hand across her nose. "I'm going to see if Mom and Aunt Pris are done in there."

"Yeah, of course. Sure."

He watched her disappear inside the old house, but couldn't summon the strength to follow her. Something about her words, her posture of defeat, struck a chord of fear in him, but it didn't scare him away.

It made him want to dig in his heels and love Josie Martin all the more.

Though Maggie claimed she could have made us dinner at her place while Josh took the twins to baseball practice, I insisted on taking my sister out.

We chose a local favorite, Fresh & Co., and sat outside the quaint restaurant at a table with a wide wooden bench on each side.

Maggie looked over the simple menu. "Thanks, Josie. It is nice to get away for a little. I feel like we have a lot of catching up to do."

"I practically had to sneak out of the house, though. Lizzie would have understood, but I'm still on Amie's bad side, I guess. I think she would have been hurt not being invited."

Maggie swirled her straw in her lemonade. "Amie still has some growing up to do, I think. She's not as mature as we were at her age, and I think Dad's death affected her harder than she lets on. She is the baby, after all."

"Yeah," I muttered. "With all the preferential treatment to go with it."

"Josie...give her a chance, okay?"

"You're right. I'm sorry. This isn't about the girls, anyway, it's about us. "How's things going with the ready-made family? Any better than when I left?"

Maggie's face softened into a smile. "The boys have completely captured my heart."

I noticed how Maggie's first sentence wasn't about her husband, but I stayed quiet. "They still dream about their mother?"

Maggie nodded. "It's getting better. I think my appearance into their life stirred some memories."

Josh's ex-wife had been a recovering alcoholic when a relapse one winter night had her driving drunk on icy roads with the boys unbuckled in their car seats. Though the twins had been little more than infants and miraculously survived unscathed, something within them remained scarred. Maggie had told me they often had nightmares of their mother's death, and suffered an insatiable fear that Maggie would leave them just like their birth mom did.

I squeezed my sister's hand. "*You're* amazing. You love those boys so well. It can't be easy."

"It isn't. But they're worth it."

Once we ordered, Maggie slid a paper from her purse and pushed it across the table to me. "What do you think?"

I scanned the brochure. For some reason, seeing it in print made it all the more real.

"It's just a rough draft really. We'll have to adjust things as we decide, but it'll give Aunt Pris an idea about what we're aiming for."

"Maggie, you did this?"

She nodded.

"It's incredible."

The elegant and romantic font she'd chosen for The Orchard House Bed and Breakfast, the picture of Aunt Pris's home and the orchard, the brief descriptions of the estate, the luxurious yet-to-be-finished rooms, and the gourmet five-course breakfast was enough to make me dizzy with pleasure.

I grasped my sister's hand. "We're *really* doing this."

She grinned. "I think so."

"And now I know what our secret weapon is."

Maggie shook her head, forehead wrinkled. "What?"

"You. If you can accomplish this in a couple days while managing all you do, imagine what you can do with a website. And marketing? This copy is fantastic, I can't think of one word to improve it. The entire layout and design is gorgeous. I didn't realize all you got out of that business degree."

She sat straighter. "I had fun doing it. It's nice to feel creative again, you know? To do something not just for the family, but for myself."

"And you clearly have a gift for it. I promise once we get things swinging, you'll be on the payroll."

"Let's just worry about getting Aunt Pris's go-ahead before we start thinking about payrolls."

I waved a hand through the air. "She's sold on it."

"I wouldn't be so cocky. The old lady has given us a surprise or two in the past. I wouldn't be certain anything's set in stone until she lets Colton Contractors onto her property. When—and if— she allows them to start putting hammers through walls, then we can consider ourselves safe."

"I think she's ready for a change. And maybe she's lonelier than we realize. Maybe she actually wants us around." I sat back so the waitress could place our meals before us, filling the table with scents of seafood, garlic, and French fries.

"Stranger things have happened, I suppose."

I forked a bite of lobster ravioli, my mouth watering, but caught Maggie staring at me. "What? Oh right, grace."

Maggie shook her head. "No, that's not it. It's just...you know, you really took us all by surprise proposing this whole bed and breakfast thing. I mean, none of us saw it coming. And you're intent on seeing it through, aren't you? Enough to take online classes in the fall?"

"I think so."

She dipped a crispy fry in ketchup, studied me. "What's going on, Josie?"

I ignored her stare and forked another bite of moist lobster in pink sauce. "What do you mean?" I'd planned on confiding in Maggie, but not before I enjoyed my food. The thought of spilling my guts to my sister made everything more real—the first step in disappointing nearly everyone.

"I mean how you're suddenly willing to give up what you've been working toward all these years."

"Lots of graduates take online classes." I spoke through a mouthful. "It makes sense with everything going on."

She forked a mussel off its shell, brought it to her mouth. "But have you made sure things were going on...so you wouldn't have to go back?"

I put my fork down. "Are you accusing me of having ulterior motives in starting the B&B?"

"Something just doesn't add up, that's all. You've wanted to become a psychologist for as long as I remember. You've put your heart and soul into getting into the program at NYU. It's your dream."

"Some dreams change, I guess. Didn't you say that just last week?"

"Josie..."

I pushed aside my plate, my appetite soured. "Okay, you're right. I was going to tell you later, but since you're intent on ruining my meal—"

"We can eat first. I didn't mean to rush—"

"I'm pregnant."

Maggie's face paled.

"Maggie, say something." But I couldn't look her in the eye, too scared of the disappointment there, too frightened of the shame I'd brought upon our family. Instead, I stared at her fingers shredding the napkin in her hands.

"How...is it Tripp's?"

"No! It's—it doesn't matter who the father is. He's out of the picture. I'm—I'm scared, Maggie. I need help. I don't know what to do."

Maggie came around and sat on my side of the bench, put her arm around me. "It's okay. It's going to be okay. We'll figure this out. We will. Together."

I sank into her words, laid my head on her shoulder. "I know you're disappointed in me. I'm disappointed in myself. But what's done is done. I wish I could take it all back. I really cared for him...I don't know, maybe I loved him. I thought we at least had a future." I swallowed my emotions.

"Josie, tell me. I'm your sister, and I love you. You need to let it all out."

"Professor Becker."

Her arm stiffened around me, then she pulled it away. "Dad's Professor Becker?"

I nodded, my misery compounded by the look of disbelief on her face.

"But he's...he's almost twenty years older than—"

"Fifteen," I said weakly.

Maggie shook her head, bunched her napkin again. "I have half a mind to go to New York and tell him to—"

"This is just as much my fault as it is his." As good as it felt to have my sister want to hang Finn upside down off his apartment fire escape, it wasn't justified. "He didn't hold a gun to my head. It just kind of...happened."

"But he knew Dad. How could he...it's just despicable."

"Then I am, too." My shoulders slumped. "You remember Finn, don't you? He's dynamic, handsome, intelligent. I've always been drawn to him—when Dad brought him home for Thanksgivings, when he taught my first psychology class...and this past year.

We started talking and I got swept up in him, Maggie. He seemed like everything I've been striving for. I wasn't thinking. I couldn't think. It was like he sucked the air out of the room and I was content to drown in him forever."

"You didn't tell him about the baby?"

"I did. He told me to get rid of it."

The napkin had disintegrated in my sister's hands. "He has no right to tell you what to do with—"

"I know. And I didn't. But he doesn't want to be a father. He didn't want me after I refused to have an abortion." My last words trembled, and a small sob escaped. How easy it was to not think of Finn when I was planning the B&B or immersed in a new Kristin Hannah novel. But here, baring my heart to my sister and closest friend, the pain washed over me afresh, along with the horrible truth: I still had feelings for Finn. After all he'd done, after the limitations and restrictions he put on his love for me, I still cared about him. What was wrong with me?

"Oh, honey." Maggie wrapped her arms around me again, squeezed tight. "He should be put in front of a firing squad for abandoning you."

"Or drawn and quartered." I forced a laugh.

Maggie sobered. "How far along are you?"

"Almost fifteen weeks."

"A baby. My goodness, you're having a baby."

"I don't know if I'm going to keep it, you know?"

"Whatever you decide, I'll support you. We all will, Josie. You know that. We love you, and we'll love this little child, too."

A small smile curved my lips at the thought of Maggie spoiling my baby with hugs and cuddles and kisses. I straightened. "So now you know why going back to New York would be...complicated."

"He has to support you in this. If not emotionally, then financially. If you decide to keep the baby."

"And that's a big 'if.'" I swiped at my eyes. "Part of me feels this is so far from the plan I made for my life that it's a no-brainer. This child deserves better than what I can offer. Being adopted worked out well for Dad, you know?"

"And the other part?"

I pressed my lips together, looked at the small wooden planter filled with red geraniums on the side of our table. "The other part of me feels this child is *mine*. That I'm what's best for him or her despite my flaws and mess-ups, that I will forever regret handing my baby over to another family."

Maggie moved back to her side of the table, tucked her shredded napkin beneath her plate. "It's a big decision, and only you can make it. Being a mother is wonderful and hard and amazing and impossible. I can't imagine doing it on my own, but Josie, if anyone can be a single mom, it's you. And you wouldn't be alone. We will always be here for you. I'm sorry you're hurting so much, though."

"Thanks, Mags, but I have no one to blame but myself." I reached for my fork. "Our meals are getting cold."

We ate a couple more bites before I spoke. "Mom's going to flip, right? I mean, I'm an adult and all that, but this is going to really throw her for a loop."

Maggie swallowed another mussel, and I could see her formulating a careful response. "She'll be surprised, but she's your biggest fan, Josie. In all things. Even this. Maybe especially this. When I decided to marry Josh, to become a mother to four-year-old twins, she was the one who cheered me on, more than the others. Mom's not about loving you for your perfection, she's about loving you in the unexpected muddle."

Maggie's words soothed my soul. She was right, wasn't she? I breathed a little freer for the first time since the appearance of those double pink lines.

"You won't say anything to anyone yet, will you? Even Josh? You know how this town can be. I want Mom and the sibs and Aunt Pris to find out on my terms, okay?"

She nodded. "I wouldn't wait too long, though. And while I hate to be the voice of reality, I can't help but wonder if having a baby in Aunt Pris's home come fall will be a game-changer for the B&B. If you decide to keep it, that is."

I groaned. "Of course. I hadn't even thought of that. Here I was thinking I had another several months to decide the fate of my baby, but that's not true at all." Even if I was determined to be the best single mother ever, it wouldn't be on my own. I couldn't afford my own place, especially if I planned to attend classes. If I could work my way onto the payroll of the B&B, assuming it went forward, that might not be until the beginning of next year. My baby would be a couple months old by then. "Maybe I should be looking for a job to support myself instead of planning this crazy idea."

"Hey, The Orchard House B&B is a brilliant idea. I just think Mom and Aunt Pris need to have all the information if you're planning to live together. Something tells me Aunt Pris isn't up for more surprises."

"Tell me about it."

"And if you decide to keep the baby, Finn's legally responsible for child support. That's how it works, and it's only fair."

I swallowed and nodded, but the thought of a confrontation with Finn over child support was enough to send me sinking below the table.

"Tripp doesn't know, does he?" Maggie scrunched up her face, seeming to half expect me to throw something at her.

I shook my head, wanting to deny that it didn't matter. That he didn't matter. But the fact was the news would break his heart all over again. How did I put up with myself? "I am not looking forward to that conversation."

"Just make sure he doesn't find out secondhand, okay? He's still hopelessly in love with you. Josie, he'd probably marry you tomorrow, pregnant with another man's child and all, if you just said the word."

"You think I don't know that?" I snapped. "He's such a frustratingly decent guy."

"That's a bad thing?"

"I don't deserve him, and he most certainly doesn't deserve me and my mistakes. I love Tripp, but it's not like it was with Finn, all steamy and—"

"Lustful?"

I fought the heat climbing my neck. "We had chemistry. Don't you have that with Josh? Don't you think that's important?"

Maggie leaned forward. "You're telling me you didn't like it when Tripp kissed you even a tiny bit last summer?"

I did. I had. Only then, I hadn't been looking for someone to fit a grief-sized hole in me. I'd planned for school and a career to fit that hole, not a man. Turns out that didn't work either.

"So you had chemistry with Finn, great. Where did it get you? Knocked up and alone."

"Maggie," I chastised, surprised by my sister's brashness.

She leaned forward, grasped my hand. "All I'm saying is there's different kinds of love, and not all of them are true. When affection and devotion disappear when it's not convenient—that's not the kind of love you should be pining for."

"So you think I should just throw my arms open to Tripp because I need a man?"

"No." Her voice stood firm. "You, Josie Martin, of all women I know, do not *need* a man. But I do think Tripp deserves your honesty. If not as a love interest, then as your best friend."

I blew out a long breath, thinking of the hard conversations before me. Maggie was right. I didn't have all summer like I thought. This baby wasn't just about me and my mess. This baby would affect the entire family one way or another.

I thought about Tripp's words a couple nights before, of him prompting me to open up and let him in. Could I do that, thinking of him as the friend he was and not as the love interest he'd always wanted to be? And what if Maggie was wrong? What if Tripp was wrong? Maybe there were some things about me even he couldn't abide. I'd not only spurned his proposal, I'd practically run into another man's bed. Tripp was good, but he wasn't a saint. And I refused to take advantage of his good-natured friendship.

Quite likely, none of it would matter anyway. Quite likely, Tripp would make sure he was far out of the picture by the time October—and Finn's baby—made an appearance.

If only the thought didn't feel like the final nail in the coffin of my own undoing.

❧ 12 ❧

I inhaled the scents of bacon and eggs and cheese as I trod down the stairs, rubbing sleep from my eyes. Dressed in a baggy t-shirt, it seemed my belly had grown twofold overnight. I didn't think I could blame it on the lobster ravioli.

As I lay in bed that morning, staring at the small mound of skin and running my fingers over it, I spoke to the child within. I asked him or her what I should do with their future. In one scenario, I imagined myself a mother. In another, I imagined handing over my newborn babe to strangers.

As Maggie pointed out, I didn't have time to vacillate. But then, why should I have to feel rushed because of the B&B? This wasn't as simple as choosing waffles or eggs for breakfast—this was my life and the life of my child. I refused to be hasty.

But Mom and Aunt Pris did have a right to know about the possibility of a baby playing at least a small part in The Orchard House B&B.

I turned the corner to see the dining room sparkling. "Whoa. What's the occasion?"

Candles, woven placemats, two wine glasses at each setting—one filled with orange juice and another with water, and elegant china. On the center of each plate sat a dainty bowl of blueberries, a sprig of mint in the middle. Beside that, a plate of Mom's famous coffee cake. My mouth watered.

"Morning, honey," Mom called from the adjoining kitchen. "Aunt Pris should be by in a few minutes. I promised her a sample of our five-course breakfast and figured I'd give the same treatment to everyone. Spinach Quiche or Stuffed French Toast this morning?" She stopped in the middle of cracking an egg over a bowl. "What's the matter?"

I tried to fix my mouth into a smile, but it wouldn't come. Had I duped Mom into all of this only to ruin it for her with news of a baby? Was I really so horrible?

I shook my head. "Nothing. Maybe we could talk sometime soon, though? Like today?"

She gave me a soft smile. "Of course. Are you worried about the estimate Tripp sent over? I have to admit it stopped me in my tracks, too."

"An estimate?" I reached for my phone. "He didn't text me."

"He emailed it early this morning. Copied you on it."

I opened my email, my heart tripping over itself. "Is it that bad? I mean, I knew it would be steep, but I hoped we'd have enough left over to put some elegant touches on it all. You know, high-quality sheets and towels, maybe organic coffees and teas."

"No, that's not it at all. It's actually a lot less than I anticipated. I'm not sure what magic that boy worked, but I have a horrible feeling he's letting us take advantage of him."

I opened the document, skimmed to the bottom line. Then, assuming the number was a single price for the kitchen, or the bookshop, kept skimming. Nothing. I looked up. "It has to be a mistake, right? I'm not knowledgeable about construction costs, but—"

"I know. I'll talk to him, or I'll go above his head and talk to Ed."

"Don't get Tripp in any trouble, okay? He's obviously trying to

HEIDI CHIAVAROLI

help us out." My insides threatened to burst at Tripp's generosity. "I'll talk to him."

"Okay. But please make it clear we're not accepting charity. If that means we have to work a little harder, so be it."

I nodded. "Got it."

She mixed the eggs with enough force to send them into whipped mounds of whites. "I mean it, Josie. I will not have this hanging over my head."

"Don't worry, Mom. I'll talk to him first thing after breakfast. And I'll take the Stuffed French Toast if you're still offering."

"I am. Now what'd you want to talk with me about?"

"It can wait. Maybe we could take a walk after dinner tonight?"

"Sounds lovely."

Another set of steps on the stairs. "*What* is that most holy and divinest of smells?" Amie collapsed beside me, squealing at the picture perfect place setting.

I chuckled at her melodramatics.

"This is superb, Mom. Your presentation is phenomenal. All this attention to detail...it's art is what it is. Pure and simple. A masterpiece. I'm super impressed."

Mom grinned over her shoulder. "Thanks."

Lizzie rushed into the kitchen through the back door, holding flowers in her hands. "Will these do for the sides of the plates? I thought a little sprig of lavender would be nice."

"Perfect." Mom grabbed a pan from the oven, and worked over it while I finished the blueberries and started on my coffee cake.

"You ready for your finals, Amie?" I asked.

"As ready as ever. What I'm really ready for is my cap and gown."

"What are your plans for the summer? Partying it up before officially entering the adult world?"

She rolled her eyes. "If you call a few college classes the adult world and hanging out with Becky partying, sure."

"You still thinking of teaching art?"

"I'm not sure anymore."

I stopped mid-bite. Had Dad's death changed her future plans as well?

Mom put a plate of artistic culinary delight before me. "Avocado toast with pickled onions, cashew cream, dijon mustard, and greens."

"There is no way Aunt Pris is going to turn us down with food like this." I bit into the toast, the crispness of Mom's homemade bread contrasting with the cream of avocado and the sweetness of pickled onions bursting on my tongue. "This is impeccable."

Lizzie sat down with a plate of coffee cake. "I agree. Mom could make the Royal Queen grovel at her feet with this food."

"You all are spoiling me with your praises, but I'm not saying I don't appreciate it." Mom winked at us, looked up toward the whistling coming down the stairs. "Morning, honey."

Bronson put his hand on the banister, swung around the last step. "Morning." He surveyed the table and gave a low whistle. "This looks a bit fancy for me, but if there's food involved, I'm in."

"Oh, there's food." Amie poked Bronson in the side. "Enough to fill you up, even."

Bronson turned his baseball cap around, stretched his neck, cracked his knuckles. "I think I'm up for the challenge."

"You look like you're headed out to work. Painting with Matt again?" Mom asked.

"No, I took a look at Aunt Pris's orchards yesterday. They're still alive and well, beneath all the weeds. I'm going to try to clean a few trees up, see what's under there."

"Watch out for poison ivy."

"And ticks," Lizzie said. "I have some spray I've been using while hiking if you want to borrow it."

"And make sure to drink enough water. It's going to be hot today," I added.

Bronson wrinkled his nose at us but forked a piece of coffee cake, cinnamon strudel crumbs falling onto his plate. "Just remember, ladies, it's the food that's keeping me here. The food and only the food."

"Oh, you love us," I said, and we all laughed, knowing that in some ways Bronson had it the toughest. We all doted on him, watched him with a mixture of fondness and wonder. No doubt he sometimes felt suffocated with our attentions.

The doorbell rang and Lizzie went to answer it while Mom put more avocado toast in front of us and brought the next course out. "Now, no word to Aunt Pris on Tripp's estimate until we talk to him, right?"

"Right. I'll clear it up quick and hopefully we'll have it ready to bring to Aunt Pris by tomorrow." I looked at the dish before me—Mom's homemade granola, Greek yogurt, and bananas all in a beautiful parfait. "But after she eats this meal, there's not going to be much convincing needed."

"Aunt Pris." Mom kissed the older woman's cheek when she entered the room. From my great-aunt's giant purse, Cragen yapped at us. "You look lovely today."

I studied the older woman, her hair in tight gray curls, foundation a bit heavy on her face. She looked the same as ever to me, but I didn't doubt Mom's authenticity.

I pulled out a chair. "Here, Aunt Pris. Sit beside me."

Cragen snarled. "No use trying to butter me up, girl."

I bent over, kissed her cheek in an uncharacteristic display of affection. "Oh, you enjoy it."

She grunted, and my heart went out to her. I couldn't deny my gratitude, no matter our past. Giving us a chance to fulfill Mom's dream rivaled the charity of paying for my graduate degree. I'd give her a kiss every morning if this all went through.

Aunt Pris surveyed the table. "You'll be doing dishes all day, Hannah."

Mom poured Aunt Pris a glass of orange juice. "It would be a big cleanup, but I think it'll be worth the atmosphere we create to make guests feel pampered."

Aunt Pris spooned a bite of blueberries into her mouth, eyeing Amie's avocado toast.

"We should have everything ready to go over with you tomorrow," I told my aunt.

"Tea time will be fine."

I swallowed down a bite of banana and granola, a thickness starting in my throat. If we intended to give Aunt Pris all the information, that meant *all* the information. Including the possibility of a baby-on-board. How had I not seen how wretched this would all appear before we started down this path? Underneath all those hard edges, Aunt Pris must be excited about our endeavor. If she wasn't, she would be after we fed her marvelous food and showed her extravagant business plans and beautiful flyers. More than likely she'd agree—how could I throw in the possibility of a squalling newborn as part of our bed and breakfast deal?

"And here is course number five. Josie chose the Stuffed French Toast, but I'm planning to offer guests a half plate of each entrée option if they choose." She placed a pillowy mound of golden brown toast before me. Confectioner's sugar sprinkled the top like snowflakes, cream cheese oozed out the middle. Sprigs of lavender adorned one side of the plate, two crisp bacon pieces decorated the other.

As wonderful as it looked, I fought a rising sense of nausea. Waves of nerves tunneled through me. I thought I'd been doing something good, something right for a change. But maybe I'd just twisted this entire thing to be self-serving while brandishing the sword of Mom's dreams as my excuse for it all.

The Orchard House Bed and Breakfast gave me an excuse to stay away from New York. It gave me an excuse to become closer to Mom. It gave me a distraction from the grief of losing Dad, the sorrow of losing the father of my baby. But what if this was all a selfish move on my part?

What would Mom think? What would Aunt Pris say? This baby...in New York it had been my problem alone. But here, surrounded by those I loved, it was so much more complicated. They deserved to know. They all did.

I vowed to tell them by the end of the day.

𝕾 13 𝕾

Tripp backed his work truck up to the job site, shoved a hat on his head, and walked over to where the crew was building an in-law apartment onto the side of a modest colonial. Since he'd finished the Martin estimate early that morning, he decided to reward himself with some time in the field performing one of his favorite aspects of construction—framing.

Pedro whistled. "Watch out, boys. The boss is coming down from his office to strap on a tool belt today."

Tripp grinned at his friend and foreman. "Thought I'd show you boys how to frame without taking all week."

Pedro's jaw grew slack, his dark skin shining in the sun. "All week? Boss Man, I was going to have this done in three days, tops." A slight accent punctuated his foreman's words. Pedro had come over with his parents from Portugal as a young adult with a wife and two little girls. He worked hard and never compromised on the job—or with his family, something Tripp very much respected.

"Well with my help, maybe we can get it done in two."

Pedro pointed the back of his hammer at Tripp. "You're on."

Tripp inhaled the scent of fresh lumber coming from the pile of two-by-fours and two-by-sixes on the ground beside the foundation. His fingers itched to get to work. "You got the plans?"

Pedro gestured him over to a makeshift table made up of a sheet of plywood and two sawhorses, but not before he caught sight of August with three other guys, gesturing to his phone and laughing.

Tripp jerked his head toward the group. "How's the crew?"

"If you mean your little brother, I think the word is inconsistent. The beginning of the week was rough, but he was spot on yesterday doing trim at the Learneds'. When he's into it, he's into it. When he's not...well..."

"I'm not paying him to be into it. I'm paying him to do a job. You think he needs to go, Pedro? I respect you. Just because he's family doesn't mean he gets to fool around."

Pedro shrugged. "We always seem to have a lagging laborer here and there. You see what you think today. Or maybe put him on Landon's job and see how it goes." Landon was Tripp's other foreman.

"Okay, thanks." He looked at the plans. "You want to cut for me?"

Pedro nodded. "Let's get to it." He turned to the rest of the crew, shouted out directions.

Compressors jumped to life. They arranged the lumber on the side of the yard. Tripp pressed his nail gun against the wood and pulled the trigger, satisfaction growing as first the floor and then the walls took shape. By mid-morning, one wall stood, and they took a break, the sun already beating hard.

Tripp sat in the shade of a tree near the fence of the property, opened up his water bottle, and took a long swig before he spoke to the crew. "You guys are on top of it today. Good job." He looked at August, wondered if his presence had made the kid work harder. Today, he'd seen what his brother could do. Follow instructions, use his brain, keep the phone in his pocket. Small things for some, but it made Tripp proud.

"Oh hey, August!" A feminine voice called from the neighbor's yard.

Tripp turned to see Jenny Simcock leaning over the fence, her low-cut, tight shirt not leaving much to the imagination. He bit back a groan, returned to minding his granola bar. Known as the biggest gossip this side of the Appalachian Trail, he knew from experience that any attention would only encourage her. About a year ago, he'd politely held the door open for her as she came out of Hannaford's. Once in the parking lot, she'd cornered him against his truck, fishing for an offer for a date.

August stood. "Oh hey, Jenny. Didn't realize you lived here."

Jenny fluttered eyelashes too long to be real. "I sure do. Been watching you handsome fellas work hard all morning."

August looked back at what they'd accomplished, and Tripp could have sworn he saw pride on his brother's face. "Yeah, it's coming along I guess."

"Hey, Tripp!" Jenny leaned into Tripp's line of vision. "I like your truck. Is it new?"

"Had it for a couple years, Jenny."

"Well, it's real pretty. And oh, I just heard, Tripp! Congratulations on the baby. That's super exciting."

Tripp's granola bar turned to sawdust in his mouth. Whatever false news Jenny intended to spread, it best stop here. "Pardon?"

Jenny's face was pure innocence. Tripp didn't buy it.

"My sister mentioned it this morning. I'm sorry. I didn't realize it was a secret."

Tripp started to stand to confront whatever messed-up thoughts the crazy girl had clinging to her brains, but changed his mind. He refused to credit her words with a gesture as important as standing. "I'm afraid Lilly's mistaken. Best set her straight right away." He looked at the crew, ready to leave this corner of the yard once and for all. "Let's get back to it, guys."

But Jenny's eyebrows rose, her head cocked to the side. "But my sister said Josie was talking about it last night at the restaurant. Lilly got a job at Fresh just a few months ago."

Tripp looked at the girl. Josie *had* mentioned plans to go to the restaurant with Maggie. But surely Lilly heard something wrong.

He didn't appreciate meaningless gossip and rumors at any time, but when they involved Josie, he really wasn't a fan. What happened in high school with Alan Ash, groundless as it was, had been enough to drive him crazy. Josie didn't need any of it. And neither did he. What's worse, the baseless gossip was being spread in front of his employees—men he wanted respect from.

He scrambled for an answer that would shut those little puckered lips up once and for all. "They were probably talking about Maggie's kids. Those boys are something. Now, if you'll excuse us, we have a house to frame." He picked up his water bottle.

"Hmmm..." More finger tapping on the fence post. "I'm quite positive she said Josie was pregnant. And she heard your name more than once."

Tripp grit his teeth, mind swimming. "And I'm quite positive that Lilly has her information wrong. Have a good day, Jenny."

She waved, a look on her face that said *Tripp* was the one with the wrong information.

They returned to framing, the quiet crew grating on Tripp's already taunt nerves, the easy banter gone. He threw himself behind his nail gun, connecting two-by-fours with lightning speed. But although he sank into the work, Jenny's words haunted him. They were ludicrous and vicious. Ridiculous. Josie, pregnant. He could more easily imagine Grandpop announcing intentions to join the circus. Josie had told him she didn't want to be with any man, that she only wanted to concentrate on her studies. She was above reproach, not one to let her heart—or her hormones—get carried away.

At least not when it came to him.

The thought caused a crushing weight to press against his chest. He remembered her silence the past year, the broken look in her eyes upon returning to Camden, her announcement that she might not be returning to New York after all, the way she'd rested a hand on her stomach when they'd gotten into her car after visiting Aunt Pris that first time.

The sun grew hotter, and he fought a wave of dizziness. He pushed through the haze, relishing the simple, satisfying work. He had half a mind to go next door and give Jenny a piece of his mind. He worked hard to be a man of integrity and character, and he didn't need her botching it up with nonsensical blather.

By lunchtime, they had raised two walls, complete with two jut-outs for a walk-in bathroom. His phone dinged, signaling a text, and as the crew sought out their lunch coolers, he saw he'd missed a handful of phone calls from Landon, and one from Josie. She'd also sent him a message.

Can we talk ASAP?

His heart leapt in his throat.

He tapped back. *Where are you?*

He waited, the dots on her phone signaling a response.

Home, doing some research. Are you at the office?

No, can we meet up in the library amphitheater?

His phone rang, Josie's name lighting up the screen. He pushed the Accept button. "Hey."

"Hey. I don't want to interrupt your day. I think a phone call would do, or we could meet up later."

He sank into her voice, feeling foolish that he believed Jenny's gossip for even a minute. But all of a sudden, more than anything, he needed to see Josie, to assure himself she was well—to hold her even.

He ran a hand over his face and stifled a curse. He was turning sappy.

"Actually, I'd really like to talk in person. Can you get away?"

"Sure. I'll meet you in ten?"

He glanced at the crew. "Better make it fifteen."

He hung up, walked over to the guys. "I gotta cut out."

"Office duty calls, eh man?" Pedro bit into a tuna sandwich. "It was nice working with you while it lasted. You did good today."

Tripp smiled, his friend's compliment shining light into his spirit. "We worked well together. All of us. Nice job, guys. I'll be by tomorrow morning with some iced coffees. Maybe we can finish this up."

He chanced a glance at August, who looked exhausted but happy. Maybe his little brother just needed some time to get acclimated to hard physical labor.

Tripp headed to his car, where he changed into a fresh shirt. To his dismay, he caught Jenny eyeing him from her porch next door. He pulled his shirt over his head, and she looked away.

Trouble, that's what she was. No doubt she knew his feelings for Josie—didn't the entire town by now? Maybe she was still sour over Tripp turning her down that day at the grocery store. Who knew what went through that girl's head?

He put his truck in drive and rolled the windows down, breathing in the thick air. In less than an hour, his world would be set straight again. He should be embarrassed to even doubt Josie. Could one woman's words so clearly dissuade him of her character?

And yet, perhaps he placed Josie on a pedestal she didn't deserve. Did he honestly believe she would never want a man if it weren't him?

Yes, he supposed he did.

And maybe that was his problem.

FINN SCREAMED AT THE TOP OF HIS LUNGS, ALLOWING THE LOUD rush of the wind to compete with the echo of his voice, his diving partners several hundred feet from him imitating his bellow.

To test one's audacity to stare fear in the face at sixteen thousand feet was nothing short of empowering. To jump out of a plane with no way to turn back, to conquer the fall, to harness the wind...how had he lived before this?

Hurtling one-hundred twenty miles per hour toward the ground felt like flying, and in the moment, he was unconquerable. Untouchable. On top of the world. If he could do this, he could do anything. The cushion of air beneath him pillowed his body and pushed against his face, taking his breath away in the most fantastic of ways.

He realized then how skydiving could become an addiction. It took away all his cares, grabbed hold of him with a tenacity that demanded his full attention—so much so that all else faded away. Almost a spiritual experience, an awakening to the bigness of the world.

His parachute snapped open, creating instant, sacred quiet compared to the volume of wind that had rushed in his ears moments before. With the exception of the soft flapping of the canopy overhead, the world—and its busy, fractured way of life—lay quiet below him. This high up, he knew his place on earth. All that stuff he lived day to day, all that craziness of life, it didn't really matter. Compared to this—the vastness of the sky and the horizon, the green of the world—everything else proved junk. Man-made drama. He'd let too much of it consume him.

Without warning, a story from the Bible came to him. Jesus, getting up early to go on a mountain to pray. Jesus, seeking to rise earlier than the mess of humanity and press of people who needed Him, the demand of those who sought answers in His teachings. He wondered if Jesus had lived today, if perhaps He would have gone skydiving instead. Prayed on the way down.

Finn shook his head at the ridiculous thought. Jesus skydiving.

Get a grip, Becker. This was *his* escape. And he was ruining it by thoughts of a God he didn't even believe in anymore.

As he approached the ground, he looked at the horizon to gain a sense of his height as well as to ensure no other divers planned to land at the same time. He spotted his target, felt the wind pulling him toward it, his speed giving him a feeling of weightlessness. He calculated the entry point of his landing pattern, his goal to land on his target within ten feet. The last several times he'd flared too high, causing his canopy to stall and leaving him too high to touch the ground at target which made for a hard landing.

Though his gut told him to flare, he waited an extra moment to avoid the hard landing. It paid off. He landed five feet within target.

A moment later, Sven stood beside him. "Best landing I've seen from you, yet."

He clasped hands with his friend. "Thanks, buddy. It felt good today. Real good." Yes, indeed. Time to look forward, to embrace the future, and not allow guilt to weigh him down.

He accepted Sven's invitation to get a drink with some of the other jumpers, one a dark-haired beauty with flirty eyes. Closer to his age than the last couple of women he'd dated, he couldn't help wondering what it might be like to share his hobby with a love-interest, a partner.

At the bar, he finagled his way to sit beside her at the group's table. Come to find out, Katrina was a lawyer for the NFL who hated the drama of having girlfriends and chose to unwind on the weekends by skydiving. After a couple of drinks, they broke from the group and sat by themselves against a quiet wall chatting about jumps, work goals, and the many museums they both wanted to see in the city. When Katrina asked him back to her apartment, he couldn't think of a single reason to say no.

He'd promised himself new beginnings, after all. The past behind. The future ahead.

So when he woke in the middle of the night in the unfamiliar apartment beside Katrina's enticing figure, he simply couldn't make sense of the tears that were once again flowing, soaking her high-end sheets. How could these tears possibly belong to him?

He'd had an amazing day, the best in a long time. Why then, wasn't that enough for some inner part of him that still couldn't move past Josie Martin?

❧ 14 ❧

I stretched out my legs, allowing the sun to warm them from where I sat on the top step of the library's backyard amphitheater. I loved the quiet here, almost sacred. The scent of honeysuckle, the boats bobbing in the harbor, the expanse of green grass centered below.

Aunt Pris had gushed—as much as Aunt Pris could ever be capable of gushing—over Mom's breakfast that morning. Once I cleared up the estimate with Tripp, I didn't see anything stopping us from getting the go-ahead.

I caught a form out of the corner of my eye and stood at the sight of my friend. His hair stuck up at odds and ends as if he'd recently doused it with water and ran his fingers through it. Dirt crusted the thighs of his jeans. A pull of attraction started in my belly, spiraling to the nerve endings throughout my body. Without warning, my thoughts turned to that day last summer—the bench overlooking Curtis Island, the pain of losing Dad coupled with Maggie's marriage. How I had sat alongside that bench with Tripp, openly sulking.

I had mumbled against Tripp's shoulder, hiding against him when the tears failed to stop. "Everything's changing. I feel like

I'm not just losing my sister, but my dearest friend." I brought my knees to my chest, rested my chin on them.

Tripp wriggled his hand beneath my own. "You've got me." His voice was quiet, solemn. "I'll stand by you all the days of my life, Josie."

I tugged my hand from his. "Don't, Tripp. Please. Not now."

"Yes, now." He said the words with resolve, surprising me.

"What?"

"I've loved you forever, Josie. Even when I tried to help myself, I couldn't. I've tried to show you, and you won't see. I've tried to tell you, and you won't hear. Things are changing, yes. Why don't we change with them?"

I moved to stand, but he kept hold of my hand until I couldn't help but meet his gaze. "You're not running away this time. I want you to hear, and hear me good."

"Tripp...."

"Josie, I want you. More than I've ever wanted anything. I know I don't deserve you, but I'll work hard all of my days to deserve you. For the rest of my life if you'll have me. Be with me forever. Marry me, Josie." He tilted his head, questioning, pleading.

Oh, how I wanted to lose myself in those sincere dark eyes, to accept his offer of love and security and friendship for life. Yet, those weren't my plans. Career first, love second. In that order, no exceptions.

If I were to become Tripp's wife, I'd lose myself. He'd expect me to stay in Camden, to never find a bigger purpose outside of our quaint town, never fulfill my dreams. The dreams I planned before I was old enough to ride a bicycle. See the world. Befriend learned men and women. Make a name for myself. Help humanity.

I could do none of it by staying in Camden. By becoming a wife. Quite simply, I loved my liberty too much to give it up for any man. Even one as winning as Tripp Colton.

"You are too good for me. I wish I could give you what you want, but I can't. I can't be this next step into adulthood for you. I can't go and settle down yet, Tripp. You know I can't. I won't."

His guarded eyes lay shadowed in defeat. "Then you don't love me?"

"I do. I truly do."

And then his warm mouth covered my own, lingering, tasting in a way that produced a thundering heat in my limbs. If I were honest, I could admit to having fantasized about such a kiss on occasion. But never had I imagined the depth of force it created within me. The world spun, turning itself upside down. Tripp was my best friend, not someone who was supposed to make my knees weak. Not someone who was supposed to kiss like *that*.

I felt his passion grow as he moved in deeper, pulling me closer against his muscled chest, and Lord help me, I wanted him. I wanted to love him.

And if it didn't mean entirely losing myself to do so, I would have. But I couldn't. I had to be strong.

So I'd pulled away, refusing to let myself get lost in a man.

"Please, never do that again."

His dazed look appeared still half caught up in our kiss. He shook his head. "What?"

"Tripp, I'm so sorry. I do love you, but I can't marry you."

"Josie, you don't kiss a man like that and then throw his proposal out with last night's garbage."

"*You* kissed me."

"And you liked it."

I closed my eyes, breathed deep. "That doesn't have anything to do with anything."

He threw up his hands. "It has everything to do with everything!"

"So I should dictate my life on pure emotion, then? On the temptation of sex?"

He bunched his fists at his side. "Is that the only thing you think I want you for? Sex? Josie Martin, I consider myself a humble man, but let me tell you, there's more than one woman in this town who would stoop to having sex with me."

I straightened, my anger matching his. How dare he send us spiraling in this direction, how dare he kiss me. And how dare I allow my own feelings to spiral out of control. "Then maybe you should go find one of them!"

He grabbed my arms again. "I don't want any of them. Josie, my Josie...I want you and only you."

I pushed back against his hands, but he refused to let go. I fought back the wetness pressing at my eyelids. "Tripp...look at us, we can't even have a conversation about love without arguing."

"I know you love me. Why can't you just admit it? Forget the proposal, even. Just tell me how you really feel about me."

I grew still, quiet, knowing my answer couldn't change. Tripp was not a part of the future I'd created for myself. "I'm sorry."

He released me, and I stumbled backward. We stood there, like frozen statues in time. Had I led him on? Had he tried to show me his feelings in the past, but I'd written them off as simple friendship, as just Tripp being Tripp?

"I'm sorry," I repeated. "Don't be angry. I simply can't love you in that way."

"That's bull, Josie. I know you...I know you."

He'd turned, walked away, and a part of me wanted to continue our fight just so he wouldn't leave. I racked my brain for something to yell at his back, searched the ground for something to throw at him. He had no right to take our perfectly comfortable friendship and turn it into something else. He had no right to make me feel these things for him. Dad had died only months ago, Maggie was off with her new family, everything was changing, and I hated it.

I watched his retreating back, and I let him go without another word.

The next time I saw him was just a few weeks ago, on the day of Mom's retirement party.

Now, as he walked toward me, the wind whipping off the harbor and sweeping over the secluded steps of the amphitheater, I appreciated that we had gained back some of our easy friendship despite our time apart. He smiled as he drew closer and it, combined with the memories of that summer day, nearly melted my heart. If only I had responded differently all those months ago. If only I'd admitted my feelings. Maybe I would have stayed in Camden. Maybe I never would have gone out for that drink with Finn. Maybe I never would have cemented that jagged crack in my heart with all the wrong things.

I straightened my spine and breathed deep, shaking off the memories and giving Tripp my full attention. "You look like you were down in the trenches today."

He dusted off his jeans, sending a plume of dirt through the air. "You could say that. What's up?"

I squinted up at him. "You probably already know what I need to talk to you about."

He lowered himself to the flat rock beside me. "I-uh, no, I'm not really sure."

"Tripp, the estimate? Mom's not too happy with you."

A look of relief washed over his face. "Oh, the estimate. What doesn't she like about it?"

"The number. It's low. Too low. What'd you do? She refuses to hire you if you're purposely taking a loss for the sake of a neighbor."

"Who said anything about taking a loss?"

I shook my head. "I don't see how you can operate a job this big without making a profit."

"Hey now, we're all about profit at Colton Contractors. This endeavor is only going to add to the charm of the town. We want to be a part of it. That's profit for the town and for the business."

"Not enough to be worth your time, though. Give us another price, Tripp. We demand it."

He shook his head. "No can do."

"So you'd rather us go to another contractor?"

"You aren't that foolish. No one will do a better job than Colton Contractors, and you know it. Besides, I'm dying to get my hands on this renovation. Would you really deny me this?"

I kicked my flip-flops off, planted my feet on the cool grass. "Mom said she was going to talk to your grandfather if you didn't agree."

He chuckled. "Tell her good luck."

I groaned. "Fine, then. I'm leaving it in her hands to decide. If she decides to go with Stanley Construction..."

Tripp made a look of pure disgust. "Charles Stanley is a lowlife who ogles your Mom every chance he gets. No chance in Hades I'm going to let that guy botch up this job."

I smiled at his profile, inhaled the spicy scent of him. "You really are a good guy, you know that? We'll probably show Aunt Pris everything tomorrow. Pray for us, okay?"

"Sure thing." His face grew serious.

"What's wrong? I actually think Aunt Pris might go for all this."

"It's not that. It's nothing, really." He shrugged. "I just heard something this morning. About you."

"Okay..."

"I felt bad for even entertaining it, but you should probably know anyway."

Something clenched in my chest. The amphitheater swayed before me. "What should I know?"

"There's some sort of rumor going around about you. About us."

I expelled a long breath. "Like that's anything new. People will talk, especially in a small town. Don't let it get to you."

He grew quiet. Too quiet. Finally, "You're right. But when

Jenny Simcock congratulates me on being the father of your baby, it's hard to suck it up and keep quiet."

"M-my baby?" I felt the color leach from my face. How had Jenny found out? Only Maggie knew, and my sister would suffer torture before betraying me, especially to the likes of the town gossip.

I wasn't ready for this. I planned to tell Mom tonight, my family soon after. But for the entire town to know? For Tripp to know? To have to face this on top of any heartbreak I'd already caused him?

"Josie, say something." He knelt in front of me, placed his hands on my bare knees, searched my eyes. "You're not..."

I pressed my lips together hard to keep from crying, to keep from speaking. If I never spoke again, Tripp would never have to know. I closed my eyes. When I opened them, Tripp's hands dropped from my knees, and he sat back down on the grass, as if paralyzed.

"You're pregnant."

I inhaled deep. There was no use denying it at this point. In another month or two my swollen abdomen would say more than I ever needed to. "I am."

"How—who?"

"It was a long year," I began.

He cursed—an unfamiliar, ugly word on his lips. I couldn't summon any fortitude to correct his ill manners. Not now. Maybe not ever.

"The entire thing was a mistake. A horrible, horrible mistake."

"A mistake? A mistake? The girl who could never give herself to a man..." He stood, raking his hand through his hair, a sound of pure frustration and anger erupting from him and echoing on the harbor. "You have to be kidding me. Please tell me you're kidding."

A tear slid down my cheek and for a moment I saw myself through his eyes and hated myself. I opened my mouth to make excuses—to tell him I was lonely, I was duped, that Finn seemed like everything I wanted for my life. But the words didn't make it past my throat. What did it matter? What did any of it matter?

"Where's the father now? Does he know?"

"He knows," I whispered.

"And?"

"And nothing. I haven't decided if I'm keeping the baby after it's born."

Tripp paced in front of me, his anger and energy palpable, humming through the air between us. I sensed his gaze heavy on me, but I couldn't meet it, didn't want to witness the intense disappointment directed my way.

"I can't be here right now. I have to go."

I felt as if he were saying *I can't stand the sight of you.*

He turned, walked a few steps away from me, then turned back, the depth of hurt in his dark eyes searing me deep. "There really never was a chance for us, was there?"

Even now, I couldn't affirm his words, even if I should. If I said no, there had never been a chance for us, he'd probably be better off. Yes, it would hurt, but it would push him forward toward a new life, one that didn't include me. But I couldn't lie to him. Neither could I tell him how close I'd been to succumbing to his love that day last summer, how close I'd been many times since. For I'd given myself to another. What kind of a woman was so wishy-washy to think herself in love with two men?

So I said the only heartfelt thing I could say. "I'm so sorry, Tripp."

And I was.

Sorry for ever laying eyes on Finn Becker. Sorry for not believing Tripp's love would be enough for me. Maybe I was even sorry for returning home, for breaking his heart all over again. Sorry, sorry, sorry.

I watched his retreating back once again and curled myself over my belly. I'd never felt more alone. And now, half the town knew of my transgressions. I could only imagine the talk floating around....

Poor Hannah, losing her husband at such a young age....

Poor Martin kids, wearing their hand-me-down clothes....

Poor Martin family, trying to start yet another project while raising a bastard of a child....

Why did we want to stay in Camden anyway? Even if Aunt Pris would still give us a chance, maybe fate—or my own bad decisions—doomed us all to failure.

❧ 15 ❧

Someday, the pain would stop. Someday it would ease, dissipate from the massive sting of hurt clawing his insides —his very soul—to something far more manageable. Maybe a trickle, a pinprick of pain.

Someday. But not today.

Tripp careened into his grandfather's drive, noting that neither Grandpop's nor August's vehicles were parked in the drive or the garage. Once inside, he took the stairs hard up to his bedroom where he changed into a pair of gym shorts, tore his shirt off, and threw it on his bed. By the time he entered the basement and donned his boxing gloves, he breathed heavy, could barely see past the red fury in his mind. He planted his feet on the ground and pounded out his frustration on the punching bag.

One, two, three, four, hard and fast. Knuckles flush with the bag. One, two, three, four. No pain. No pain.

If he kept telling himself that, would it be true?

He rested his head against the bag, gave it some hard hooks, jabbing it over and over again until sweat poured down his face and chest, until he felt he might pass out from the exertion. And still, the pain clamored at his heart, shaking it with an intensity he'd never known.

As much as he hated to admit it, he still held hope for him and Josie. He might be a fool, yes, but he simply couldn't imagine loving another, couldn't imagine them not being together. Who else could he laugh with, fight with, cry with, love with? Who else could he picture by his side into old age? Who else could he love enough to have his children?

He let off an especially hard punch at that last thought, felt the bones of his knuckles explode, cracking with his anger and frustration. He swore, tore off the gloves, saw his knuckles bruised and red, the bones of his right hand seeming to be in the wrong place on his hands.

He stumbled up the stairs and to the kitchen, grabbed a bag of frozen peas from the stainless steel freezer and plopped it onto his sweaty hand. He gulped down a glass of water, but it didn't satiate the need within. He walked into the dining room, sought out Grandpop's liquor cabinet. While Tripp indulged in an occasional beer or cocktail now and then, he usually stayed away from the hard stuff as a means to dull pain. But this afternoon, he couldn't think of one good reason not to sulk with Jack Daniels.

He took the bottle out, twisted off the cap, and poured himself a shot. And then another. He sat heavily at the dining room table, knowing his actions went against his convictions. He'd never been so weak. He was supposed to be holy and blameless.

He thought of Josie again. Holy and blameless, his backside. Well, what was good enough for the goose, was good enough for the gander. He took another shot, felt the room spin, and pushed the bottle aside, soaked in the fog of oblivion.

Who knew how much time passed, but from somewhere far away, the doorbell rang. He ignored it, but it wouldn't stop. Then a persistent knock, louder and louder in his ears.

He stumbled toward the door. If Josie stood on the other side, he didn't think he'd be able to take it. And what would she say, seeing him like this? Then again, who really cared? Who gave a flying leap what one girl thought of him?

"What do you want?" He wrenched open the door.

"Tripp." Ashley Robinson stood on his doorstep, fresh as a daisy in a summer dress that modestly highlighted her curves, a book in hand. If he'd had an elementary school teacher half as sweet as her, he might have done better in grade school. She shifted from one foot to the other. "I—I hope I'm not bothering you. I stopped by to leave this on the doorstep, but I saw your truck running. When you didn't answer, I got worried."

His truck running? He peered around her into the drive where the door of his truck stood open, the engine idling. He hadn't shut off his truck? How'd he get in the house, then? Had he used the key beneath the planter?

He couldn't remember. He put his arm above his head against the doorframe to steady himself. "Thanks. Thanks, Ashley. I'll go get the keys in a minute."

He followed her gaze to his bare chest. A surge of desire pulsed through him. And why shouldn't he feel such things? An image of Josie alone in the amphitheater flitted through his thoughts, but the alcohol held it at bay. Just a floating thought associated with a cloud of pain he no longer felt the need to claim as his own.

Ashley shoved a book out to him. He tried to read the title, but the letters blurred.

"I told you I'd let you borrow it at our last group session?"

He shook his head, didn't remember anything about a book. "I don't really read. Josie makes fun of me for that."

"Okay...well, I guess I'll go if you're okay. Want me to grab your keys for you before I go?"

"You want to come in?" He didn't know what he said. But he knew Ashley liked him. Why not explore that? Why should he be so blindly faithful to a woman having another man's baby?

"Um, before I get your keys?"

He shrugged.

"Tripp, are you drunk?"

"I had a couple of shots. Got some bad news today."

"I'll be right back." She walked to his truck, grabbed his keys, and came back. He lingered on the curves of her beneath that dress, felt his body responding to what it might feel like to give in for once. Who was he waiting for anyway?

Ashley handed him his keys, but not before seeing his hand. "Your hand. You need to go to the ER, Tripp. Come on, I'll take you."

He took her arm with his opposite hand, pulled her into the house, but started to stumble. "Don't want to."

She led him to the sofa, helped him sit down. He pulled her onto his lap, felt her soft skin against his arms, the thin fabric of her dress against his chest.

She resisted at first, but not very hard. "Tripp, this really isn't like you. You need to sleep this off."

He lowered his lips to her neck, trailing them along her skin. He'd wanted to do this to Josie. Blast it all. Why couldn't she love him? Why couldn't she want him as he knew Ashley did? Why couldn't she sink into his arms like this?

But no, he refused to go there. Instead, he trailed his lips up to Ashley's mouth, tasted her. She responded to him, but when he tasted salt, he opened his eyes and pulled away.

"Why are you crying, Ash?"

"Because I've wanted this for so long, but I know it's not real and I know we need to stop whatever this is. You'll wake up from this stupor and wish this hadn't happened and I'll want it to happen all over again. Only next time with you not drunk."

"I'm an idiot." He sighed, felt himself sober up a notch. "I'm so sorry."

She gave him a sad smile. "You'll never be over her, will you?"

He shifted, lifting her off his lap. "I wish I could be. Ashley, you don't deserve this. You don't deserve me, that's for sure. I really am sorry. I should have never played with your feelings."

Of all people, he understood how that felt.

"Let me take you to the ER?"

He looked at his knuckles. "I'm fine. Really."

She stood. "Okay."

"Ashley, I know I don't deserve what I'm about to ask but—"

"You're right, you don't." A small, sad smile broke over her face. "But it doesn't matter, I'll give it to you anyway. I won't say a word about this, to anyone."

"You're a good friend," he said.

"Remember that, Tripp Colton."

And then she was gone, leaving him to sleep off the haze of drunkenness he'd stupidly drowned himself in.

"Man, you smell like you took a bath in a tub of Jack Daniels after running a marathon."

Tripp peeled open his eyes. A sharp pain split the side of his head and he winced, closing his eyes again.

Another insistent tap on his arm. "Come on, Bro, we got to get you off the couch before Grandpop gets home. No hope for this couch but to steam clean it, anyway."

"August?"

"You expecting Princess Leia? Come on, up and at 'em, Tiger."

With much effort, he allowed his brother to help him into a sitting position. He pressed a hand to his head, then winced at the throb in his knuckles.

"What'd you do, get in a fight with Grandpop's liquor cabinet?"

Tripp groaned. "Something like that." With his left hand, he pulled up on August's arm until they both stood.

"Can you make it up the stairs?"

"Don't have much choice, do I?"

"Not if you want Grandpop to keep you up on that pedestal of yours."

Tripp worked his way up the stairs, his head throbbing with each step. He was a royal idiot and a half. And August finding him like this....

Lord, what have I done?

With crashing realization, he remembered Ashley, and then his horrible conversation with Josie. He stumbled a few feet from his room, fresh pain sucker punching him in the gut.

Once upstairs, August grabbed Tripp a couple of ibuprofen and a glass of water, then dumped him in the shower. The hot water cleared his head some, but as he recalled the fool he'd made of himself, he wished for the haze again.

He shut off the water and wrapped a towel around his waist, then went into his bedroom where August sat in his desk chair. "She's really pregnant, huh?"

Tripp pressed his left hand to his still aching head. "How'd you know?"

"Can't think of much else that would send you to Grandpop's liquor cabinet."

"I shouldn't have done that, August. It was stupid. I'm a—"

"Hey, I know. Just—try not to be the big brother or the boss right now, okay? I'm trying to help you for once."

"Yeah...about that, thanks." Tripp ducked back into the bathroom to hang up his towel and throw on a fresh pair of shorts and some deodorant.

"I'm assuming you're not the father."

"You're assuming right."

August clasped his hands over outstretched legs, shook his head. "Man. *Josie.* I could have seen Amie getting knocked up, or maybe even Maggie, but not Josie. She always seemed to know where she was going and it never had anything to do with getting caught up in men. What happened?"

"I thought you were trying to help." Tripp lay on his bed, allowed the breeze from the open window to calm him. The smell of lilacs floated in. Mom had loved lilacs. He thought of her in heaven, and for a split second felt a moment of peace. He wasn't in control, of any of this.

He should have tried telling himself that before he broke into Grandpop's liquor.

Who did he think he was, anyway? Hot shot contractor, in charge of the thriving family business, father figure to his younger brother, moral, faithful, God-fearing man...yeah, right. He'd really proven his worth today, hadn't he?

"God, I'm such a mess. Help."

August came over, sat beside him, jabbed him in the ribs. "Hey, aren't you always telling me that God loves us even when we're at our ugliest?"

Tripp couldn't contain a small smile. "You were actually listening to me?"

"Maybe here and there."

Tripp breathed deep around the lingering pain in his heart. God loved him at his ugliest—and if the last few hours were any indication, he was a colossal ugly. Yet, he would survive. He would get through.

And God loved Josie at her ugliest, too. Now. She was in trouble and alone. Not truly alone, he knew, for Hannah and her siblings would never leave her side.

But he had.

He thought of the rumors circulating in town. People thought he was the father. For once, he wished the gossip were true.

With renewed pain, he remembered Ashley sitting on his lap. How far would he have let things go if it hadn't been for Ashley's tears? And how would he feel going to Josie with such a confession, only to have Josie turn her back on him as he had done to her today?

He groaned again. He claimed to love Josie forever and ever, and yet he'd abandoned her when she needed him most. Of course, no one expected him to sit around and keep up the puppy love habit, but he was her friend, and he sure hadn't acted like one.

And though it hurt like Hades, it also didn't change the fact that he loved her. Well, now was his chance to prove it: love despite the ugly. The kind of love that was much more than a nice, fuzzy feeling. More than lust. But genuine compassion. Willing the good of another. Being prepared to sacrifice.

"Uh-oh. I know that look. What are you planning, Bro?"

Tripp shook his head. He had a lot of thinking and praying to do before he saw Josie again. He had a call to make to Ashley, an apology to utter. And probably somewhere in there, he needed to see a doctor about his hand.

He sat up. "Nothing but a lot of reevaluating. You up to driving me to the hospital so I can get this hand looked at?"

August grinned. "Sure. You know, if you wanted to get out of framing the rest of that in-law apartment, you could have just said so. You're the boss after all."

Tripp didn't have the energy to put his brother in a sleeper-hold today, but soon, very soon, he would.

And then he'd thank the daylights out of him.

❧ 16 ❧

There was something to be said about ripping the Band-Aid off fast.

Tripp's reaction to my misdeeds hurt. It caused me to grieve my choices anew, but now I could stop wondering how he'd take it all. I was done with secrets. Thanks to Jenny, there wouldn't be any left anyhow. Best to set the town straight before my sins harmed others.

Like my family.

I entered the house, quiet except for the gentle hum of the dishwasher. A flutter of movement in the backyard caught my attention and I opened the door to the patio, where Lizzie was planting larkspur and pink pansies in a pot. I sat on a chair beside her. "Those are pretty."

She pulled back, surveying her work. "They are, aren't they? I've been planning some pots for Aunt Pris's porch. Thought about it a lot on my hike this morning."

"Where'd you go today?"

"Maiden Cliff. I wanted to work on a song."

"Hopefully not a morbid one."

Lizzie smiled, her face at peace. I remembered Dad's name for her, then, thought it suited. Little Tranquility.

"I've always been drawn to that place, the story of that girl."

A large white cross marked the top of Maiden Cliff in memory of the eleven-year-old girl who had fallen from it more than one-hundred fifty years ago. I wasn't sure how healthy Lizzie's preoccupation with her was. Whether it be this girl, Elizabeth Alcott, or Molly Mello, a fifteen-year-old from our church who had recently died in a tragic car accident, my sister tended to dwell on those who had gone too soon. I often wondered why Mom and Dad had named us after the *Little Women* characters—and why they thought it okay to name Lizzie after the one whose outcome had been...well, morbid. Of course, Lizzie's brush with cancer didn't help any.

"You're always one for deep thoughts." I smiled at her. "You look good. Really good."

"I feel good. I'm on a new thyroid medication that's making all the difference. I've never had so much energy."

I could tell. She actually glowed. Beautiful. I remembered sitting in the hospital waiting room after they'd taken out her thyroid, my own shorn head cold from the unfamiliar chill of the exposed air. I'd appreciated my sister anew then. The thought of losing such a gentle spirit, the simple beauty of her self-forgetfulness that brought such brilliant light to our own family, was more than I could take. I wondered when she woke what she would say about my bald head. She'd think I'd done it for Rose Hornwell, of course. Rose shared a room in the hospital with Lizzie and had a much more serious form of cancer and was already deep in chemotherapy.

The day before her surgery, Lizzie lay amidst crisp white hospital bed sheets, her old favorite doll Johanna, laying by her side, almost enveloped in the large sleeve of her jonnie. "I wish I could do something for Rose. She's devastated about losing her hair. I'd shave my own head if I could to make her feel better."

I'd tugged at my sister's smooth brown locks. "Let's get you through surgery before you start planning such things." But as they rolled Lizzie away to surgery, I knew something I could do to encourage her—and of course, it hadn't anything to do with her at all.

I still remembered Tripp's look of horror when he first saw me in the waiting room, then his warm arms around me and soft lips upon my shaved head as I explained in tears why I'd done what I'd done. "You're still beautiful to me." In that moment, so very frightened to lose my sister and her gentle spirit, Tripp's warm embrace comforted my sore heart, led me nearer to the Divine arm that would truly uphold me in my worries over the weeks and months following Lizzie's surgery.

Later that night, Tripp bought me a soft green knitted cap with a handwritten note that said, *Lizzie's not the only one with a heart as big as the moon. You are amazing, Josie Martin.*

He'd loved me even then. Why hadn't I had the eyes to appreciate it?

Lizzie cleared her throat from her spot on the patio. "Speaking of deep thoughts, you're awfully quiet." She pressed her gloved hands into the sides of the pot, the gentle color of the flowers swaying beneath her ministrations.

"I have a few, I suppose." My breath wobbled at the thought of what I needed to say.

"Out with it then." She pivoted to give me her full attention.

The front door slammed, making me jump. "Josie!"

"Out here!" I called, already dreading the urgent pitch of Amie's voice.

She rushed out the back door, spilling her books onto the patio table. "Tia Graber is spreading the most ugly rumor about you and Tripp. It's all over school, and I almost socked that pretty little nose of hers off her face for insisting it was true."

"Oh, Amie." Lizzie sat up straighter. "You cannot get in

trouble with only a few days left of classes. They could ban you from graduation, you know."

Amie looked at me. "Don't you even care what they're saying? I mean, I know you all might have gotten used to everyone talking about us over the years, but I for one am so ready to be done with this school and this town. And them bringing Tripp into it…" Her face reddened. "It's not right."

"I'm surprised a bunch of high-schoolers care about us old folks." I attempted to joke, but it fell flat.

"Well, what's the horrible rumor then?" Lizzie asked.

I breathed deep. "I already know what they're saying."

"You do?"

I bit my lip. "I spoke to Tripp this afternoon."

Amie flopped onto the double patio swing, pushed her legs against the cobbles. "So it's already gotten around town. Great. Poor Tripp."

"What about poor Josie?" Lizzie pinched the fingers of one of her gloves and slid it off.

I shook my head. "It's not poor Josie because—"

"We having a pow wow?" Bronson, covered in grass clippings, came around the side of the house and sprawled out on the shade of the cobbles in the far corner, clumps of dirt sticking to the bottom of his work boots.

"Josie was just going to tell us why there's a big rumor going around that she's pregnant with Tripp's baby." Amie crossed her arms over her chest.

Bronson shot up. "What? I'll kill him. I don't care if he's older and bigger than me—"

Lizzie lay a hand on his arm. "It's not true, Bron. It's just a rumor."

Amie squinted at me. "But rumors usually start with a shred of truth, so what gives, Josie? Are you and Tripp back together again?"

"We never *were* together to begin with, so—"

"Guys, can I have some help with the groceries?" Mom called through the window. "I think I went overboard, and—" She looked at all of us, came outside the door. "What's the matter? Do I need to sit down? Tell me if I need to sit down because I think I've handled my quota of shocking news for a lifetime in the last eighteen months."

I rubbed my hands over my eyes. Poor Mom. Blow after blow for this family. Never simply a time to rest, to enjoy peace. "You better sit down, Mom."

Lizzie and Amie turned wide eyes toward me. Mom lowered herself beside Amie on the swing.

There was no easy way to say this, no easy way to deliver my news. Best to deliver it quick and fast, face the consequences of my shame head-on.

"I'm pregnant."

I expected a lot of reactions, but Mom laughing wasn't one of them.

I stared at her. "I'm not joking."

The laughter on Mom's lips died and her mouth fell open.

"Josie," Lizzie whispered.

Amie stared at me, shook her head back and forth, back and forth.

Bronson stood, heading for the door. "I'll kill him. Acting all high-and-mighty, badgering you to high heaven. He's—"

"Tripp's not the father, Bronson."

"Then tell me who is, because I'm not above killing strangers, either."

I could only stare at Mom, suddenly preoccupied with the pattern of cobbles at her feet.

"Mom, say something," I said.

"Okay. It's okay. We'll figure this out." She pushed her feet against the cobbles to rock the swing.

"I told Maggie last night." Not pertinent information, but something to fill the silence of the patio, the void of disbelief suspended in the air. "I don't know that I'm going to keep the baby, but I had an appointment last week, and I'm due in October." I lifted my gaze to my mother's. "Mom, I'm so sorry. I know you didn't expect this, I know you'll be disappointed in me—I'm disappointed in myself. But all the same, I'm sorry."

She swallowed, held her hand out to me. "Honey, you are a grown woman and I will always be proud of you. This doesn't change that. I just—well, you always had such big career plans for yourself. A baby...oh my, a baby."

"I know it complicates things. That's why I needed to tell you all now. I'll have to tell Aunt Pris before she gives us her final answer, too."

"But if Tripp's not the father, who is?" Amie asked.

I shook my head. "That's not important. He was a man I knew in New York, a man I got wrapped up in. A mistake."

Lizzie placed a hand on my knee. "I'm so sorry, Josie."

I didn't deserve such words and tears pricked the back of my eyelids.

"I was stupid. Even now, I feel like I was in some alternate reality. That's not an excuse. I made decisions, and now I need to face them. I don't know if I can keep this baby, I don't know if I can be a single mother. I don't know if I can afford to live on my own while paying for childcare. I don't know if I'm what's best for this child."

"If you keep the baby, the father has to pay child support. He can't just walk away because he's a man. I mean, what kind of lowlife does that?" Amie's face turned red.

"He knows, doesn't he?" Lizzie slid her small hand into mine.

I pressed my lips together before speaking. While I needn't tell them Finn's identity, I could tell them the facts. "He knows. He wants nothing to do with the child. I'd rather move on and pretend he doesn't exist."

"He sounds like a winner." Bronson's sarcastic words stung.

Not because they weren't truth, but because they pointed to my own bad judgment.

"Right now, that's where I'm at. Maybe once the baby arrives and I know for certain what I'm going to do with it, I'll be able to face him. But right now, it's still too painful."

Bronson sat back down on the cobbles, arms slung loose over bent knees. "If the father refuses to be involved, then maybe giving it up is what's best. There's lots of couples who actually want a baby—"

"And who's to say Josie doesn't want her baby?" Lizzie said in her quiet way. She turned to me. "I'd help you, Josie. I know I'm not a father, but I would love your baby like he or she was my own."

"Oh, Lizzie..."

"This is a big decision." Mom rubbed her temples. "It's not one to be made lightly or by others, and certainly not in one night. This is Josie's decision. But honey, we are family and we will support whatever you decide."

A chorus of nods and affirmations.

"Thank you." I hadn't expected anything less, but to hear it caused a burden to lift from my chest.

Bronson stood, took off his hat, and slapped it against his thigh. "I still want to kill the guy."

He wasn't the only one.

"I'm going to go shower. Maybe...you think we could pray for you?"

"Only if you add in a prayer for your murderous heart as well." I joked, but didn't mind the offer of prayer as much as I usually bristled at such things. Here, it seemed a show of support, a solidarity in beseeching a Help I very much needed.

"Done." Bronson placed his hand on my shoulder. He prayed for the unborn babe within, for wisdom and guidance for me in making the decision I would have to make for my child. He even prayed for the father of my baby.

I tried to pray alongside my brother on that one, to put aside my ill will toward Finn. Really I did.

When Bronson finished and the chorus of "Amens" had died down, he bent over and kissed my cheek. "Let me know if you need anything, okay?"

"Thank you."

Amie stood and gave me a hug. "If the girls at school ask, I can just tell them it's none of their business."

I sighed. "You're right, it's not. But the truth will be apparent before long, so whatever, Amie. I'd rather Tripp be spared from the rumors, though."

She smiled. "I'm pretty certain Tripp can handle himself."

"You didn't see him when he got the news."

Her face fell. "He was real upset, wasn't he? Of course he was."

"He's always loved you, Josie. Too bad..." Lizzie's voice trailed off.

"I know. Too bad I hadn't made a slew of other possible choices this past year."

Lizzie shook her head. "That's not what I was going to say." She stood. "If you need to talk, I'm here, okay?"

"Thanks, sweetie."

My two sisters left the patio, leaving me alone with Mom and the fresh scent of soil from Lizzie's recent plantings. Mom patted the spot on the swing Amie had vacated. I sat, allowed her to put her arms around me even as they called forth tears.

"I'm sorry, Mom. I feel like a broken record, but I am. I let everyone down. You, Dad, myself, Tripp. I'm a mess."

"Oh, honey. Never be afraid to come to me. We all have a mess or two of our own, don't we? You've always been super hard on yourself, so I think it makes it more difficult for you." She squeezed my shoulder. "But don't you dare think Dad's up in heaven shaking his head over you, hear me? If he can see us at all, it's with the clearest, most perfect vision. He's seeing this as the turning point it is for you. He's also seeing how God's going to orchestrate it all out for good. I just know it."

"I wish I had your faith."

"It's not my own, that's for sure. I find it the more I fall into His arms and the less I depend on human power and wisdom. It's about the falling...and trusting that He will do the catching. That He will be the very best of friends."

I sniffed.

"Honey, you will never be fatherless."

I tried to sink into that fact, that assurance, but the old worries crowded in. "I have to tell Aunt Pris, don't I?"

She smiled, pulled her arm out from around me. "Afraid so."

"She's the last one on my list, so maybe I'll head on over there now and get this over with."

"You want me to come?"

I shook my head. "I didn't need your help getting into this, so I best handle it on my own. I just...if I decide to keep the baby, Aunt Pris might not want me living in her home. I don't know a lot about babies, but I know they're messy and they cry a lot. I'm not sure if that would be a game-changer. If it is, I promise I will figure something out on my own. I will not let this dictate whether The Orchard House Bed and Breakfast will happen."

Mom took my hand in hers. "We'll work something out. Who knows, maybe you're not giving Aunt Pris enough credit. She's certainly surprised us so far."

I closed my eyes and leaned back into the swing. "The funny thing is, I feel like I need this B&B as much as you do. How crazy is that?"

"Even if you decide to keep the baby, it doesn't mean you have to give up your dreams."

"Do you think dreams can change?"

"Of course."

"Did yours?" I asked.

She smiled. "I was never as headstrong and determined as you.

Yes, I dreamed about a B&B, but most of all, I dreamed of having a family. And we did a great job on that one if I do say so myself."

Dreams of a family. All this time I'd been telling myself Mom had sacrificed her bed and breakfast dream for us. But no, her real dream had been *us*.

Was that the sort of happiness I wanted too?

She elbowed me. "Are you changing your mind about your major?"

I shrugged. "It's like my past experiences this year in New York and with...everything, soured me on the idea of becoming a psychologist. Like all I want now is home and you guys."

"Dreams can certainly change, and I think during big life decisions it's natural to seek the place we feel most secure, but Josie, you were meant to fly, my girl. Whether that's in the field of psychology or not, take some time to really think and pray about where your passion's leading you. *Your* passion, honey. Not your father's, or your baby's father, or Tripp's or any other man's or mine...but yours. Let the Lord speak to your heart."

I relaxed into that thought for a moment, caught a brief glimpse of unfamiliar freedom in it before it floated away. Had I been chasing after everyone's dreams but my own?

She hugged me one more time. "Until then, I am very much looking forward to running a bed and breakfast with you."

"Me too, Mom. Sure hope Aunt Pris feels the same way."

Mom ran a hand over my hair, a gesture she hadn't performed since my early teens. "You always were my brave girl."

Brave? If only I felt such a thing.

🞋 17 🞋

"Pardon me, young lady?" Aunt Pris bristled from where she held court on her Queen Anne sofa for tea time.

Esther grabbed my aunt's arm, and leaned closer. "She said she's pregnant, Priscilla. A baby. Don't you just love babies?"

"I'm afraid I don't," Aunt Pris snapped.

I looked at my aunt's faithful friend, grateful for her presence.

"The only reason you don't like babies is because you don't know what you're missing!" Esther exclaimed.

Maybe not the best approach. Had Aunt Pris ever wanted children? She hadn't even taken in her own nephew when he'd found himself an orphan.

Esther shimmied onto the edge of her chair. "Babies bring life to a house—almost how dogs do. Can you imagine this home without your Cragen?"

I glanced at Cragen, ever faithful on my aunt's lap but eyeing me with suspicion, a low growl in his throat. If babies were anything like Cragen, I may just have to throw in the towel now.

"Aunt Pris, I don't know that I'm keeping it, but I thought you should know about the possibility if we all end up living with you, that is."

She eyed me over the top of her glasses. "And you're not getting married?"

"No, I'm not."

Her hand fluttered at her throat. I hoped she wouldn't have a heart attack here and now.

"You are determined to raise this child on your own, then?"

"Or I will give it to a family who wants a baby."

She sat up straighter. "Well, I'll cast my vote for that idea."

"Priscilla!" Esther's dark brow wrinkled. "A baby!" As if those two words could make everything okay. "One of God's greatest blessings." She smiled at me. "Oh sure, the circumstances aren't as He'd intend, but this innocent babe *will* be a blessing."

The surety of her words almost made me believe them. Maybe it was time I started thinking of this child as a blessing instead of a curse—instead of a symbol of how Finn had abandoned me in the end.

"Aunt Pris, I don't want this to affect our bed and breakfast endeavor. If you are not comfortable with the idea of a baby beneath your roof, and if I decide to keep him or her, then I will find a way to live on my own. There's plenty of jobs I'm suited for, and I'm a hard worker."

"But who will run the bookshop, then?"

"I haven't thought that far ahead. Perhaps we don't open the bookshop until later, when we can afford someone to run it, if that can't be me." My chest squeezed at the thought of giving up the bookshop. I'd been waking all hours of the night, planning. How the store would look, how I wanted plenty of space to face the books outward so shoppers could see the beautiful covers. I'd include all things bookish as well. Journals and bookmarks, bookish jewelry and bookish clothes. Books on the history of Camden and New England, books on the Alcotts and their Orchard House. Maybe a small nook for coffee and tea, a few chairs and tables to add to the welcoming atmosphere.

"Absolutely not," Aunt Pris said. "I will not have a stranger handling part of the family business, handling our money."

"Okay. I want to run the bookshop, Aunt Pris. I'm very excited about it, so I understand."

"And what's to become of this degree I'm paying a hefty penny for?"

I blew out a slow breath. No turning back now. "I thought to transfer to online classes so I could be home. Less money as well, but same degree."

"And you'll have time to run a bookshop, take care of a baby, and attend school?"

"As I said, I'm not certain I'm keeping the baby. I need some time, Aunt Pris."

She didn't seem to hear me. "Perhaps we take some of that money you all plan to use to tear apart my kitchen and build a small apartment above the bookshop. That way we can all have a bit of separation between us and that child."

Should I be flattered or offended? "That's nice of you to offer —I think. But again, I don't know if I'm even keeping the baby. And Mom needs the new kitchen...although Tripp's estimate came back much lower than expected. Maybe we could do both if it came down to it and if you were open to more construction."

"What's one more thing at this point?" She threw up her hands. "Now tell me about this estimate. Why haven't I seen it?"

"Mom and I planned to show you everything tomorrow. Is there a time that works for you?"

"Eleven will be fine."

Esther beamed. "Yes, eleven is perfect."

Though I didn't remember inviting her, I appreciated her presence. She tended to soften Aunt Pris's hard edges.

Aunt Pris stood, spilling Cragen off her lap. "Now, if you'll excuse me, I need the restroom. I'll see you tomorrow, girl."

I blew my bangs out of my face as my aunt left the room. "I think that actually went well."

"Of course it did!" Esther smiled in that innocent way of hers. "A baby!" She crooked a finger at me until I came closer and bent at the waist to hear her words. "Don't let her fool you. She's just as excited 'bout the idea of this bed and breakfast as you are."

I straightened. "She is?"

"Yessiree. She's been lonely, poor dear. Why else do you think she lets me hang around? She couldn't stop talking about it at our quilting club meeting this past Saturday. Going on and on about the grand plans. She likes to pretend she's put out, but I can see it clear as day beneath all that fire and brimstone."

I cocked my head. "See what?"

"She's proud of you all. To have you, to have this home be filled again with purpose and laughter and family."

I kissed Esther's cheek. "Thank you, Esther. I needed to hear it."

"And don't forget what I said before, either. That baby is a blessing, child. You'll see."

⚜

JOSIE: *Hey, Captain. Not sure if you're still talking to me, but if you are, we're having a celebratory picnic tonight at Aunt Pris's. She signed off on our plans! Hope you'll come. Bring Grandpop and August too. 5:00*
TRIPP: *Good news. We'll try to make it.*

⚜

TRIPP PULLED UP THE DRIVE OF ORCHARD HOUSE, NOTING A large section of the blooming orchard trees closest to the house grew uninhibited by tall grass and weeds. It looked good, really classed up the place.

He ignored the knot in his stomach as he shut the truck door and greeted Grandpop and August, who had pulled in behind him. Procrastinating at the office hadn't helped his taunt nerves. He wondered if Josie set the truth straight with her family, or if some of them still believed the rumors flitting around town. Did any here wonder if he were the father of Josie's child?

Hannah waved and came over, her face glowing. She hugged Grandpop then Tripp. "I'm still not totally sure whether I should thank you both or scold you."

Grandpop kept a hand on Hannah's elbow. "Gratitude hurts less, so I vote for that, dear."

Hannah planted an impromptu kiss on Grandpop's cheek. "I want you all to come for a meal as often as you like, okay? You're a part of this. You're family."

Grandpop blinked fast. Was the old man growing emotions in his ninth decade?

Tripp gestured to the Victorian. "We can't wait to see your business alive and booming."

"Me neither." Her smile lit the evening, making her prettier than he'd seen her since Amos died. She was happy. If only Josie could get her smile back, too.

"We have shrimp cocktail and spinach-and-artichoke dip just out of the oven. We're about to break open the champagne."

"Just a simple picnic, huh?"

"Nothing's ever simple when it comes to cooking with Mom." Amie sidled up next to Hannah, her gaze settling on Tripp. "Glad you guys could come."

"Hey, Amie." August gave one of his dashing, dimpled grins to the youngest Martin. Was his little brother putting on the charm for her? "You almost out of jail?"

She rolled her eyes. "If you mean high school, yeah." Her gaze fluttered to Tripp. "And boy, I can't wait. The last couple of days have felt especially prisonish."

Tripp excused himself and walked toward Josh, who refereed a race between the twins. Out of the corner of his eye, he glimpsed Josie pouring champagne into dainty wine glasses at the picnic table. He hurried in Josh's direction.

Maggie's husband straightened at Tripp's arrival and held out a hand. "Hey, man. How's it going?"

"Good to see you." Tripp held up the three fingers of his right hand and shrugged. He'd broken his outermost knuckle during his tantrum the other day, which was stuck in a splint for the next four to six weeks.

"Hurt on the job?"

"Went a little too hard on the punching bag the other night."

Josh winced. "Ouch. Right-handed?"

Tripp nodded. "Yup. I only have myself to blame, though." He looked at the two boys barreling across the green grass toward them. "You recruiting them already?"

Josh chuckled. "Can never start too young. They come to as many meets as Mags can get them to. You should see them yelling at the kids on the sidelines. They can be just as loud as me."

"How's the old place? The high school, I mean. Amie just compared it with a jail, so maybe not much has changed."

Josh's grin put Tripp further at ease. "I guess like anything else, it's all in what you make it. Tough when your sister's the topic of gossip, though, especially when you should be reveling in your last days of senior year."

"Amie's sister?"

Josh jerked his head toward the object of Tripp's affection and pain. "Josie. It appears this town doesn't have much else to do besides gossip about the Martin family."

His jaw tightened. "I heard firsthand myself. I don't know what it is, but this family has always been a source of fascination for folks."

The twins raced in, barely catching their breaths before arguing about who won. "Davey won this time, boys, but it was close." Josh pointed toward the rectangle table Hannah had adorned with a tablecloth. "Go see about getting a drink over there."

"Soda!" They raced off.

"Water!" Josh yelled back. He laughed, turned to Tripp. "Business good?"

"Great." He nodded toward Aunt Pris's home, standing grand and historic beside them, its many gables and turrets regal in the afternoon sunlight. "We're excited about this project, thinking of hiring on a few more, actually. You know of any graduates who are handy with a hammer?"

"I could check with the shop teacher for you. But you know, I've been looking for some summer work myself."

Tripp tilted his head to the side. "You?"

"I've swung a hammer or two in my day. Helped my uncle after high school and through college. Demo, framing, roofing and shingling, some finish work. It's been awhile, but I think I could hold my own."

"You guys okay...you know, financially?" The question felt a bit intrusive, and maybe it was, but like he'd told Hannah, this family was his. If he could help, he wanted to.

"We're fine. More than fine, really. We can pay our bills, contribute to the boys' college and retirement a little, all the good stuff." He shifted, and Tripp followed his gaze to Maggie, who knelt down by one of the twins while twisting open a bottle of water. "I just—I guess I want to give Maggie more. She deserves more."

Tripp clapped Josh on the back with his left hand. "Listen, man, I've known Maggie since we were kids, and she has never been happier than she is now, with you and those kids. I know she likes a few nice clothes here and there, but don't you think she'd rather have you with her and the kids for the summer rather than a few extra wardrobe accessories?"

Josh smiled. "A little extra never hurts. The boys' mother was —" He shook his head. "Never mind. Maybe something part-time, even? How do I apply?"

"If you're set on it, come down after school tomorrow, and we'll give you some paperwork."

Josh gave him a hearty, left-handed handshake. "Thanks, man."

Maggie approached and held out a champagne glass to each of them. "You two look awful serious over here. Come on, we're about to have the toast."

They walked toward the shade of the massive weeping birch in the front of the house. Josie poured a small amount of bottled water into her empty glass. She caught his gaze and smiled tentatively. He lifted one corner of his mouth in an attempt to make peace. She beamed, sending his insides tripping over themselves. She would forgive him. And he would forgive her. It's what they did. Argue, then make-up. Swear to hate each other forever, then find out they couldn't live without the other's friendship by the next day.

Hannah held up her glass. "I'd like to propose a toast!"

They gathered in a circle around Hannah, each holding up their glasses.

Hannah turned to Aunt Pris, who sat on a wicker chair they'd brought down off the porch. "To Aunt Pris, for braving an adventure with us." She turned to Grandpop, then Tripp. "To Colton Contractors for their excitement and contribution to this project." She looked fondly at Josie, her eyes sparkling along with the contents of her glass. "To Josie, the brains and brazenness of the idea." She raised her glass around the circle. "To each one of you for supporting this endeavor and not thinking it foolish. I am so excited to see what God's going to do with this place. Cheers!"

They clinked glasses and sipped their bubbly before Hannah urged everyone to help themselves to the food. Tripp ducked behind Josie and grabbed a paper plate.

She looked up. "Hey. Glad you guys could make it."

"I'd never miss your mom's chicken salad."

"She made some without walnuts and cranberries this time." Josie grabbed a snack size bag of potato chips and put it alongside her sandwich.

"Good news. That stuff's too fancy for me." He piled a scoop of potato salad on his plate, then followed it up with a separate bowl of salad greens.

She walked to the wide steps of the porch and sat. He followed, seeing that August and Grandpop sat with Bronson, who gestured to the orchards.

"Can I sit here?"

She moved over, though not out of necessity. The steps ran three times longer than a normal set, creating the elegant look that followed throughout the veranda. Curved porch rails and massive columns ensured plenty of shade and room enough for a party. Hannah would probably buy more wicker furniture and tables to ensure enough room for multiple guests to enjoy the area while maintaining some privacy.

He sat, balancing his large plate in his hands. The wind coming off the harbor carried the scent of the sea. "This place is going to be booming in no time."

"We're grateful for your help." Her voice sounded stiff, and Tripp hated the wall between them. But Josie had never been good at shallow and pretend. She was good at real, and that had always been right fine by him.

"Josie, I'm sorry for how I reacted the other day. It was rude and inconsiderate. You don't owe me anything, and yet, I've been going on like you do. Can you forgive me?"

"You're wrong about one thing."

He studied her profile. Really studied her. How much of her did he actually know, and how much had he made up for himself in his mind? "What's that?"

"I do owe you something. Friendship. I haven't been much of a friend this past year. Not responding to your texts. Kind of pretending you didn't exist. I'm sorry."

He forked a cubed potato covered in mayonnaise, but felt his stomach curdle. He put his plate on the step beside him. "It's not like I made it easy with what happened last summer. But can you understand? I couldn't keep my feelings a secret forever."

The corner of her mouth curved upward. "We've always been truthful with one another."

"Despite what you might think, you were never an easy answer for me. You were never my next practical step to achieving manhood. You were—you are, my heart."

She let her head fall in her hand. "Tripp—"

"No, hear me out. I don't want any awkwardness between us. I just want to tell you how it is."

He hadn't planned to say this at a family picnic. But blast it all, he needed to be out with it, especially with Josie so contemplative this evening. This was a new beginning for her—this baby, this B&B. He couldn't afford not to lay it all out on the table here and now.

Despite the inevitable pain of her continued refusal.

Despite his continued hurt surrounding the rumors and his reputation.

Despite his fragile and bruised broken heart.

"I have not stopped loving you, Josie Martin. And I can be whoever you want me to be. Husband, friend, you name it. I can also be whoever you want me to be to this baby. You know what my heart wants—it wants you, and if a part of you is another man's child, then I'm up for the task. And I swear to you, I will be the best father on the entire east coast if it means waking up beside you every day."

Her bottom lip trembled. "Tripp—"

"No, let me finish. Please. I've thought about this. I've prayed about it. This is tricky stuff, but love doesn't run away from the tricky." He licked his lips, fumbled for words. "The ball's in your court, for however long you need. If you'd rather me be honorary uncle to this child rather than father, if you'd rather me be your friend—it might kill me, Josie-girl, but if it makes you happy—I will be that."

A tear rolled down her cheek. "Tripp, you *are* too good, just like I thought all along." She stared down at their laps in silence, then gestured to his hand. "What happened?"

"My temper."

"Through a wall?"

"No, plain old punching bag."

"I guess you are human." She bit into her chicken sandwich.

"You don't know the half of it." He sighed. "So, are we okay?"

"You mean will things be awkward between us?"

"Yeah."

She smiled. "Let's make sure they're not."

"Deal." He'd take what she would offer, even if he did feel ignored by her, even if her continued rejection felt like the pouring of salt on his open and wounded heart.

"After all, we're going to work together an awful lot over the next few months. You have your work cut out for you here." She waved behind them at Aunt Pris's home.

"You're good at changing the subject when you're uncomfortable, you know that?"

She straightened. "What do you want me to say, Tripp? That you're the saintliest, most decent guy in the world and that I can't win no matter what? If I turn you down yet again, I'm the stupidest girl on the planet. If I let you fix everything, I'm the most indecent, life-sucking person that's ever lived—someone I really don't want to be."

She tapped her foot on the step. "I was supposed to be the one with all the answers, don't you understand? Not someone who leeches the life out of her best friend—"

"Are you serious? You don't leech life out of anyone, Josie. Just look at the life you've breathed into your Mom and Aunt Pris in the couple weeks you've been home."

"Tripp, if we got married now, wouldn't you question my motives? You look like the easy answer, after all. Steady, secure, loaded. Do you honestly expect me to hurl myself at you? You deserve so much more."

Didn't he just say he loved her authenticity? Well, here it was. Real Josie, laying it all out on the table. Could he love Josie Martin, marry her even, if she didn't want his heart? If she married him for a home, security, a father for her child? Was that what he wanted? Would it make him happy?

No, he wouldn't be satisfied. But he'd take the risk. Because love—real, unconditional love—didn't decide itself based on the other person's response. Love, quite simply, loved. End of story.

He wondered if Josie put some effort into it, if she *could* love him. For the millionth time since he heard her news, he wondered about the New York man who stole her heart. He must be sophisticated, probably read all the books Josie read, probably never stooped to reading a comic in his life. He probably hired other people to fix his door when it came loose from its frame. He and Josie probably paraded around the city going to wine tastings and poetry readings, laughing at the same inside literary jokes Tripp never got. They probably made passionate love on the bare rug of the guy's extensive library.

Tripp grit his teeth, felt his anger rising again even as he tried to tamp it down.

He had one thing over this mystery man, at least. This so-called father of Josie's baby.

Tripp had staying power.

In whatever capacity Josie wanted, he would be there. And if he never got to take her in his arms and show her how he cared for her, if it killed him until the end, he would keep on staying, keep on pursuing, keep on loving. As long as she didn't choose another man that would change his role, he would be here.

Because that's what scandalous, unconditional love did.

And that's where the scales fell in Tripp's favor.

🎐 18 🎐

Three Months Later

"I thought you were going to flare high again, but you landed it today." Katrina pushed her watermelon Greek salad aside, half-finished as always.

Finn lifted his glass of Bourgogne Blanc to his lips and took in the view of the Hudson River from his seat at the Pier i Café. "You, too."

They'd locked hands while freefalling this time, the experience and bond they shared that high up pure ecstasy. He knew from experience it would only fuel their time in the bedroom later. And, if he were lucky, the tears wouldn't come tonight.

Katrina had noticed them a month ago, said they were signs of a mid-life crisis or testosterone deficiency. Finn had snapped at that. Who did she think she was, anyway? He was the psychologist. She needed to stick to her law degree.

She hadn't mentioned the tears anymore after that, but also stayed away from him for the next four days, her message plain—his tears were weak, and if he didn't get a hold of himself she'd find someone more capable of doing so.

Her independence had drawn him at first. Even in the beginning, she spoke of not wanting to be tied down. She probably saw other men here and there. He told himself that was okay.

But it wasn't.

Bottom line was, he *wanted* to be wanted. *Wanted* to be needed.

No matter how weak that made him.

Three hours later, Finn sat at the large in-ground pool of Bill White, head of the psychology department at NYU, chilled beer in hand. Beside him, Katrina sipped her margarita and spoke to Bill's wife, advising on how to handle a landscaper who, according to Mrs. White, didn't hold up his end of the contract.

Nancy Rutherford, who had an office next door to his at the university, walked over and sat down at the edge of the pool to dip her feet. She pushed dark sunglasses onto her head. "Good summer, Finn?"

"Yes, ma'am. You?"

"Had a lot of time with the grandchildren, so can't beat that. And it's Nancy, Finn. We're colleagues and I can't be more than ten years older than you."

Don't remind me.

Finn's fortieth birthday fast approached, throwing a dark shadow over his days. During the summer, he'd distracted himself with jumping, lazy trips to Long Island with Katrina, late nights in her arms. But sitting here with his colleagues and starting classes this past week filled him with thoughts of his own mortality, of how fast the seasons came and went, of how fast half his life had already passed.

"I'm looking to hire on a graduate student for my office." Nancy swished her feet in the clear water. "Someone dependable with good organizational skills. Good pay with lots of potential for growth. I was thinking of Josie Martin—she was in my psychopharmacology class last year. I tried to look her up, but it appears she's not enrolled this semester. Any idea what she's up to?"

His skin grew hot, then cold, the beer glass slippery in his hand. Maybe he was having a midlife crisis, after all. "W-why do you think I would know?"

Nancy sipped her fruity drink. "You were acquainted with her father at one time, weren't you? Just thought I'd ask. She's been on my mind for this position."

"You must have her contact information if she was in your class last year."

"I do, but I thought it odd she didn't come back." She shrugged. "No matter. I'll reach out to her myself. Though if her plans have changed, it might not matter."

Bill carried a framed photograph over to their group. He stooped over Nancy and pointed at the various faces behind the glass, reciting whose children belonged to whom.

Finn excused himself and stood, going to the far corner of the outside bar. His right hand began to tremor, and he commanded it to still.

Josie wasn't coming back.

While he'd seen her name absent from his own roster, he assumed that was intentional. But quitting or transferring altogether? NYU had been her dream. It had been Amos's dream for her. She'd worked too hard for those scholarships and grants. Accepting money from her great-aunt hadn't been easy, either. This degree, this career, meant too much to her.

That could only mean one thing—she'd decided to have the baby. Did she plan to give it away? Shouldn't she have at least informed him of all this?

He raked a hand through his hair. The echoing laughs of his colleagues behind him grated on his nerves. They spoke of their grandchildren as if they were life's finest fruits.

Irrational anger bubbled up from his gut. He needed to get

out of here, take a run, get himself rip-roaring drunk. Anything to take the edge off.

It wasn't until later that night, after the alcohol had worn off, after he'd woken yet again to tears on his pillow, that the truth settled upon him with a fierceness that rattled.

He was angry, all right. But most of all, he was angry with himself.

Clearly, he didn't have closure when it came to Josie Martin. He'd text her tomorrow, throw out a mention of Nancy's proposition, feel out what she'd done about the baby. Maybe she'd gotten rid of it after all. Maybe she'd chosen to pursue a degree at a college closer to her family. She'd struggled after Amos's death—it made sense she'd stay close to home after a year away.

Maybe all his tears were simply for nothing.

❧ 19 ❧

The sound of birds woke me, the splash of sunlight from my attic window kissing my face. I stretched, turned on my back, and placed my hands over the mound of my belly. Little Mouse, as I'd taken to calling the babe, twisted and turned within.

When I'd first felt movement, I'd resisted the urge to put my hands on my stomach, to communicate and attach myself to the tiny human. If I were to give up my baby, it would only be harder if I bonded with him or her.

My resolve hadn't lasted long, however. It was simply too impossible not to touch the child. And why shouldn't it know love while it grew within me? Whether I kept it or not shouldn't dictate the child's need to feel cared for, even in my womb.

"Good morning, Little Mouse." I rested my hands on my large belly and turned to look at the ultrasound picture propped against the lamp of my nightstand beside the journal I'd taken to writing in. I didn't know the sex of the baby, again feared that knowing would make it all the more concrete, all the more difficult to release the child to another mother's arms.

And yet, with each day that passed, with each doctor's

appointment, and with each Lamaze class I attended, I felt a surety within me, a perception I couldn't quite explain, that I would indeed keep this baby. I'd kept my intentions quiet. For the most part, my family gave me time and room to make my own decision—not that they weren't busy enough with their own endeavors.

The B&B was in full remodeling swing and we'd accepted an offer on our house two weeks ago. Between boxing up our belongings, planning the decorating scheme for each guest room, and having Aunt Pris live with us while Tripp and his crew completed the work on the kitchen remodel, it seemed that what I did with my baby come October was the last thing on everyone's mind.

I rolled out of bed and pulled on my favorite—if one allowed for such a gross oxymoron when it came to maternity clothes—pair of jeans and a t-shirt that didn't make me feel like a beached whale.

I came down the stairs, the sweet scent of something in the oven a normal part of my morning. While Mom didn't prepare five-course breakfasts every day, she loved trying out new recipes. It also seemed to be the secret weapon in keeping Aunt Pris happy.

"Morning." I grabbed the kettle to heat up water for my tea. Every day, the kitchen grew barer and barer. First the curtains vanished, then the decorative wall hangings. Now, the hutch lay empty, cardboard boxes beside it. I'd offered to clear Dad's study, but Mom insisted on doing it herself. I hadn't argued, though I had grabbed a few of our favorite books from the room before she began. Maybe I'd even use some for decorative purposes in the bookshop.

"Morning." Mom pulled a pan of fluffy goodness from the oven. "This has to be eaten right away, so grab a plate."

I did so, letting her serve a piece on a small plate before placing it in front of Aunt Pris. "What's this?"

"German Apple Pancakes. My mother's recipe." She handed me another plate.

I took it and sat. "I'm really not sure if I'm gaining weight from the baby or all this food."

Aunt Pris glanced at my stomach, then at the rest of me. "You certainly have filled out everywhere the last couple of months."

I glared at her. "Baby's tend to do that."

Mom pat my shoulder before she sat with us, a slice of pancake on her own plate. "Josie, you're beautiful. That's all there is to it."

"She needed some weight on those bones, looked like a colt before—all skinny arms and legs. I wasn't insulting you, girl."

Nice save, Aunt Pris. I lifted a bite to my mouth, the tangy sweetness causing a moan to escape my lips. "This is heavenly."

She smiled, sipped her coffee. "We're headed over to Orchard House today so we can check on the progress. Want to come?"

"Absolutely. I'm in awe of all they've gotten done so far. It looks amazing." Tripp planned to hang kitchen cabinets this week, countertops would be installed next along with upstairs bathtubs and sinks.

Tripp's special project had been the balcony off the largest bedroom—what we'd decided to name the Alcott Room. Mom and I purchased portraits of Louisa May Alcott and her family to frame and hang in the room. Amie planned to paint an owl on a branch below the mantle of the fireplace, as well as calla lilies on the wall beside my personal favorite furniture piece—a simple half moon desk inspired by the very one Louisa had written *Little Women*, just like the one still on display at the Alcott Orchard House in Concord, Massachusetts.

Mom and I had studied her historical room with great care and had even taken a trip to Concord to view the home last month. We strived to bring as many touches from Louisa's old bedroom into the Alcott room as possible, while making it a bit more elegant for a modern-day guest seeking escape.

We'd done the same with the other rooms, duplicating the sleigh bed, white sheer curtains, and rich scarlet color of Emily Dickinson's bedroom and choosing some bolder, deeper colors for the Frost and Emerson rooms. I loved the Hawthorne room, situated in a corner turret and done in pale yellows with a grand four-poster bed. The Thoreau room would hold more of a rustic, log cabin feel, but with two comfy chairs by the fire and a claw foot tub.

And the bookshop...well, I hadn't seen the bookshop yet because Tripp demanded that I not set foot in it. He said I always managed to ruin any surprises, and I sure better not ruin this one. Which, of course, made me all the more curious.

Tripp. He'd been an absolute dear this summer, working hard on Orchard House, speeding things along even as his hand healed. Once the splint came off, he labored like a madman, toiling late into the night, many times alongside Josh and August. We hung out now and then, but I'd kept my distance, too frightened of his words at the celebration picnic, too scared to trust my own emotions any longer.

"Have you decided anything about it, girl?" Aunt Pris's voice cut into my thoughts. I blinked to see her pointing at my stomach as if it were an alien. "Hannah says it's in the budget to do a small bedroom and bathroom—no kitchen facilities—above the bookshop, but Ed will need to know sooner rather than later."

I blew out a long, unladylike breath while folding my napkin into accordion-like creases.

Mom cut in. "We really don't want to rush her, Aunt Pris."

"Seems Mother Nature is doing that already." Aunt Pris smirked, and Cragen started licking my ankles.

I pushed him aside with my tennis shoes. "I hope you're not planning on letting your precious pup around our guests. If so, he'll need to learn some manners."

"Josie." Ever the peacekeeper, Mom gave me a look.

Aunt Pris only hooted. "Oh, don't discourage her, Hannah. I

get all my fun from this girl, believe it or not. The rest are too proper to speak their minds around me."

I hid a grin, as Aunt Pris and I grew quite comfortable the last couple of months with one another's presence—and with speaking our minds.

"Aunt Pris, you'll be the death of me." Mom turned in my direction. "We're going to get an early start. You want to ride with us or meet up over there?"

"As much as I love sharing the backseat with Cragen, I'll meet you there."

Aunt Pris cackled again. I cleared my plate and met Amie on the stairs. My plan to get closer to my younger sister hadn't exactly materialized these last few months—in fact, more often than not, a simmering anger seemed to stew below Amie's skin. The only one in the family who'd voiced disapproval of me keeping the baby. Once, she'd outright stated my child would be better off given a stable start, insinuating the obvious—that I wasn't it.

Couldn't really argue with her there, but still, it hurt.

"How's your night class going?" I asked.

"Fine." She continued down the stairs, the brushoff apparent. Maybe she was still sour over this entire bed and breakfast thing. She'd been last to get on board with the idea of selling the house, and her mood diminished rapidly when she'd had to share a bedroom with Lizzie in order to make room for Aunt Pris. She complained about college, how she'd wanted to go to Boston or New York, but like all of us Martin children, was short on funds.

"You have a good day, too," I muttered to my sister, unable to keep the sarcasm from my tone.

Amie had so many opportunities before her. Just as I had before I squandered them.

I pushed the thought aside. I didn't need bitterness. I could still sign up for online classes next semester, could still give up this baby and never think of him or her again.

If such a thought didn't threaten to shatter my heart to pieces, I just might consider it. But lately, the thought of not thinking of my baby ever again felt as easy as cutting off a finger and forgetting about it.

Maybe once we moved into Orchard House, maybe once things settled, maybe once the baby came, Amie and I would find some common ground. Until then, I tried like mad to practice something I wasn't naturally good at—something Tripp showed me during that celebration picnic months earlier.

Giving grace.

THERE WAS NO USE DENYING IT: I WAS IN LOVE. LEGIT, IN love.

"So, what do you think?" Tripp stood beside me, thumbs slung in his pockets, an unsteady grin on his face.

I grasped for words.

He laughed. "Wow, now this is something I've never seen—a speechless Josie Martin."

I shook my head, drinking in the bookshop. *My* bookshop.

Tall, wide windows ran along one wall, splashing the entire room, including the beautiful rustic beams overhead, with amazing sunlight. Gorgeous, soaring bookshelves and a large front-end counter. A walnut ladder that moved on wheels to reach higher shelves. A small nook for coffee and tea, a cozy sitting area with a rustic gas fireplace, and a door leading to an outside patio area overlooking the orchard. My gaze settled on the spiral staircase running up to a small second-story loft with additional shelving. Wow. Just, wow.

"It's not what we planned." I ran my hands over the smooth rungs of the walnut ladder.

"I thought I'd take a chance and get a bit more creative."

"Tripp, this is definitely out of our budget."

He shook his head. "I pulled a lot of the shelving off another job. It was all destined for the dumpster but nothing a good sanding and a few coats of stain couldn't fix. Even had the staircase from the Hillside Mansion renovation a couple years ago."

I shook my head, tears welling. I blamed them on the baby. I never cried until these blasted hormones made an appearance. "I couldn't imagine anything more perfect."

"Good. I wanted to do it for you, to make this a place you'd want to be every day."

He'd succeeded. I could just imagine myself behind the desk, planning inventory. Stocking the shelves with my literary friends. In a way, bringing them to life. And maybe, after closing time, I'd sit with my journal beside the fire, daring to coax my own story to life with pen and ink.

For some reason, this bookshop, this B&B, gave me space to dream again. To live without heavy expectations, to explore new beginnings and hope.

Without thinking, I placed my hands on Tripp's shoulder, stood on my tiptoes, and planted a kiss on his stubbled cheek. His hand came lightly at my waist, and he grinned down at me. "I guess you like it, then?"

"I love it. Thank you."

A moment passed where neither of us moved. Ever so slowly, he dipped his head, as if testing if I would pull away.

I didn't.

That magnetic pull I'd felt that day last summer had only intensified the last few months. While aware I'd never felt more vulnerable in my life, that Tripp's steadiness and offer of love quite likely caused my increased attraction, I didn't wish to resist it any longer. He'd kept his distance as far as any possibility of romance, but like the steady waves of the ocean, his continued offer and patient persistence drew me. In small words and deeds, in bigger ones like the attention to detail of the bookshop. It seemed he'd never give up on loving me. On pursuing me.

And I was falling.

So unlike my experience with Finn. Not quick and filled with lust—a needy kind of searching to cement that hole of grief inside me—what I felt for Tripp was steady, real, tender, and more powerful for its authenticity and the history of friendship we shared. Maybe it would never be fairytales and love at first sight for me and Tripp, but it was genuine, if not ideal. Bound to be filled with hiccups and bumps, I couldn't think of someone more worthy to love.

I wanted to give in. More than anything, I wanted to surrender to the press of feelings I'd pushed back all these months.

"Josie," Tripp breathed, as if asking permission.

I looked into those eyes, dark with want, and answered him by leaning in just a bit, my heart beating against my ribcage, as if asking for release.

His warm lips met mine in gentle restraint, tender, as if testing, tasting. I sank into them, my willingness all the encouragement he needed to sink deeper. His mouth covered mine, searching hidden places within me, and I lifted my fingers to the taunt muscles of his broad arms and shoulders, pressing in closer.

His arms came around me, firm fingers pulling me tight, creating heat in every inch of my body, causing me to forget time and space and reality.

He broke away all too soon, ran a thumb over the curve of my cheek. "Did that really just happen?"

I smiled. "I think so."

"And you're not pulling away from me yet. Josie, what does this mean? I sure hope it's more than just a thank you for the bookshop."

I bit my bottom lip. "I want it to be more, Tripp. And yet I feel selfish that I do."

He shook his head. "Don't. Please, don't. Don't pull away or think you're not the very best thing for me. Ever. Real love...it takes work and sacrifice. It needs tending, like a seedling."

"Now you're a gardener?"

"I am when it comes to this. No one stands by a new plant and watches it scorch in the sun without watering it, right? Love takes water, Josie. I have bucket loads for us. All I'm asking is for you to contribute a couple cupfuls to help us along. It's work, but when has work ever scared you?"

I inhaled a breath that echoed on a tremor. "I haven't told anyone yet, but I'm keeping the baby. I don't know if you were hoping for something different."

He traced my bottom lip with his thumb, stirring a fierce desire within me. "I was hoping for nothing but you and all that comes with you. I meant what I said back in May. I will love this baby as my own, I swear it. Part of me already does. He or she is a part of you. I'm ready to move forward if you are. No more dwelling in the past."

I pulled away, my head swimming. "I don't want to rush anything, okay? No proposals or plans of a future forever together just yet. Let's just explore this, see where it takes us. See how you feel when the baby comes. See how *I* feel when the baby comes."

He cupped my face in his hands, stooped down just a bit. "It's not going to change a thing, at least when it comes to my feelings for you. But I think we could have a lot of fun with this...exploring." He lowered his lips to mine again, and I welcomed his soft mouth, the feel of his lean body alongside my own. While the prominence of my stomach should have made me less desirable, Tripp's insistence in pulling me closer assured me he would indeed welcome this baby.

When we parted, I caught my breath. "That was new for us."

He laughed. "I hope it's just the beginning."

From within my womb, Little Mouse gave a hard kick. I gasped, pressed my hand to my side.

"You okay?"

"Yeah, either he really likes you or he's telling you to back off."

"He, huh?"

I shook my head. "Aunt Pris is insisting it's a boy. I think she's gotten into my head is all."

Tripp held out his hand. "Can I?"

I took his hand and guided his fingers to the spot in my side where Little Mouse pushed. I studied Tripp, waited until I felt a shift within my womb.

Tripp adjusted his hand. "Whoa, that's amazing."

"Right?"

He kept his hand on my stomach, waiting for more, but the babe went still. He turned his hand so our palms met. "So I'm really the first one you told?"

"I'm going to tell my family tonight, whoever's around on a Saturday night, that is."

"So, since you're not ready to get hitched, you think Aunt Pris is going to insist on us starting the apartment upstairs?"

"Like you all need one more thing to do around here."

"We'll make it work. I'm going to miss Josh's help though. That guy isn't just talented at teaching. He caught on quick and has the work ethic to match his brains."

"I'm not sure Maggie will miss him working so much. She had quite a summer with the boys."

"They okay?"

"Oh yeah, I just think she thought they'd get a lot of family time this summer. Didn't really happen."

"Josh could have taken vacation whenever. We both know this is temporary. I appreciate his help."

I squeezed his hand. "We all do. And what you've done for us...."

He chucked my chin. "Whether or not you ever agree to marry me, Josie Martin, your family will always be my family, too. I mean that. Grandpop gave us a physical home, but you, your parents, and your siblings, gave me and August a family. Not to mention the fact that we would have starved our teenage years if it wasn't for your mom's meals."

I smiled. "That was Dad. Give your neighbor the shirt off your back even if you don't have a spare. Even if they *do* live in a mansion next door."

"You miss him, huh?"

I looked around the bookshop, the empty shelves waiting to be filled with adventures. "It's not as poignant as it used to be, you know? I miss him, but in a weird way I feel he's such a real part of all this. Did I tell you what Mom's planned for the opening?"

"What?"

"She wants to have a big ol' open house, invite the entire town, with a special invitation to those staying at Dad's mission. She hasn't been very involved with it since Dad passed, but she thought it would honor his memory to have some of our first visitors be those that will probably never be able to afford to stay here. She's going to serve up a buffet style meal with plenty of desserts, maybe make it a regular thing if it goes well."

Tripp took my hand. "Your father would have loved to see it."

I placed my other hand on my stomach, wondered at the miracle that had gotten me to this moment. Somehow having this baby grow within me, knowing Tripp's offer of love, and anticipating not only Mom's dream of a B&B, but my own...somehow it seemed the spiritual side of things wasn't so very out of reach anymore. Maybe, if God allowed, Dad would be able to see the opening of this place.

"I better get back before Mom and Aunt Pris wonder where I went. Mom and I are going shopping downtown for some deals, trying to get a few last-minute touches for the rooms."

"Can I kiss you one more time?"

"I think so."

Though not as long, it lingered just as sweet, and when I said goodbye and walked out of the bookshop, a pleasant heat rippled through my body. I stopped myself from skipping up the side stairs of the main house and told Mom I'd meet her at home.

"Aunt Pris wants to stick around." Mom gave me a wink. "I think she's secretly in love with the new kitchen."

"Who wouldn't be?" Bright and airy, white cabinets against sea-green granite countertop, Mom hadn't made her gushing as quiet as Aunt Pris.

"Shall we drive down together from here, then?"

"Sure. I just need to grab my purse from the car." I walked outside, a lightness to my spirit I hadn't felt since childhood. I inhaled the lingering scents of summer—the brine of the sea combined with the fading Roses of Sharon.

I opened the door of my car and sat in the driver's seat to grab my purse. From within, my cell phone dinged and I slipped it out. Probably Lizzie. She wanted to come shopping with us if she finished teaching her music classes at the middle school in time.

I pressed the button on my phone. My blood ran cold at the sight of the name. Not Lizzie at all.

Why, just when I felt ready to put him behind me for good and embrace a new future, would Finn Becker pop into my life again?

✸ 20 ✸

I stared at Finn's name, denial washing over me along with a thousand other emotions.

Among them anger, that he would reach out after months of silence and after how we'd left things that last day. Curiosity, over why he contacted me now. Fear, for how he held the potential to disrupt my new life. And something else. Something fierce welling up within me that I couldn't name—a vicious motherly instinct to protect my baby from him at all costs.

For a split second, I considered swiping my thumb over his message, deleting it—and him—from entering my life and the life of my child. My heart ached as I thought of Tripp, of what he offered us and how Finn threatened it all—not because I was tempted by him, but because for all intents and purposes, he *was* the father of my child.

With one leg hung out the driver's side door, I tapped my phone to open the message without debating the issue further. My hands trembled, pulse throbbing at my temples.

Thinking about you today. Nancy Rutherford mentioned a position at her office she had in mind for you, but saw you weren't enrolled for the semester. Hope you are okay. Would like to talk when you are able.

I read it again, and again. *Thinking* about me? Hoping I was okay? He was about eight months too late to be all sorts of concern now.

I mumbled a few choice names for him beneath my breath as I swiped his message away. I hoped he saw that I had read it. I hoped he felt guilty for casting me aside, though quite honestly the word *guilt* and *Finn* didn't even belong in the same sentence together. Finn believed guilt to be almost useless, a flaw imbued in us by our superego and rigid moral upbringings. Though in some circumstances he thought the emotion could be used to better ourselves, on the whole he believed more in claiming comfort in his own skin than in berating himself for past failures.

That was the draw of speculative philosophy, I supposed. And I couldn't pretend I'd been immune to its convenience and seeming freedom as it unraveled the world as it deemed fit, putting it back together without the help of faith or scripture, dependent on the god of intellect alone.

Only when it failed me had I doubted all I'd begun to build my world upon. Only then had I revisited the comforting truths of my childhood.

Mom came down the stairs of Orchard House, and I slipped into the passenger side of her car, trying to wipe Finn's message from my mind as easily as I'd done on my iPhone.

But it was no use. I thought of Professor Rutherford, of how I'd admired her teachings in my psychopharmacology class last year. I would have given anything to work under her, to gain professional experience in the field under her guidance and mentorship, to work alongside her in some capacity in the years ahead.

Little Mouse moved within me, and I rested my hands atop my abdomen, the old dream fading. I leaned back against the headrest, looked toward the elegant windows of the bookshop, the orchards ripe with fruit. Bronson had harvested what he could, intent on learning how to care for delicious, pesticide-free apples.

I thought of Tripp's kiss, and my heart ached.

I closed my eyes. I had changed a lot in a year. I didn't want New York. I didn't even really want a psychology degree. I wanted to help people, but maybe not in a counseling office. Maybe I could help them by putting the right book in their hand, by creating a space where all felt welcome to come and browse and read and learn and grow. Maybe I could help my child by being the best mother I could be.

Mom opened the driver's side door. "All set?" She stopped short. "What's wrong? You look pale."

I forced a smile. "I'm okay."

And I would be. Maybe I should even thank Finn for texting me, for putting some things in perspective once and for all.

❧

"MAGGIE, THIS IS BEAUTIFUL! IT'S REALLY COMING TOGETHER. Wow." I pointed at the scrolling pictures on Maggie's laptop where we sat at Mom's dining room table surrounded by half-packed boxes labeled with black marker. The picture on the screen showed Aunt Pris's Orchard House in the background, deep blue hydrangeas in the foreground. The next showed Mom's Eggs Benedict garnished with flowers, a cup of delectable fruit, and a fancy glass of orange juice in the background.

"I'm going to add more once the rooms are final and we have the sign in front of the house." She clicked over to a page that read *Our Area*. "I've started listing things to do and see—hiking, lighthouses, food, kayaking, art, history, culture, festivals, seasonal events. If you two think of anything else let me know."

Mom shook her head. "You outdid yourself. And these photographs are superb."

"Amie's to thank for that."

"What am I to thank for?" Amie came up behind us.

"These pictures." Mom put an arm around my younger sister. "They're exquisite."

She grinned. "Thanks. Did you order the sign for out front yet? And the plates for the bedroom doors? I could get some nice ones and take some pictures for our home page."

Mom nodded. "Street sign's ordered. Josie said she was going to try her hand at wood burning the door signs."

"No way." Amie glanced at me. "You remember what happened the last time you used the burning tool, don't you?"

"Come on, Amie, give me a break. That was over nine years ago."

"And my favorite jewelry box is still ruined."

I offered her a weak smile. I'd thought it a swell idea to personalize her precious wooden jewelry box by wood burning her name on it for her ninth birthday. It hadn't turned out so well. "It's a memory, right?"

"One I'd rather forget." She sat in a chair and placed crossed arms on the table.

I tried not to bring up *her* art-inspired mishaps. Her own wood-burning endeavors had left a few well-loved marks on the railings and beams of our home as well as the stench of burning wood pervading our living space for days. She'd made so many clay figures they came tumbling from shelves to endanger the lives of all who lived in the Martin home. Traces of her mud pies still dulled the back of Mom's favorite white sweater from a sloppy hug.

"We'll let Josie give it a go, and if we're not satisfied with the result, we'll order some, okay?" Mom turned back to Maggie's laptop. "We need to finalize prices for the rooms. I've been researching other inns in the area. I want to be comparable, but take into account the full-service breakfast without being overpriced."

Maggie nodded. "I've been meaning to look too, but things have gotten busy with Josh working so much."

"He started school this week, right? And cross-country must be in full swing."

"It is. Only he's insisting on helping Tripp on nights he doesn't have meets. I thought working for Colton Contractors was a summer thing, but he doesn't want to give it up. Meanwhile, I feel like a single mother over here." Her gaze fluttered to me. "Sorry, Josie."

I waved her off. "Come on, Mags. You know I'm not that easily offended. Did you talk to him?"

"By the time he gets home, I'm dead to the world. This morning, I woke up to make him breakfast, but he was kissing me goodbye before I turned on the Keurig."

Mom closed Maggie's laptop. "You've been working hard too, honey. You two need some time away. Why don't you let me babysit this weekend?"

My sister shook her head. "I can't let you do that. Look at this place. There's still so much to do before closing. Not to mention all that's left with the B&B."

"Then let me," I chimed in. "Those boys need some fun with their Aunt Josie. Maybe Tripp will even help out."

Maggie bit her lip, the bags beneath her eyes noticeable. "Really? You think so? Maybe just one night...but the boys haven't been without Josh since Trisha died."

"They'll be great. It will be fun."

Maggie leaned back in her chair. "It would be nice to get away for a little. I think I'm more stressed about the fact that I'm not pregnant yet. We've been trying for months."

"Maybe you should ask Josie for pointers." Amie spoke from the couch.

"Amie!" Maggie and Mom said in unison.

My younger sister winced. "Sorry. I was trying to be funny. I guess that came out kind of rude."

I glared at her, but Maggie hid a smirk. "It's okay. We know you didn't mean anything by it."

Huh, sure.

Mom squeezed Maggie's arm. "It will happen for you, honey. You've been through a whirlwind this past year with those boys and now helping me out. You need to relax, spend some time with your husband. Josh will probably jump at the chance to be alone with you."

My sister didn't look convinced, but in the end, we finalized a time for me to watch the kids next Friday, then chatted about prices for each guest room, along with tentative dates for the open house.

"Josie and I can work on a press release for some of the local papers to stir up some hype," Maggie said.

Mom tapped her chin. "If everything falls into place, we might be able to plan an open house Columbus Day weekend, catch some of the leaf-peeping tourists. Oh, I can't wait to decorate for Christmas! Lights and greens. Red roses, white chrysanthemums, trailing vines, a glittering tree."

"It sounds divine." Amie sighed. "It'll be tough saying goodbye to this place, but it *will* be grand and romantic living in that old house, won't it?"

Maggie stared at me. I knew her thoughts to be the same as mine. Still, I wasn't sure if I was ready. Finn's text had shaken me up more than I cared to admit.

She didn't stay silent. "You could have the baby by then. Have you given any more thought to...you know?"

The room grew silent, tension thick, as if everyone held a collective breath as Maggie touched the nearly untouchable topic of these last couple of months. Ready or not, I'd decided. And ready or not, I was going to be a mother.

My stomach danced a nervous jig, and it had nothing to do with Little Mouse doing somersaults fit for an Olympic floor exercise routine. I dragged in a breath. If only Lizzie were here, but she'd gone for another hike, taking advantage of the cooler September afternoon.

"I've decided to keep the baby." I exhaled the words all in one breath.

"Oh, honey." Mom wrapped her arms around me. "I was ready to support you no matter what, but I just know this baby is going to be a blessing—just as Esther insists. And I've been eyeing the cutest little baby socks down at Jo Ellen Designs."

We laughed.

"I think a baby will be the perfect addition to this family—and to the beginning of our new endeavor." I didn't miss the tiny spark of sadness in Maggie's eyes.

My heart went out to her. She was such a great mom. She deserved children of her own. I, the one who'd messed up royally, should not have the privilege of having the first Martin grandbaby—the first one to carry Dad's blood.

"Am I the only one who sees how hard this is going to be?" Amie leaned forward. "How will you provide for this baby, take care of it while working? It's not a pet like Scrabble that you can just dump on Mom whenever you need a break, you know."

I grit my teeth to contain my anger. Leave it to Amie to bring up our only pet—a stray dog I'd brought home on a cold winter's night that neither Dad nor I had been able to take to the pound. I'd neglected him all too much, forgetting to feed him or take him out. More often than not, Mom had picked up the slack. But that was years ago. I was not a child anymore.

I struggled to rein in my temper, but one look at Amie with her upturned nose and judgmental attitude—with her jabs at my attempts to wood burn or be a mother or do anything right—fed the fire growing within me. A fire that included all the wrongs she'd ever done me. Emptying my bureau drawers onto my floor when I was in middle school. Always tagging along with me and Maggie or me and Tripp, never giving me a moment of privacy in early high school. Always clinging to me just to correct me.

Words tumbled out before I could bother to stop them. "I don't understand why you have to keep throwing all my faults back in my face. You're all hoity-toity, aren't you? Perfect little golden child. Well, don't worry, I don't want you having anything to do with my baby, okay?" Even as the words left, I knew they were wrong, filled with rage, childish. But Amie knew how to push my buttons good. She always had. My retaliation had always been to push her away, hard and forceful.

Amie stood, leaving the throw pillow she'd been holding to fall at her feet. "Well, that's just fine! You always think everyone will be ready to jump and cater to you, but I'm not. I don't want anything to do with you or your bastard child!"

I didn't think, I lunged. Reaching for yellow hair, seeing red, arms holding me back.

"Amie, go to your room," Mom said.

"I'm eighteen. You can't just—"

"Go to your room!" The entire house grew silent, for I couldn't remember a time Mom raised her voice. It hit its target, for Amie stomped up the stairs, mumbling murderous threats along the way.

I let my head fall in my hands. "I'm sorry. I got angry. But who does she think she is—"

Mom quieted my words by smoothing my hair. I expected some sort of lecture or platitude. *A kiss for a blow is always best* or some such nugget of wisdom. But nothing. Just the calm stroking of my hair.

The gesture had the desired effect, for the next thing I knew, my shoulders shook with sobs. "She's right, isn't she? I can't even control my temper. How will I ever be a mother? Maybe I'm wrong to think I'm what's best for this child. All I ever do is screw up."

"Josie, no...." But Maggie ran out of words.

Mom continued stroking my hair. "My dear girl, God doesn't require us to be perfect to be mothers."

Maggie let out a small laugh. "Isn't that good news."

"I should say so." Mom tugged my hair until I looked at her. "You can do this, Josie. You must do this if you're feeling the pull. If not, you will forever wonder if you made the wrong decision. But I can promise you, if you keep this child, you will never wonder. He or she will grow you, just like you kids did for me. You gave me the best gift of all. Showing me the depths love can go, growing and molding me into a person who isn't perfect, but one who knows she can't do it on her own but by leaning on the Lord."

I sniffed. "I haven't been leaning much."

"Me neither." Maggie slumped in her seat.

"It's never too late." Mom draped her arms around us and squeezed my shoulder. "I hope you and Amie can work out whatever it is that's between you two."

"If I knew what was between us, that'd be helpful," I muttered. "For now, I think we both need to cool off. I'm going for a walk."

Amie and I both ran hotheaded. More alike than our other siblings, we were driven, passionate, and opinionated—probably why we clashed so much. I'd talk to her soon. But not today. Maybe not even tomorrow. She'd been bent against me keeping this child from the beginning. Why couldn't she just support my decision? Her hateful words about my baby resounded in my head, the newfound mother-bear inside of me clinging to them instead of brushing them off.

As I walked toward Curtis Island Overlook, I sank into a prayer. More of a monologue really. A beseeching on behalf of my child, a plea for wisdom.

I turned left onto the path, my feet throbbing, my swollen belly heavy. A ding sounded in my pocket and I scooped it out.

Finn's name again. I closed my eyes in defeat and stopped walking. It had been almost a week since his first text. I thought that if I ignored it, he would get the hint—he wasn't welcome. Not in my life, or our baby's.

Our baby's.

I groaned. Like it or not, I couldn't cut Finn off from our child. Or couldn't I? He'd squandered any rights when he'd demanded I get rid of the babe, when he cast me aside *because* of our child.

I didn't need his presence now. It was just too much trouble.

I walked to the end of the path, sat on the empty bench, and looked across the harbor to the lighthouse, clear and white. I sighed. No use putting off the inevitable. I clicked into Finn's text.

Can we talk, Josie? Please? Call me anytime.

The unfamiliar, vulnerable tone caught me off guard. I couldn't ignore him forever, even if he did deserve it. Trying to summon some of my residual anger toward Amie and fuel it toward Finn, I hit his name at the top of the phone, and lifted it to my ear, ready for a fight.

Lord, help me.

If ever there was a time to lean, it was now.

❧ 21 ❧

Finn jumped at the hollow sound of his phone vibrating against the coffee table. His pulse ratcheted at the sight of Josie's name. In truth, he hadn't expected her to call, and so soon. But the sight of those five letters forming her name caused ten kinds of longing and regret and fear within him.

He swiped the button to accept the call and paced his fifth-floor apartment. Katrina would be here soon. They planned to go to the Museum of Modern Art, browse a bit, then have dinner at The Modern, an upscale restaurant with spectacular views of the sculpture garden.

All of that could wait.

"Josie, thanks for calling." His words came out in a rush. He needed to speak his piece before she changed her mind and hung up.

The nightly tears continued. A single text to Josie hadn't stopped them. Almost like a part of him was crying out for something only Josie could give—closure of sorts, maybe a cleansing of guilt.

"I really don't think we have much to say to one another." He almost didn't recognize her strong, firm tone.

"I—did you get my text last week? I thought you might be interested in Professor Rutherford's offer."

"I'm not, but thank you. I plan to stay in Maine."

He swallowed, unsure he wanted to hear her answer to his next question. "Are you in school?"

A long sigh. "What do you want, Finn?"

"I've been thinking about you. I guess I've been kind of worried about you."

"Nice time for you to grow a conscience."

He sat on his sofa, tapped his socked foot against the area rug. "I-I was wondering if you...you know."

"No, I'm afraid I haven't the slightest clue."

He silently cursed. She wasn't planning to make this easy for him, of course. "If you were still pregnant."

"Not for much longer, but yes, I am."

He released a trembling breath. She hadn't gone through with the abortion. Of course she hadn't. But now, what did this mean for him? He hadn't thought this far ahead. Only knew that reaching out to her had been what he needed to do.

"Then we need to work this out." He almost didn't recognize his words. But was there any other option? He'd never get peace again. The nightly torment may well last forever. Was he really the kind of guy to walk away from his child?

"Work *what* out, Finn? Don't worry. I'm not going to come hounding you for child support or to be a part of this baby's life. You made your feelings abundantly clear and, quite honestly, I think we'll both be better off without you."

Her words pierced something deep inside of him—that new feeling, that part of him that longed to be wanted.

He imagined a baby, *his* child, and the thought caused pride to fill him, whereas eight months earlier it'd only produced disgust.

What happened to him? Was he getting weak with age? Was the idea of turning forty causing him to change what he'd previously thought about life, purpose, and his role in it all?

He raked a hand through his hair. "I want to do what's right, Josie. I want to be a part of this child's life. Monetarily, yes. But maybe even an active participant. I've missed you. Do you think —well, is there any way...." Behind him, the door of his apartment opened. Blast it all. "Listen, I have to go. Can we talk more some time? I don't—"

Katrina entered the living room. "Ready to go, Finny? I could really use a glass of chardonnay, or a couple. The Dowley case kicked my—" She stopped, saw he was on the phone, quieted her voice. "Sorry."

"Is that your latest conquest, I suppose?" Josie's voice on the other end of the line. She didn't sound angry though. Not even a bit jealous. Just stating facts. Facts he hated about himself in this moment. For how would she take his proposition to start things back up between them while he had another woman in his apartment?

"I think it's better we keep our distance, Finn," Josie said.

"Can we just talk again? Please?"

"I don't think so." A brief pause. "I can let you know when the baby's born, though, if you want."

"Yes—yes. Thank you."

"Goodbye."

"Bye." He hung up the phone, let his arm fall on the sofa before remembering Katrina. Great, more guilt. "Sorry. That was —well, she and I were—"

Katrina slapped him on the shoulder. "Really, Finn, you don't have to explain."

He squinted up at her. "I don't?"

She flung herself on the cushion beside him, propped an elbow against the top of the leather couch, her dainty hand resting on her dark hair. "Nope. That's what's great about our relationship. I can totally be myself with you. Who I am is not dependent on me being the only woman in your life, and who you are isn't dependent on being the only man in mine, right? I like being with you, living for the moment. It's kind of like jumping. That's enough, isn't it?"

"Uh, yeah. Sure." So much for being wanted, being needed. By Katrina, by Josie, by his unborn child. But he'd chosen this path. Hadn't he wanted to be what Katrina described? Independent, assured, fully comfortable in his own skin—whether that included a significant other or not.

She stood, held her hand out. "Ready to go?"

"I—I'm actually not feeling well all of a sudden."

She lifted a hand to his forehead. "You don't feel warm." She studied him. "This girl really got to you, didn't she?"

He could tell her about the baby, couldn't he? But why should he? She wasn't invested in any part of his life—in *him*. She'd just said as much. Why bare his heart if he was just another passing pleasure to her, one of many men in her pocket.

The thought churned his stomach. He pulled away. "Forget it, Katrina."

She flipped her hair over her shoulder. "Fine, then. I'll find someone else to accompany me tonight."

"I think that's a good idea."

She stomped out of the room without another word, but her anger spoke volumes about how much he did indeed matter to her. How could you spend time with someone, go through the bond of jumping hundreds of times, of laying in one another's arms in the darkness of night while the city lay quiet, and tell yourself they didn't matter to you?

Before she reached his door, he called out. "We still on for tomorrow's jump?"

Her expression softened. "Sure, Finny. Whatever you want. Let me know how you feel in the morning."

And then she was gone, leaving him more confused than ever.

He sank back on the couch.

He was going to be a father. A *father*. He cursed, put an arm over his eyes.

God, help.

It had been a long time since he'd thrown up even a 911 prayer to the God of his childhood. But then again, it had been a long time since he'd felt this unsure about himself, this lost.

Turn from evil and do good.

Good. What was good in this situation? Sending Josie a hefty check to help with medical bills? Going to her, groveling at her feet to let him have a second chance, to let him be part of this child's life?

My grace is sufficient for you, for my power is made perfect in weakness.

He tried to push the words from his mind. Didn't he believe in the inherent goodness of self, as Rousseau taught? Why then did he battle with his goodness? Why listen to words from a dead book? Besides, he'd never understood that verse, even as a child. Why should it come to him now? Even Josie's father put more emphasis on the doing parts of his faith rather than an emphasis on weakness to obtain power. What did it all mean?

He closed his eyes, exhausted. Perhaps he should give up while he was ahead, throw himself into his work and his jumping, find meaning in concrete things.

His eyes grew heavy. Either way, his dreams would tell him. His body wouldn't rest if there was more for him to do. Over the last several months, he'd gotten good at listening to the tears.

❧ 22 ❧

The war cries curdled the air as Tripp ducked behind a hydrangea shrub. The paint on his face cracked from the sun.

He was ready for battle.

"Found him!" Davey blasted him with a round of Nerf bullets while waving his brother to the site of capture. "Come on, Little John. The Sheriff of Nottingham is no match for us!"

Tripp dove out from behind the bush, rolled onto the grass, and landed at the foot of Josh and Maggie's small porch. He climbed up the stairs on all fours, pretending exhaustion, then popped up beside a laughing Josie. He hooked an arm across her shoulders, pointed his small Nerf gun at the boys, who stood wide-eyed at the bottom of the steps. "What'll ya do now, ya fine Merry Men? I've caught ya lovely Maid Marion. Surely, you wouldn't risk striking her for the likes of me?"

Isaac looked sideways at Davey, a bit unsure of himself. Though only four minutes older, Davey was the apparent leader.

The older twin straightened his back—and his resolve. "You can't hide behind the maid forever. We will wait you out!"

"But Aunt Josie—I mean, Maid Marion...is she scared? We

can't leave her, we should rescue her!" Isaac raised his Nerf gun in the air.

Tripp leaned his head toward Josie's ear, felt her hair against his cheek. "What say you, lovely maiden? Are you scared?"

Josie made a show of waving her hand wildly at her throat. "So scared! You must do something now, Merry Men! I feel I may swoon if you don't!"

Isaac's eyes grew wide. "Davey, she might *swoon*!" He elongated his o's in the word *swoon* to get his point across.

Davey fell out of character for a moment, looked at Josie, his face wrinkled in distaste. "What's swoon?"

Tripp stifled a chuckle.

Josie lay her forearm across her head in dramatic show. "Faint! I will faint straight away if something isn't done!"

Tripp didn't miss her sly smile just before she grabbed his gun and whirled out of his arms. He stared down the barrel of the Nerf Rival Takedown XX-800 Blaster.

"But since I'm a modern woman who doesn't need to stand helplessly by while I wait to be rescued, I will help the Merry Men out. Sheriff of Nottingham, do you surrender to these fine gentlemen?"

"Never!" Tripp lunged off the stairs, running toward the boys.

"Get him, Merry Men!" Josie shouted.

The boys pummeled him with Nerf bullets. He jolted his body, howled in mock pain as they continued their assault.

"Boys!" Josie shouted. The Nerf guns grew quiet. Tripp gave up his howls for soft moans. "Punishment without trial is bad form. Though we know this scoundrel to be guilty of all kinds of injustices, we must give him a fair trial."

Davey grabbed Tripp's arm, pointed toward the house. "To the trial!"

Isaac scooped up his other arm. They paraded Tripp into the house, sat him at the kitchen table. Josie paced before Tripp, then put both hands on the table and leaned over him. "And how do you plead, Sheriff?" The corners of her mouth tugged upward, and he wanted nothing more than to kiss those sweet lips.

"Guilty." He made a slow study of her face. "Wholly and terribly guilty."

Josie straightened, slapped her hand on the table. "He's confessed, boys!"

"Can we shoot him now?" Davey asked, gun raised.

Josie tapped her finger on her chin. "Hmmm. Do you really think he deserves death for his crimes? Is that not a bit harsh?"

"Then what can we do to punish him?" Isaac seemed disappointed that Tripp wouldn't get his due.

"I know!" Davey jumped up and down. "No cookies before bed!"

"No cookies!" Isaac chimed in, grinning.

Tripp fixed a frown on his face. "Please, sirs. Not that, anything but that. All that chocolaty oatmeal goodness! I beg you to reconsider. For the sake of my stomach and my taste buds."

"If not the withholding of said chocolaty goodness, then what would you have us do?" Josie cocked her wrist in the air.

"I think I should be made to…kiss a girl." Tripp shot a wicked grin in her direction.

"Ewwww!" the boys said in unison.

Josie shook her head, but Tripp was on his feet. "What do you say, Merry Men? Do you think the punishment fitting?"

"But Aunt Josie's the only girl here, and she's Robin Hood's wife." Davey stuck out his bottom lip.

Uh-oh. Tripp hadn't expected the kid to make such a quick connection. "Then perhaps just a quick kiss on the cheek."

"Like how we have to kiss Aunt Pris?"

Tripp shared a giggle with Josie. "Exactly like that."

Davey sat at the dining room chair, legs dangling, arms on the table, fingers tapping. "I guess that *is* punishment. Okay, go ahead."

Tripp swept Josie in his arms, lowered his lips to her soft cheek for but a second. "There. Debt paid."

"Now we can have cookies, right?" Isaac asked.

"Cookies all around!" Tripp marched to the plate on the counter.

"Hold up, Sheriff." Josie fell hot on his heels. "These Merry Men need to wash up before they indulge themselves."

Tripp turned direction. "To the bathhouse!" He marched toward the bathroom, the boys following close behind.

When they returned, they all sat at the table, plates and glasses of milk at each setting.

Isaac reached for a cookie. "Grandma makes the best cookies."

Tripp grabbed up two to put on his plate. "She does. I'm glad I'm not withheld from the chocolaty goodness." He winked at Josie. While babysitting twin boys with your pregnant girlfriend —if Josie would allow that label—was not your typical Friday night date, he couldn't imagine anything better.

"When you guys have your baby, we'll make him a Merry Man too, right, Uncle Tripp?"

A cookie crumb caught in his throat. Though he did consider himself part of the family, he didn't remember Maggie or Josh ever referring to him as "uncle." Yet, what was the harm, really? Half the town already thought the baby was his—something he struggled over. He strived to live with honor, and the gossip among the town diminished his reputation. But he'd take it any day if it spared Josie even a little disrepute. He looked at her now, wearing out her bottom lip with her teeth over Davey's question.

"You know, boys, this actually isn't Uncle Tripp's baby. It's just Aunt Josie's, okay?"

The words shouldn't have stung with such intensity. She was trying to protect him, but somehow it felt like pushing him away.

Davey shrugged. "Okay."

They chatted about the boys' kindergarten class. Isaac said he'd show Tripp his LEGO mini figure collection.

Josie stood. "Bath time and pj's, boys."

"Then a story, right?" Isaac asked.

"That's right. What'll it be?"

"Midas and the Golden Touch!" Davey shouted.

Josie hauled the boys off for their bath while Tripp cleaned up the plates and cookie crumbs and empty milk glasses. She peered around the corner at him a half hour later. "Boys are in bed, waiting for story time."

He smiled, threw down the kitchen towel. "Good, don't want to miss it."

"I didn't think you would, it being a book with nice big pictures and all."

He pinched her arm and followed her up the stairs where he knelt on the floor beside Davey's bed, the two boys on either side of him, Josie in the rocking chair in the corner. "I guess I'm being nominated for this one?"

She shrugged. "They wanted you to read it."

He turned the brightly-colored hardcover book to the first page. "Once upon a time, there lived a King named Midas who loved gold. King Midas had a daughter named Goldie who he loved with all his heart...."

I thought my heart may very well break in two for the tender scene before me. Of course Tripp was a natural with my two energetic nephews. He would make a great father someday.

I pushed my feet against the hardwood floor of the boys' room, tried to rock away the emotion climbing my throat. Why did the thought of Tripp being a father sadden me when only a short time ago it nearly made me giddy with hope?

But I knew.

Finn. Finn's call changed everything. And I hadn't the guts to tell Tripp, either, had instead made that careless comment in front of the boys about Little Mouse being just my baby. Yet, what else should I say? I didn't want them to assume a picture-perfect family that wouldn't materialize. Nor did I want them inadvertently solidifying the rumors of Tripp being the father. Hadn't I told Tripp I wanted to take it slow? For reasons like Finn. To give Tripp an easy-out if that's what he preferred.

I leaned my head back, listened to the story of the king who found out the hard way what really mattered. When Tripp finished the story, we tucked the boys into bed. I smoothed their hair back from their foreheads, kissed them, and told them goodnight.

"Aren't you going to pray with us?" Davey asked.

"Mommy always prays with us. Daddy too when he's home." Isaac clutched his bed covers with a tight fist.

My mouth grew dry. "I-um, sure."

Tripp squeezed my arm. "Don't worry, my modern day damsel-in-distress, I can take this one."

I rolled my eyes, knowing I'd never hear the end of my little speech as Maid Marion.

He sat on the edge of Isaac's bed, and I sat on the end of Davey's. "What should we pray for then, men?"

"That Mommy and Daddy will get home safe." Isaac's voice trembled and I put a hand to my chest.

Davey sniffed. "Our real Mommy died in a car accident."

Tripp looked thoughtful. "So you're afraid the same thing might happen to your new mom?"

Both boys nodded.

I swallowed. "Oh boys, I can understand why you're scared, but just because that happened does not mean it's going to happen to either of your parents now, okay?"

Tripp shifted on the bed, crooking one leg. "You want to hear what I do when I'm scared about something?"

Davey giggled. "You're big. You're not afraid of anything."

"Sure I am. You know those spiders with the really long legs?"

"Daddy long legs?"

Tripp nodded. "Those things scare the daylights out of me."

"But Mommy says they don't even bite you!"

Tripp pretended a shiver. "Anything with legs that long deserves to put the fear of God in a man, in my opinion."

We all laughed.

"So what do you do?" Isaac's eyes grew wide in the dim light of the room.

"I write what I'm scared of on a piece of paper and then put it in a box. As long as it's in the box, it's God's to handle and not for me to worry about."

"Does it work?"

"You want to try it?" Tripp asked.

The boys nodded. I opened their closet and searched for a shoebox, finding the boys each had a pair of dress shoes stacked neatly in their boxes, a polaroid picture of the shoe taped on the outside. I wouldn't expect anything less of my sister.

I dumped one pair on the floor, certain Maggie would forgive me for a good cause. Meanwhile, Tripp secured pencils and paper from Davey's desk and helped the boys write out their worries.

"Now, fold them up." They both did. "And put them in the box. But wait—" My nephews looked up at him, faces glowing and expectant. "This is serious business, men. When you place that fear inside the box, you are really putting it in God's hands. You can't take it back. Are you ready for your mission?"

They nodded, and Tripp gestured to me. "Aunt Josie, will you please do the honors?"

I slipped the lid off the box and went first to Isaac, then to Davey as they each placed their wrinkled paper inside. Then I shut the lid tight. Tripp knelt down beside the boys and placed a hand on each arm. He prayed the most beautiful prayer of protection over my sister and her husband, over the boys and me. His rhythmic words lulled me into a state of peace, and when I opened my eyes to his final "Amen" I saw that both boys lay asleep.

We tiptoed out of the room. I carried the box downstairs where I placed it on the kitchen counter. "That was the most amazing thing I've ever seen."

He wrapped his arms around me. "Those are two amazing little guys."

"I didn't know that about you—that you write down your worries and put them in a box."

"A guy's got a right to a few secrets, doesn't he?"

I cocked my head. "What other secrets do you have?"

"Would you believe me if I told you I read the most popular memoirs, literary fiction, and political books Amazon recommends to me?"

I shook my head. "Nope."

"Can't blame me for trying, right?" He planted a kiss on my forehead. "You know, I've enjoyed playing house with you." He trailed his lips to my mouth, creating pleasant prickles along my skin.

"I can't make out with you while my nephews are upstairs sleeping."

"Even if I say you make one beautiful Maid Marion?"

I laughed. "I'm a regular whale of a tale, that's for sure."

He gave me a chaste kiss on the lips, pulled me close to lean his chin on the top of my head. I sank into it, closing my eyes, imagining this was our life. Not having to say goodbye at night. Having children upstairs. It surprised me how much I wanted it all.

Unless Finn pushed his way into it.

I opened my mouth, breathed through a quivering breath. "You know...there's been something I've been meaning to tell you."

"There's more cookies, isn't there? I knew you were holding out."

I shook my head. "No, I…" But I couldn't push the words forth, couldn't ruin this moment by speaking of Finn. "I really don't know why we haven't done this sooner." I stood on my tiptoes to capture his mouth with my own, sank into him, relished the feeling of being loved.

There was no use in bringing up my baby's father. Finn was unpredictable. He could have been drunk when he sent those texts. No more stable than the wind, flitting this way and that with whatever philosophy or emotion suited him at the moment. Quite likely, I wouldn't hear from him again. And while I would keep my promise to let him know when the baby was born, I doubted it would make a difference.

In the words of Toni Morrison, love was only as good as the integrity of the lover. Finn Becker only cared about one person— and it wasn't me, and it wasn't our child.

It was himself.

23

"Josie, these are great!" Lizzie gazed at the name plaques for the guest rooms I'd painstakingly wood burned onto stained pieces of pine. Their beveled edges gave the otherwise rustic pieces an elegant flair. She picked up the one closest to the edge of the dining room table—the Hawthorne Room— and ran her fingers over the indents in the wood.

"Mom liked them. We'll have to see how they look on the doors once they finish painting everything."

"It's all so exciting." She panned the room, the many boxes piled high around us, waiting for our move in just two days.

Tripp's crew was still working on the painting and trim of the B&B, as well as the small apartment above the bookshop. We'd use the next two weeks to get settled into our new living space and decorate while waiting for our occupancy permit. We'd hang our sign, advertise as best we could online and through various newspapers, and plan the open house as soon as we got the green light.

Oh yeah, and somewhere within that time frame I'd be having a baby.

I gathered the plaques. "How's teaching? Kids aren't giving

you any trouble, are they?" How my shy, introverted sister commanded a class of rowdy middle-schoolers was beyond me, but she loved it and did it well.

"Classes are good, but there's talk of cutting the music budget in the new year."

"Would they do that?"

She shrugged. "I suppose if it came down to it. Music and art always seem to be the first on the list when it comes to budget cuts."

"But that's not right. So many kids find an outlet through those classes. A talent they might not otherwise find." I thought of my own secret vice of writing when I was younger, of the half-filled journal upstairs that I'd written in each night for the last several months. A story. A creative release, a way to unwind and let the world fade away. Some people had a glass of wine at the end of the day, others had a television show; I had my writing. How many children would miss out on finding their outlet if the budget was cut?

"I know." The corner of Lizzie's mouth tightened. "I don't see how I'm ever going to work full-time at this rate, either. Good thing Mom can use my help at the B&B. I'll never be bored."

"As long as we get reservations, you won't be." I'd been so certain of the worth of my idea, but what if it didn't take off? What if Mom didn't make enough to make ends meet? What if we couldn't live long-term with Aunt Pris without killing one another?

Lizzie rubbed my back. "We will get reservations. Maybe the first few months with winter and all will be slow, but people will come. You're worrying for nothing."

The mention of worrying made me think of Tripp's worry box. Maybe I should start one of my own.

The door squeaked, followed by Mom bustling in with bags. "Oh good, you girls are home." She placed the bags on a chair and dug into one, pulling out a soft yellow baby bath towel, a duck face on the hood. "Isn't this just the cutest thing? I think I'm getting addicted to baby clothes."

I reached for the soft material. "It's adorable, Mom. But you're already spoiling this child."

Lizzie ran her thumb and forefinger over the towel. "Someone has to since you're dead set against a shower. I don't see why you won't let us throw you one, Josie."

I blew out a breath that fanned the hair above my face. "Don't you think we have enough going on? Besides, I'm just not comfortable on display, sitting in a chair I barely fit in while opening presents in front of a group of gabby women who don't approve of me. I've dipped into my savings for some of what I need, but the rest will come." I'd purchased a car seat and a stroller and some diapers. Bless his heart, Tripp surprised me the week before by setting up a crib in the bookshop. We'd move it upstairs once the apartment was finished. "I'm not one of those mothers who thinks everything has to be perfect before the baby comes. I've winged this whole thing so far, don't see why that should change once the baby's born."

"Okay, then. We get it." Lizzie turned to Mom and shrugged. "I know it's early, but I was at the craft store today and there were these beautiful red berries on sale. I think they'd be perfect for decorating inside for Christmas. You want to check it out tonight?"

"Oh honey, I'd love to, but can I take a rain check? Aunt Pris asked me and Maggie to go over a few details on the website. She saw it for the first time yesterday and was both impressed and appalled, I think. She wanted Maggie to make some corrections on the *History* page, and I didn't want to send her over alone."

"I could go with you," I said to Lizzie. "If Mom trusts me enough for a second opinion on decorating themes." I'd missed too much last Christmas. We all had, it being our first without Dad. But this new season of life made me hunger for the holiday that held so many fond memories.

Mom and Lizzie exchanged glances.

"What?"

"No gaudy neon lights, Josie." Mom planted her hands on her hips.

"I loved those ornaments on the tree when we were growing up."

"And each year, I flinched when I walked into the living room."

Lizzie laughed. "I just put on a pair of sunglasses. It wasn't so bad after that."

Mom turned to Lizzie, put her hands on both shoulders. "Lizzie Martin, do you solemnly swear to be strong enough to withstand Josie's persuasive and winsome ways? To put your foot down in the name of all that is beautiful and tasteful about Christmas?"

A smile crept over my sister's mouth. "I do."

I rolled my eyes. "Whatever, you two. Who says Christmas has to be tasteful, anyway? If there's ever a time to get loud and bright, it's December."

The doorbell rang and Mom turned toward the front. "But we don't want to blind our guests, dear!"

Lizzie and I erupted into giggles. I looked at the corner where our Christmas tree stood for as long as I'd been alive. Now, a stack of cardboard boxes filled its place. I sighed and finished gathering the name plaques for the rooms. "Hard to believe we're really saying goodbye to this place, isn't it?"

"It is. But you know, I've been thinking that it sort of feels like cleaning out the old to make way for the new. Like maybe God's asking us to trust Him in this so He can do something amazing."

That was Lizzie, always seeing the hopeful side of things. I winked at her. "I'm trusting you're right. And when the time—"

"Finn!" Mom's excited greeting split through the air. "It's been too long. What an amazing surprise!"

My knees grew weak, and I dropped the room labels. They

clattered to the table. Finn...my Finn? But not mine. I didn't want him to be mine. I put my hands, palms flat, on the table to steady myself, dragged conscious breaths through my nose.

"Hey, are you okay?" Lizze came to my side, supporting me.

If I had enough strength to carry my heavy body up the stairs, I would have hid in my room. It struck me then how I had gained more than my fair share of pregnancy weight, how I did not want to face Finn like this.

I couldn't believe he'd come. Hadn't I been clear when we talked? I really didn't want anything to do with him. Only because he was the father of my child did I even intend to tell him when Little Mouse was born.

Why on earth was he here?

Mom swept him into the dining room, her hand on his back, pushing him forward. It struck me for the first time how he was closer to Mom's age than mine. My stomach soured.

"Girls, you remember Professor Becker, of course. He came over for many a Thanksgiving around here."

I stared at the table, couldn't make my gaze meet Finn's. But why not? This was my turf, my home. I needn't be ashamed. He was the one who threw me away when I no longer suited his needs.

I lifted my chin, stared him down, but found myself a little swayed by those familiar brown eyes. My breath hitched in my chest. I'd had so many expectations for us. Maybe they hadn't always included the traditional marriage and family picture, but they'd been real. Authentic. How many talks over the complexities of the human mind had we discussed? How many books had we debated over? How many intimate moments had we shared?

I hated my thoughts, hated to remember his good points instead of the bad I'd clung to the last several months.

"Hello, Josie."

I didn't answer, felt Mom and Lizzie studying us. With sudden clarity, Mom inhaled a sharp breath, her eyes wide. I met her gaze with my own, and I knew she knew. She bit her bottom lip to keep her emotions at bay. I was certain if we all kept staring at one another Mom would say something she'd regret.

I gestured toward the backyard patio. "We can talk out there if that's why you've come."

He nodded, looked at Mom. "I'm sorry, Hannah," he whispered, sliding past her before Mom could manage any words.

Once on the patio, I sat on the swing, the act of pushing my feet against the cobbles helping to expend some of the nervous energy surging through my body. Finn didn't sit, but stood, hands in the pockets of his khakis, pressed shirt neatly tucked into his pants. He looked good, trim and tan. He'd always had it so together. We were complete opposites, really. Is that why I'd been drawn to him? Had I been nothing but a unique amusement to him, a way to pass time until someone better came along?

"You didn't tell them." He seemed preoccupied with the herb garden, a chaotic assembly of basil and oregano, thyme and sage, mint and parsley.

"I never expected you to show up. I didn't think there was a reason, thought it would only complicate things."

He sat down in the chair closest to me, leaned over long splayed legs. "I'm sorry, Josie. I—I should have done a lot of things differently."

"Like?"

He closed his eyes, his chest rising and falling beneath the buttons of his dress shirt. This was hard for him, but I didn't care. In fact, it satisfied something within me to see him squirm.

"Like listened to you, listened to what you wanted. I was stubborn. I tried to manipulate you into doing what I wanted. I should have known you were too strong for that." One corner of his mouth lifted. "I guess I was pretty full of myself, huh? Thinking you'd do anything—even get rid of our baby—if it meant keeping me."

"I guess so." I didn't intend the sarcasm on my tongue, but

feared if I didn't stay mad, if I didn't cling to my anger, he'd whisk me away again. Make me forget myself, make me forget everything but him.

And I couldn't let that happen. Tripp had shown me real love, not just these past few months, but all my life. Tripp, with his offer of tender security, with his patient thoughtfulness. I could not afford to get caught up in the whirlwind of Finn Becker again, and the fact that I thought it a possibility now made me all the more desperate to push him away.

"Josie, I'm sorry. I've thought long and hard about this, and I want to do the right thing."

"But isn't 'right' relative?" I asked, throwing one of his own premises back in his face.

He swallowed. "I'm not pretending to have all the answers anymore. But I'm trying. Please." He reached into his back pocket, slipped out an envelope, and handed it to me.

I turned it over. "What's this?"

"Something to show you I mean what I say."

I slid the envelope open. Inside was a check large enough to pay for a year of graduate classes at NYU. I shook my head. "Finn—"

"I told you. I want to do the right thing. In many ways, you turned my world upside-down. I've never known my conscience to be as active as it's been these last several months. Josie, please let me make it up to you."

There were times, weeks even, after finding out I was pregnant with Finn's baby that I'd dreamed of a scenario such as this. Finn, practically groveling at my feet, begging me to give him and our baby another chance. I wouldn't give in too easy of course, I'd make him work a bit, but eventually he'd win me over. And we would move forward, plan our next steps to being a happy family. Only now, the thought of being with Finn felt like bondage. I didn't want to go back. I didn't want to leave Tripp and all he'd given me—hope in a future, hope in him, hope in God, hope in myself—to go back to a lie.

"What do you want from me, Finn?" I whispered. All of a sudden, I just wanted to make peace, to say what he needed to hear so he could be on his way back to New York City.

He stood, reached in his front pocket and withdrew a square velvet box. Even as he planted one knee firmly on the cobbles beneath him and held a massive glittering diamond rock up to me, I couldn't comprehend what in the Sam Hill he thought he was doing.

I shook my head, wondering how he thought *this* could be the best solution to what was before us.

"Josie, I made a big mistake when I let you walk out of my life. I'm ready, now. Ready to be a father to our child, a husband to you. I will help you finish your classes, pay for childcare so you can pursue your dreams. They shouldn't die. Josie, will you marry me?"

FINN'S HEART HADN'T POUNDED THIS HARD SINCE HE STOOD AT the open door of the plane on his first skydiving jump. But he'd thought long and hard about this, had even prayed a little. Him, Finn Becker. *Praying.*

It was the only decision to give him a good night's sleep, sans the tears. It was the only decision that gave peace. Maybe he *could* turn over a new leaf. Be a family man. Maybe fulfillment wasn't just about enjoyment of life. Maybe it was in the work of family and love, sticking it through when the tough came along.

Yes, there was definitely something honorable about it. Something that made him stand a little straighter and sleep a little deeper. Katarina hadn't understood, not really. But she would be okay in the end. She was a strong woman, too.

His arms grew weighty from holding up the ring. He'd gone

down to Manhattan Jewelry and bought one of the largest engagement rings he could find. Something no woman would say no to.

But Josie's response didn't meet his imagination. He studied her. Rounder than he remembered, but her figure could come back in time. He'd pay for a gym membership, one with childcare, so she could run on the treadmills.

He realized his mistake too late. Josie hated running on the treadmill. She only ran outside. For some reason, this realization caused his carefully crafted plans to collapse in his head. And he knew—knew what she was going to say before she said it, was astonished to feel just a tiny bit of relief, even.

But what did that mean for their future and the future of their child?

❧ 24 ❧

Tripp whistled as he parked his truck in the Martin driveway and went around to the back door, holding a single sunflower in his hand. He told Hannah he'd take as many packed boxes over to Orchard House as he could in the next couple days.

Maybe Josie would take the ride over with him. They could grab a bite to eat, maybe some ice cream. Lately, she was always up for ice cream.

Grandpop had been by the B&B that day to inspect the work. He'd given his hearty approval, and Tripp hadn't been able to hide his pride. The Orchard House was spectacular. Alive with purpose and anticipation and history, it glittered. The rooms needed hardware and a paint touchup, and Josie's small apartment needed some work, but it would be done before the baby came, as would the bookshop.

He pictured Josie rocking her babe in the upstairs apartment, looking over the vast orchard in bloom. He wanted that place, that snatch of time, to include him, too, but Josie hadn't indicated anything long term. He refused to rush her, knew from experience it would only push her away.

He turned the corner and stopped at the sight of a dark-haired man on one knee, a ring the size of Augusta in his hand. And Josie. *His* Josie, sitting with her arms over her swollen belly, jaw open.

The sunflower fell from Tripp's hand. He couldn't move, a thousand thoughts flitting through his mind. The man looked familiar, but Tripp couldn't place him. Not that it mattered. It didn't take a high IQ to gather this was the father of Josie's baby, the man she'd fallen in love with and gave herself to, the man that Tripp wanted—with every sinew and fiber and muscle of his body —to pummel beyond recognition.

And yet he stood frozen, couldn't tear his eyes away from what would happen next. While Tripp wanted this guy far away from the woman he loved, he needed to make sure Josie felt the same. Was this man what was best for her?

Hell might as well freeze over if that were the case. But Josie wouldn't take kindly to Tripp swooping in and saving her. Besides, what was he saving her from? A marriage proposal?

Something inside Tripp came undone. Josie had loved this clown. Maybe she still did. He was the father of her baby. Was that reason enough for her to marry him?

No. He wouldn't let it happen.

He strode hard toward the patio, an awkward sound escaping his throat.

Both turned, and Tripp saw the guy was older. Not ready to apply for Medicare exactly, but old enough to already have a wife and grown children. Was Josie just the next in line for him?

Josie's eyes widened. "Tripp."

The man turned back to Josie. "Josie..."

"We need to talk about this, Finn."

"I thought that's what we were doing."

Josie's gray eyes landed on Tripp and he couldn't place what he saw there, but it wasn't welcome. Surely, not resentment? Had she been about to accept this guy's proposal?

Josie shook her head, as if to clear her thoughts. "Tripp, this is Finn Becker. Finn, this is my friend, Tripp."

She may as well have rammed a metal bat into his gut. *Friend.* Did you kiss a friend how Josie had kissed him in the bookshop? Did you entertain offers of sharing your life with a friend, of allowing a friend to be the father of your fatherless child?

Friend.

And yet, at the core, that's the relationship they knew best. Maybe he'd been a fool to believe otherwise.

He looked at the guy he despised more than any other, now on his feet. It dawned on Tripp why the man looked familiar. He had been one of Amos's charity cases. He'd spent several Thanksgivings with the Martin family when Tripp was a teen, had visited once after Tripp graduated high school.

Tripp could still remember him and Amos and Josie discussing some random theory on the human brain on that last trip, how Josie's eyes had sparkled at the conversation, at Finn's witty words. He'd wanted to make her eyes sparkle like that. He remembered how long he listened to their debate on quantum mechanics and its possible role in consciousness, how he'd searched for an opening for something brilliant to say, but how in the end, he'd kept quiet for fear of making a fool of himself. For fear of Finn looking at him in a way that said, "Best keep to the tool belt, son." Yes, he remembered the man well now. He had taught at the local college. Psychology. Had been transferred to some big wig school in New York.

It all came together. Well-respected professor preys on much younger, vulnerable graduate student. Perhaps uses his past relationship with her dead father to get close to her. To sleep with her.

Everything within Tripp clenched tight. He wanted to sock the lowlife in his pretty little face. Old man probably wouldn't be able to make it back on his feet for a comeback.

But...*friend.*

"Nice to meet you." The man named Finn held his hand out, seemed not the least bit intimidated by Tripp, didn't even seem to remember him.

Tripp ignored the hand, crossed his arms over his chest, and stood tall, taking childish satisfaction that he had a few inches on the guy. "You're the father, I take it?"

The man pressed his mouth together, creating dimples on either side of his face. He nodded.

That was all the confirmation Tripp needed. His anger bubbled hot and fast, boiling over until all he could think about was wiping those pretty little dimples off the shmuck's face. He pulled a fist back hard and fast, propelling it forward until it made a satisfying connection with pretty boy's face.

Josie screamed. The guy reeled back, cursing, holding a hand to his eye.

"Who do you think you are, coming back here after all these months? What kind of a lowlife gets his girlfriend pregnant then abandons her?" Tripp raked a hand through his hair, his body humming with something like justice, something like hurt. "Let me tell you something, buddy. This is the best woman you'll ever lay eyes on, and if you couldn't recognize that back then, you don't deserve her now."

"Tripp!" Josie's voice snapped him from his anger. He turned to see her bunching her fists and gritting her teeth. "You need to leave. *Now*."

He took one last look at the professor, then shook out his hand. Josie crossed her arms above her belly, searing Tripp with a glare.

"Sure. Whatever you want, *friend*." He walked around the house toward his truck.

He grabbed his keys from his pocket, climbed into his truck, and peeled out of the driveway.

It wasn't until he got home that he realized the damage he'd

done. All this time, he'd told himself he showed Josie unconditional love. He showed her the kind of love God gave.

But it was a lie.

Because unconditional love didn't rush in and hurl fists. It was
patient. Kind. Gave free choice. Trust.

Tripp leaned his head against the steering wheel and groaned.
Maybe he and Josie simply didn't belong together. If one woman
made him feel such crazy emotion, maybe it was a mistake to
surround himself with her day and night, night and day.

Love in the hard. He was supposed to love Josie in her chaos.

But looking at what had happened today, he'd been wrong to
think Josie was the only one who had trash to clean up.

"Finn, I'm so sorry." I led Finn toward the kitchen door.
"Let's get you some ice."

I pulled open the screen door, still shaken from the events of
the afternoon—Finn's proposal, Tripp's outburst, Tripp's hurt. I
pulled out a chair for him at the dining room table, opened the
freezer door, and scrambled for an ice tray. Miracle of miracles,
the kitchen was actually empty. I wondered if Mom planned it
that way.

I broke the ice over the sink, slid it into a plastic sandwich
bag, put a paper towel around it, and held it out to Finn.

"Thanks."

"You need a doctor?"

He shook his head. "I don't think so."

I sat down at the table and rubbed my eyes, exhaustion
creeping over me.

"He's in love with you." Finn gazed at me out of his one
good eye.

"Tripp. Yes. For a long while now, before...us."

He pressed the ice harder to his face. "And how do you feel about him?"

"I—" How was I having this conversation with Finn? And how to answer that question? Yes, I loved Tripp. I'd always loved him. But it was only recently that I'd fallen *in* love with him.

But right now I was so mad at him. Tripp had been my rock these last few months. My solid safety and security. But to have him come barreling in to save me without even asking if I needed to be saved? Would he ever be able to trust me?

Still, could I blame him for his temper when mine was enough to rival his? How often did we fall short? How often did we need to forgive one another?

Maybe that was the nature of real love.

I clasped my fingers on top of the table, knowing one thing for certain. "Finn, I can't marry you."

He placed the icepack down, stared at the worn wood grain of the table. "I know."

"You do?"

He nodded. "It's probably a good thing, actually. I don't deserve you, Martin."

I licked my lips, swallowed hard. "It took a lot for you to come here. I just think—well, we messed up. And I think this baby will be something beautiful to come out of that mess. But I don't think our child should be the reason we get married."

"And you love Tripp."

I nodded. "Yes, I do."

"I'm not sure he knows it."

"Because I haven't told him."

He put the ice back on his face.

"We can work this out, Finn. Somehow."

The eye that wasn't swollen glistened, surprising me with the sincerity that went along with it.

"What made you change your mind about being involved?"

He shrugged. "My conscience. God. Who knows? Maybe they're not mutually exclusive."

I squeezed his hand. "I will let you know when the baby's born. I'm not saying it will be easy, because it won't. My home is here now. I'm helping Mom start a bed and breakfast and—"

"A bed and breakfast, huh? Psychology grad turned hospitality specialist? Are you sure this is what you want, Josie?"

"Yes. I've never been more sure of anything." I reached into my pocket, slid the envelope with the check in it back toward him.

He shook his head. "No. That was yours regardless of your answer to me. Use it for whatever you need, or start a college fund for the baby. I'll set something up so you have regular payments out of my paycheck."

"Finn, I don't—"

"Josie, please. Let me do this."

I swallowed, in awe at the change in the man before me. I wondered what our fate would be had it come sooner. Would we have stuck it out for the sake of our child? I exhaled a breath, relief filling me. Crazy, but I was glad our journey brought us here, moving forward together, but separately. "Thank you."

The kitchen door opened and Bronson stormed in red-faced and ready to take on the world. "Lizzie told me—" He looked at Finn, chest heaving. "Josie, is this punk bothering you?"

I couldn't help but laugh at my twenty-two-year-old brother calling a forty-year-old college professor a "punk."

"Put your fists away, Bronson. He's cool, okay? Besides, Tripp already took a swipe at him."

Finn stood. "Guess that's my cue to leave."

I walked him to the door.

"I guess I shouldn't worry if you'll be well taken care of around here, huh?"

I smiled. "I've missed my family."

He looked back toward the kitchen through a hallway of

stacked boxes, a wistful look on his face. "Your family was always something special. I remember thinking during my Thanksgiving visits that if I ever had a family..." He cleared his throat. "If I ever had a family, I'd want it to be like the Martin family. Now, our child will be a part of it. That's something special, Josie."

He lifted a hand to my face, and I put my fingers over his, squeezed lightly. "You're a part of it too now, Finn. Okay? Family's more than marriage ties and bloodlines, and I want you to come visit our child as much as you want." The words left my mouth, surprising even me, but they felt right, this extending of kindness.

"I think I'd like that." He bent, kissed my cheek. "Thank you, Josie."

And then he was gone, leaving me with overwhelming gratitude and hope. As I watched him walk down the front steps on the last day I would be standing in my childhood home, I felt this was the beginning of a new chapter—a chapter I could never have written for myself, but one more creative than I could have orchestrated.

There was only one thing left to do.

25

"**S**o you punched the guy?" August leaned against Grandpop's 1941 Packard parked in the garage.

Tripp waxed the antique car harder. He came out here looking for something to build but could only glare at his workbench, finding no motivation. Instead, he'd picked up some wax and a rag. "I don't know what got into me—no, that's a lie. I do. When it comes to Josie, I'm a wreck."

August nodded. "You're a lovesick puppy, that's for sure." He placed a firm hand on Tripp's shoulder. "Don't be too hard on yourself, dude. Women mess with our best intentions."

He raised an eyebrow. "You sound like you're talking from experience."

August sighed. "I'm not coming home on the weekends because I enjoy the drive."

Tripp's brother had started classes back up more than a month ago. "You seeing someone from Camden?"

"Trying to."

"Trying? Are you telling me a woman is resistant to August Colton's charm?" Tripp feigned surprise, and his brother punched him in the arm.

222

"Just one. The one I want."

Tripp sighed. "The problem with love. Guess we're both done for, huh?"

"Guess so." August went to the workbench, scooped up a few papers. "So Big Bro, I started a drafting class this semester. Tell me what you think."

Tripp shifted toward the light, took in the drawing of the house, one elevation on each page, the proportions spot on, the design original and tasteful. He flipped the pages, his gaze sweeping over the rustic barn doors, the wide columns and extensive porch, the gabled windows. "These are incredible, August."

His brother grinned. "I'm enjoying myself. You know, I felt kind of like a drifter in my art classes until I worked for the company this summer. The building...it inspired me. Like it's a kind of art, you know? I'm thinking of taking more classes, maybe becoming an architect."

Tripp slapped his brother's back. "That's awesome. You'll have a job waiting for you at Colton Contractors, that's for sure. You tell Grandpop yet?"

"Nah. You know how he'll get. I just want to stay chill about it, see how it goes."

"Well, you're talented, that's for sure. I'm proud of you. You've really straightened up your act."

August put a hand on Tripp's shoulders, a mock look of seriousness on his face as he shook his head. "Now if we can only get you to straighten up yours."

Tripp wrapped him in a headlock but let go of him at the sound of a car door. August scrambled away and grabbed up his drawings. "Gotta run. Good luck with the missus." He scooted out before Tripp could get another punch in edgewise.

Not that he had a mind to do so with Josie standing fifteen feet from him, looking all types of surly with her hands on her hips, the setting sun like fire behind her, the sunflower he'd brought her almost wilted in her fist.

"Hey." He took a tentative step closer.

She didn't speak.

He flung his hands out to his side. "I'm sorry, Josie. Really. I shouldn't have barged in like that. I lost it. Way lost it. You have a tendency of doing that to me."

"Don't you dare turn this around on me, Tripp Colton. You're the one who screwed up."

"I—I know. I'm so sorry. I saw red. Knowing you loved another guy enough to sleep with him after you turned me down is one thing. Having an accurate mental image of the guy, of what he did to you, and with you...it put me over the edge." He walked out of the garage doors until he was close enough to touch her. "But I know that doesn't make it right. I told you I loved you with no strings attached, but then I sweep in like Captain America ready to take on Red Skull."

She shook her head. "We have *got* to get you some better reading material."

He cracked a smile, but sobered quick at the memory of the professor and his ring. "So...what'd you say?"

"What do you think I said? I'm in love, Tripp."

In love. His heart twisted. Maybe it was better this way. Josie's child would have its father—its *real* father and mother together, under one roof. No splitting the child between them for weekends and holidays. No competing between parents. Just one big happy family.

He tried to be happy for her—if he really loved her, he would be, right?

He sniffed hard, desperate to keep his emotions in check. "I—I see. Well, I hope you guys are happy together. I can't say I'm not devastated. Will you go back to New York or—"

"Tripp, shut up."

He blinked. "What?"

She stepped closer, those gray eyes holding the power of a wild sea squall approaching shore. "I'm not in love with Finn. I'm in love with you. I told him no."

He let out a sharp breath, blinked, tried to comprehend her words. He bent his knees to be eye level with her, put both hands on either side of her arms. "Wait, really? You said no? You love me?"

The corner of her mouth twitched. "All I could think about when he showed me that gaudy diamond was the bookshop, the crib you spent hours putting together, how wonderful it feels to kiss you. You opened up the door for me to hear the whisper of God's Spirit again. You reminded me why I need Him so desperately in the first place. And I do. We both do. Let's face it—together, we're a hot mess."

She blinked before looking up at him. "But you know who else I need? You. Tripp, I need you so much."

Her words sent a wave of hope and gratitude coursing through him. He was really hearing these words. She was really *saying* these words.

He scooped her up, and dipped his head, softly kissed her until her arms came up behind his neck, pressing him closer. He inhaled the smell of her—wind and lilacs and everything good in life. His body responded, warming, and all he could think to do was make her his as soon as possible.

His Josie. Bright and beautiful and full of light. He pulled away. "What does this mean? Never mind, I know what this means. We need to go ring shopping."

She stepped back. "Hold on there, Captain, I didn't say I was ready for wedding bells."

His stomach twisted. "But I thought—"

"Just because I said no to one proposal today doesn't mean I need to say yes to the other."

"You said you loved me."

She reached for his arm. "I *do* love you. That's why we need to wait. Let me have this baby first. I don't want you signing up for anything you'll regret."

"You remember all those times you walked over to my house, asked me if I wanted to do something?"

"Yeah, sure."

"Did I ever say no?"

She smiled. "Not that I remember."

"Because it didn't matter what we did. Whether we had a grand adventure getting lost in the State Park or dodging boats around Curtis Island or putting up a lemonade stand or just sitting in your apple tree, looking at the clouds. Even when Amie tagged along, or you just wanted my help with homework. It never mattered, because I was with you, Josie. Always. A baby is not going to change that. If anything, it makes me want to care for both of you all the more."

"Oh, Tripp..." She scrunched her brow. "Wait—you helped *me* with homework?"

He grinned. "Okay, maybe it was the other way around."

"I'd think so." She inhaled deep, contemplating. "Still, I think we should stick with waiting. Finn's proposal shouldn't change that. It shouldn't change us. But now, he wants to be a part of the baby's life. I don't know how that makes you feel. When you offered to love me, he wasn't in the picture. I can't pretend it won't be complicated."

Yes, he supposed it would be. "We'll work it out. And I'm okay with waiting if that's what you want. I'm going to need some time to figure out how I'm going to compete with a college professor anyway."

"Tripp, there's no competition. I was lost this past year, searching for something to fill the loss of my father. First, it was a career, then it was Finn. Now, I realized something. I realized that everything I wanted was right in front of me. Here, with my family, with you."

He ran the back of his fingers over her cheek. "I've waited forever to hear you say that."

She lay her head against his chest, her child between them.

He squeezed her tighter. "I can't wait to make you my wife, Josie Martin."

She released a sound of contentment against his chest.

"I just want to clarify one little thing."

She lifted her head. "What's that?"

"When you call me *captain*, you mean Captain America, right? Because I don't think I'm cool with my future wife thinking of me as Captain Underpants."

She ran her forefinger along his chin. "How about captain of my heart?"

"Incredibly corny, even for you, but I'll take it. Where shall we sail next, my fair lady?"

"To the edge of the horizon, as long as we're together."

"I'm up for that." He kissed her long and deep, pulling every ounce of sweetness from her lips, from the moment. "I'm very much up for that."

❧ 26 ❧

I walked up the stairs to the second floor of Aunt Pris's home. The Martin home now, too. It was all really happening.

I stopped on the landing halfway up the stairs where a generous window bench graced a bow window. I sat, waiting for the cramp in my belly to disappear. Especially active last night, Little Mouse had been quiet for most of the day, save for the Braxton Hicks contractions I'd sustained for most of the afternoon. My doctor assured me they were normal, especially in the last month of pregnancy.

We'd unpacked the last few days, the closing on our home behind us and nothing before us but the preparing of the B&B and the bookshop. Once the money from the house became available, I'd start building our store inventory.

I ascended the remaining flight of stairs and walked to the room straight ahead, the Alcott Room, labeled with the wooden sign I'd labored over for hours. Amie must have approved of it, for she didn't protest the placards. I knocked on the open door, not wanting to startle my youngest sister from her painting.

"Come in."

I peered around the door to the fireplace in the corner,

where Amie worked on painting an owl identical to the one in Louisa May Alcott's room at Orchard House in Concord. She looked up, a palette of oils on the floor by her feet. Her expression seemed to dim at the sight of me. We hadn't quite made peace over our awful argument a few weeks earlier. We were civil enough, of course, but neither of us had apologized, clinging to our pride and the very real sense that the other was in the wrong.

I supposed I should ask for forgiveness. I didn't want to bring my child into the world with this terrible thing between me and my sister. I wanted to be good and noble, a mother like mine. But it was hard. Was I under some unrealistic expectation that becoming a mother would make me more saintly?

Hardly.

I gestured at her artwork on the mantle. "That's beautiful, Amie. It looks just like the original."

She leaned back, squinted. "I think it will do. I like having it here, anyway. Gives it the Alcott authenticity, I think."

"It does. You do great work."

She went back to her painting, and I walked around the large room, ran my hand over the curves of the four-poster bed, anticipating the things that were still left to do. Window treatments and wall hangings. Comforter and television (I'd argued over that one but lost the battle—Mom insisted we'd alienate our clientele by not having a TV in each room). We already had a handful of reservations for December, and that being through nothing but word-of-mouth and the website.

I lowered myself to the chair in front of the half moon desk. I ran my hand over the smooth white paint, tried to choose my words carefully. "You know, I never should have said what I did— about you not having anything to do with my baby. That's not what I want. Not what I want at all." Another pain started, but it proved to be a gentle, slow mounting pressure that subsided in quick enough time.

My sister continued painting, silence her answer. It dragged out until I couldn't take anymore.

I grit my teeth, my anger rising along with another contraction. "What do you want from me? Seems you're always holding something against me, and I don't know why."

She dipped her brush in her colors and raised it to the mantle. "I guess I want you to stop having it all."

I shook my head, confused. "What?"

She shrugged. "First you had all of Dad's attention, then Tripp's. Then you got to go off to New York, a city of excitement and culture and art and beauty. You left him and I thought..." She bit her lip, swirled her paint with her brush. "You had everything, Josie. Everything. But you ruined it. And yet you still come out on top, don't you? Helping Mom achieve her dream, having the first Martin grandchild to carry Dad's blood, and Tripp...he still loves you. After all the junk you put him through, he still chooses you."

My mind swam. Tripp. Did Amie actually have feelings for him? I mean, sure, there were times her schoolgirl crush on our good-looking older neighbor was apparent, but he was *my* best friend. The boy who loved *me*.

She lifted her brush again, the sunlight from the window across the room streaming onto her golden head. "You did everything wrong and you still get it all. I guess I figure if Tripp can't hold a grudge against you, I'll do it for him."

"You love him..." I spoke the words softly, unsure of their value or the reaction I would receive when speaking them.

Amie sniffed. "It doesn't matter, not now. I thought with you rejecting his proposal last summer and leaving for New York... then when you came back pregnant, I thought for sure there wasn't a chance. But I was wrong. Dead wrong."

"Amie, I'm so sorry. I didn't realize. I mean, he's so much older than you and—"

"Professor Becker is just right for your age, is that it? Do birthdays really matter when it comes to love?"

My heart—and my belly—squeezed. I couldn't write Amie's feelings for Tripp off as a superficial crush. She was eighteen, old enough to hold such feelings. And she was right. Who was I to judge when it came to whose heart one chose? I could understand the draw of an older man, perhaps one she'd admired since childhood. Tripp had never been anything but sweet to her, so much more than just an older brother.

No wonder she loved him. What was *not* to love?

I swallowed, another pain building, something in me aware that they came with increasing intensity now, that perhaps I should give my doctor a call. But not yet. Not before I said one thing to my sister.

"I won't see Tripp anymore then."

She froze mid brushstroke, turned to look at me. "What?"

"Love and men, they are important. But my sisters—my siblings, this family...I won't risk it dividing us. I can't bear it." The words swam over and through me, and I thought I meant them. It was the noble thing to do, wasn't it? Move aside until Amie's heart had time to heal? Tripp had been so patient with me. What was a little more time? I couldn't imagine marrying him, blending him into the family with this thing between me and Amie.

"What do you mean?"

"I mean I'll stop seeing Tripp if it's going to hurt you, Amie."

"But...you love him."

I nodded. "I do. And it would hurt like crazy to stop seeing him. But you're...you're my sister. How will this affect our family if I don't—" Another pain clenched my belly, and this time I leaned back in the chair, put my hands over my stomach, tried to practice the breathing I learned at Lamaze classes.

Amie got to her feet. "Are you okay?"

I pushed myself to a standing position. "I probably just need to walk it off. Maybe I'll go call my doctor just to make sure."

She took my arm and guided me across the room, but not

before I felt a pop within me, much akin to a balloon bursting. A gush of water fell between my legs along with another pain, this time tearing across my abdomen with claw like force. I crumpled over myself.

"Oh no, oh no, oh no." Amie started for the bathroom, but then whirled around, came back to me. "You're going into labor!"

I doubled over, the pain now unrelenting and ten times more excruciating.

"We need to go to the hospital. Now." Amie tried to lead me toward the door, but I squeezed her arm until she looked in my eyes. I shook my head.

This couldn't be happening. I had a month. A month to prepare for this child. To get the bookshop and apartment ready. To get *myself* ready. I looked into my sister's clear blue eyes, tried to gain strength from the fact that they were the color of the ocean on a cloudless day. But it was no use. "I can't be a mother. Amie, I'm not ready to be a mother."

My breaths came fast, my chest rising and falling in rapid succession. A feeling of panic came over me, causing the pain in my middle to intensify. Hot hands compressed and squeezed, clasping the life out of me. My knees weakened, and I lowered myself to the ground, leaned back against the four-poster bed.

Amie knelt in front of me, took my face in her cool hands. "You listen to me, Josie Martin. You are the strongest woman I know, you hear me? You hear? You are going to be a *great* mother, and this child is blessed beyond words to have you." She looked at the floor, bit her lip, then brought her gaze back to me. "And Tripp...he's going to be the most amazing father or step-father or whatever he's going to be to this child, too. You both are amazing. Together. There's nothing you can't do. Now buck up, because you're about to have a baby and you *can* do this."

"Don't leave me," I huffed, the pain that just ended turning over into another. "Don't leave."

She cursed. "My phone just died. Do you have yours? We need to call the ambulance."

I shook my head, grasping for something that wasn't pain. "It's downstairs."

"Aunt Pris!" Amie shouted, rattling my head. "Aunt Pris!"

Mom and Lizzie had gone grocery shopping, Bronson was at the far end of the orchards. Last I checked, Aunt Pris and Esther were downstairs.

And then the old woman was before me and I couldn't comprehend how she'd climbed the stairs so quickly.

"She's in labor?"

Amie spoke. "I don't think we can move her. We need to call an ambulance."

Aunt Pris left and I heard her call for Esther to ring for the ambulance. An overwhelming urge to push came from within me. But no. This couldn't be happening so fast, especially not with a first baby.

Then I remembered Amie's words about me being strong. I felt certain this baby would be strong as well. That he or she was forcing its way into the world even now, ready or not.

More pain, a feeling of lightheadedness.

God, help.

Then wrinkled black hands soothed my forehead, demanded towels and a bowl of warm water and sterile scissors. Esther, as clear and focused as I'd ever seen her, told me I was going to be fine. That she helped her mother deliver a baby or two in her day and the good Lord was bringing it all back to her.

I didn't have much time to doubt the validity of an octogenarian woman with severe dementia. Another pain and the need to push. And then again, and again, Esther encouraging, Aunt Pris praying, Amie crying and holding my hand.

And then one more push and a beautiful cry lit the room. Esther called Amie to her, instructing her to cut the cord. I lifted up on my elbows, a bursting in my heart for the gift of new life before me.

"It's a boy!" Amie cried.

Aunt Pris propped pillows beneath me. Esther pushed aside the buttons of my shirt to tuck the squalling infant against my skin. I held him close, not believing this was him, my child. He turned his cheek toward my breast, and I kissed the top of his dark head.

The EMT's came in a short time later, Aunt Pris directing and ordering them to be careful down the stairs with her great grand-nephew. For once, I was glad she was on my side. Amie called Mom and Lizzie and Tripp. Amidst the excited screams coming through the phone, I gathered that they would all meet us at the hospital.

Once there, a nurse took Little Mouse to weigh and measure and clean. Tears fell down my face at having him taken from me— so small, so innocent, with me the only thing to protect him.

I knew then that I would have never been able to give him up. That maybe me having him at home, of sharing those first few moments of bonding, was somehow God's way of showing me that.

A soft knock came at the door of my hospital room and I looked up to see Mom, Lizzie, and Bronson. They all hugged me and oohed and ahhed over Little Mouse as Amie gave them an account of our eventful afternoon.

"I'm so glad she was with me." I looked at my youngest sister, felt a newfound bond between us that I hoped with all my heart was not a one-sided affair.

She squeezed my hand. "You scared the snot out of me. But I wouldn't have traded that for the world. Wow. And who would have known that Esther really knows her stuff?"

We laughed. Another light knock came at the door and Tripp entered the room, looking handsome and rugged in a Colton

Contractors t-shirt and dirt-stained jeans. He glanced at the bundle in my arms, a foreign uncertainty about him.

"Well, what are you doing still standing in the doorway, Tripp Colton?" Amie asked. "Come see this little guy."

Tripp came closer, and Amie placed my hand in Tripp's before sliding her hand from mine. My bottom lip trembled as I looked at her. She nodded.

"Thank you," I whispered, moved by the gesture and all it meant. She smiled, but it didn't quite meet her eyes, something bittersweet around the edges. She turned away.

My heart filled, and I uttered a silent prayer of gratitude and healing for my youngest sister before I smiled up at Tripp, who gazed at Little Mouse in wonder.

"He's amazing, Josie. I'm so glad you're both okay."

"The doctor said he's full term and completely healthy. We must have miscalculated my due date."

"What are you going to name him?" Lizzie asked.

I looked down at Little Mouse's wrinkled skin, tiny capped head and gloved fingers. I knew his name, thought it fitting that my entire family—including Tripp—be in this hospital room when I revealed it.

"Amos. Amos Arthur Martin."

Mom lifted a tissue to her eyes, and Lizzie put an arm around her. "That's fitting, Josie. Very fitting indeed."

Becoming a mother hadn't been Dad's dream for me, but now, gazing at little Amos, I wondered at how quickly it became my dream.

In that moment, I sensed a sort of restoration within me. I'd searched for success and approval all my life, had been too busy to look for real love. Until now. Surrounded by family and friends, with my child tucked sweetly in my arms, I felt the lavishness of love—and knew that's what really counted.

Bronson stepped forward. "Can we say a prayer for him, Josie?"

I nodded and everyone huddled in, entwining arms around one another. Bronson placed a hand on Amos's hatted head and spoke a blessing over my son and his new little life. I closed my eyes, relishing the warmth of his tiny body, savoring those I loved surrounding me—my mother, my siblings, Tripp.

This was indeed a new beginning—the beginning of something I'd never planned but something I wouldn't change for the world.

🐾 27 🐾

I t'd been too long.

Finn tapped his foot against the floor of the plane, anxious to jump again. He looked around the group that included Katrina, acknowledged the rare camaraderie their unit shared jumping that afternoon.

While Katrina had flirted with him most of the day, for reasons unknown to him, he couldn't reciprocate the dalliance.

As the plane climbed upward, Finn anticipated the last jump of the day. Their drop zone mentor had reported winds of 13 knots—not anything anyone in their experienced group shouldn't be able to handle. A little wind tested jump skills, added extra adrenaline to the rush of the dive.

Finn leaned back in his seat and closed his eyes, the engine of the plane and the rollicking chatter of the group lulling him. He thought of Josie—only this time not with guilt, but with anticipation. He would have been okay with her saying yes to his proposal. More than okay, really. For the first few days after he returned to the city from Maine, he'd sulked, lost. He'd been certain Josie would jump into his arms. Isn't that what she wanted all those months ago?

But she hadn't. He still wondered how her rejection had the power to shake him up as it did.

But one thing was certain—he looked forward to being a father. Maybe he wouldn't see his child every day like some, maybe one day he'd have to accept that Tripp would, but Finn couldn't ignore the feeling of fulfillment and purpose snuggling into his soul, the anticipation at meeting a child he had helped create.

It was a complete one-hundred eighty degree turn from where he'd been in February. What had transpired? His conscience, of course. The tears. But it was something more, that voice from his childhood he'd been hearing and leaning into. On the rare occasions he gave himself over to it, he knew peace.

Mario, a wingsuit diver in the front of the cabin asked the pilot for a ground wind check.

A few minutes later, he yelled back at them. "Manifest only saw one gust pass through—it was at twenty-four knots."

A couple of the jumpers cheered, up for the excitement. Something in Finn's middle hitched. Twenty-four knots was a steep increase in winds since takeoff.

The two-minute light came on, and a few of the divers buckled up, ready to take the "ride of shame" back down to the airport. But there shouldn't be any shame in it. Unpredictable gust fronts could throw them off their landing area by a long shot. No one wanted to land in power lines, someone's house, or the interstate.

Katrina elbowed Finn. "What do you say, Professor? You up for it?"

"I don't know..."

"Come on. You want the experience, don't you?"

He did. Nothing like a little wind to test one's limits and skills, to prove one's ability. And while he sought to keep his distance from Katrina, he also felt a sort of responsibility for her. Was it right to let her jump on her own under these conditions?

He'd wanted adventure, hadn't he? In a few weeks, he'd be a father.

A father. Who did he want to be in his son or daughter's eyes? A man who let fear mold his decisions or a man who made the most of life, letting it take him on a ride worth living?

"I'm good for it." He yelled above the noise of the open plane door.

She squeezed his knee, and they stood as the Otter emptied as one jumper after another leapt from the plane.

Finn performed his last check, slid his goggles on, and followed Katrina out, the ground clear beneath them, the horizon blue before them.

And then, peace. A pillow of air, a silence of all things unimportant as he settled in an arch position. Katrina fell below him, her bright blue jacket small in the vast sky. Maybe they should talk tonight. About what he wanted in a relationship, about the possibility of becoming more serious. Maybe Josie didn't want him, but he couldn't ignore the deep ache inside, this longing for something more.

The wind pushed at him, and he gave himself over to it. The sun shone, hovering above the horizon, a cast of pinks and oranges and yellows.

You have made the heavens and earth by your great power and outstretched arm. Nothing is too hard for you.

The random scripture verses didn't surprise or even alarm him anymore. Almost like they were a part of him, a part of his childhood he'd stuffed and buried after his mother died and his father turned to the bottle. Though he couldn't be sure it wasn't a part of his consciousness trying to connect to his long-dead mother, he only knew that instead of guilt, he now found peace in their presence.

You have made the heavens and earth by your great power and outstretched arm. Nothing is too hard for you.

The feel of the jump, the resonance of the words in his soul caused something within him to sing, to see the world anew.

Nothing was too hard for God.

The promise gave him hope. He sank into it.

He didn't want to be the man he'd been the last forty years. He wanted to be made new, filled with a purpose that mattered. No doubt part of that included being a good father to his child, but there was more to it—more pieces to fill, more mystery to explore.

And suddenly, he hungered for it.

Below him, and far to the right, he spotted a flurry of canopies open, including Katrina's. He spotted the landing area, knew if he could hit his target in this unpredictable wind he would have proven his skill.

As soon as the thought crossed his mind though, a gust pushed him with brute force farther away from the other parachutes. He struggled against it, attempted to wiggle his body like a fish to get closer to the landing zone to no avail.

The ground approached fast. He'd have to pull his chute, try to toggle himself to safe landing. Just as he was about to open his chute, another squall carried him farther away, toward a large copse of trees. He searched for an open landing, but saw none unless another wind gust came to carry him farther north.

He pulled his chute, seeing power lines in the not-too-far distance among the trees. The foliage looked beautiful—soft even —deceivingly so, for they proved a danger. Still, he'd choose them over power lines any day.

He toggled toward the trees fast. Another gust of wind had him hitting the treetop hard, branches jabbing and jarring his limbs, scraping his chest and face, catching in webbing and chute. A sharp lurch caused something in his neck to snap and then, everything went black and numb before him.

His last thought was of that awe-inspiring sunset, the verse in his head.

Nothing is too hard for you.

He supposed he would see about that.

I STARED AT MY PHONE AND THE PICTURE I'D SENT FINN TWO days ago now. Our child, eyes open and staring at the camera, tufts of dark hair sticking up. Underneath I'd written:

Amos Arthur Martin
September 18th
1:38PM
8lbs, 3 oz

I'd sent the text forty-five hours ago now, and still no response. I couldn't feign surprise or disappointment. In some ways, it'd be easier if Finn chose to be uninvolved.

And yet how could he see this adorable picture of our child and ignore it? It was one thing to try to cast off the babe while just a notion in my womb, but now, with the evidence of his glorious little fingers and toes, the small little nose, his thin searching mouth?

I turned onto my side to study my son's profile, mesmerized by his features so perfectly knit together within me. Though I couldn't wait to get home, I'd suffered some intense bleeding the day before, and the hospital staff decided to keep me another day. Tripp worked on finishing the apartment upstairs from the book-shop. The thought of bringing Amos home to our little piece of heaven thrilled me.

My phone vibrated beside me, and I scooped it up, not recognizing the number. Probably the lactation specialist calling to make a follow-up appointment. "Hello?"

"Hello, is this Josie?"

"Yes, it is."

"Hi, Josie. This is Professor Rutherford."

My mind tripped on itself, so far removed was the world of school and psychology and New York from anything I'd thought about these past couple of weeks, and certainly these past couple of days. "Professor, wow. This is a surprise."

"Yes, well it was quite a surprise not to see your name on the fall roster. I'm calling because I'm looking for help for my private office. I can't quite seem to get the idea out of my mind that you'd be perfect for the job. Is there any chance you'll be reenrolling in the new year?"

"I'm sorry, Professor. I thought Professor Becker might have told you. Unfortunately, I won't be returning to NYU."

But I didn't really mean the "unfortunately" part, did I? Before Amos was born, I hadn't questioned my decision not to return. But now, with this tiny bundle in my arms, I couldn't fathom leaving Camden for New York. I couldn't fathom wanting to chase the business of classes and school, competing for a spot on the Dean's list.

This offer only confirmed my decision.

Professor Rutherford cleared her throat. "Professor Becker... no, last I spoke to him he didn't know of your plans. Shame about his accident...but dear, are you certain I can't persuade you to return? Even if it was just for a work position?"

My mind stalled on the word *accident*, imagining the worst. Did that explain Finn's silence these last two days?

"I'm afraid not, Professor. I really am flattered you'd think of me, though. Um, I haven't heard from Finn in a couple weeks. Is he okay?"

"Oh dear, I'm sorry to be the one to tell you, but there was a complication on his latest skydiving jump. He has a lot of broken bones and a back injury. They're not sure he'll walk again."

I shook my head back and forth, disbelieving the professor's words even as I could see their truth. To imagine Finn—so active, always searching for the next adventure—bound to a wheelchair for the rest of his life, was as hard as imagining Mom without her kitchen, Amie without her paints, me without my books.

"I—I can't believe it."

"Very sad. Some of the faculty are going to visit him this week, but it won't be an easy road ahead, I'm afraid. But Finn's a conqueror. I never did know a more determined man. I'm trusting he'll be okay."

"I—what hospital is he at?"

"New York-Presbyterian in Lower Manhattan."

"Thank you, Professor. I appreciate it."

"Now, are you certain I can't change your mind about that job?"

Laying on my right arm, Amos squirmed.

"I'm afraid not, but again, I'm honored you'd think of me. I hope you find the perfect person for what you have in mind."

"Me too, dear. Now don't waste those brains, my girl. Use them up on something good, you hear me?"

I smiled, despite the fact I was still trying to come to grips with Finn and his injuries. "I will. I promise. Thank you, Professor."

"Take care, now."

We hung up, and I leaned my head back on the hospital bed, closed my eyes, and imagined Finn in another hospital bed miles away—not rejoicing over the birth of a new life as I was, but mourning the loss of the life he'd known. For a long time, I grappled with denial over such an accident. Then, perhaps selfishly, I wondered if this might change things for me and Amos.

Finn seemed intent on being part of Amos's life. Like it or not, I was tied to Finn. I needed to reach out, make an effort where I could. If not for his sake, then for Amos's.

I pulled up Finn's name on my phone and called him. It rang and rang, going to voice mail. "Hey, Finn. It's Josie. Professor Rutherford told me what happened and I just wanted to make sure you're okay." Ugh, probably the world's top ten stupidest things to say. "Sorry, that's ridiculous. Of course you're not okay. Give me a call when you can. And Finn, your son is gorgeous."

I hung up, kicking myself for my jumbled, insensitive words, surprised I cared how they might affect him. I'd been mad for so long, but here and now, I only felt pity. Pity for a man who'd searched for purpose in a variety of things that would all fail him now. He had no family—both parents long dead. Colleagues would visit him in the hospital once, maybe twice. I didn't think, with his recent marriage proposal, that he had any special love interest to help him. Finn worked hard at being independent.

I remembered the last words of our last conversation, Finn standing before me, whole and healthy, how I'd surprised myself at my offering of grace.

"If I ever had a family, I'd want it to be like the Martin family. Now, our child will be a part of it. That's something special, Josie."

"You're of a part of it too now, Finn. Okay? Family's more than marriage ties and bloodlines, and I want you to come visit our child as much as you want."

Family. Tripp had taught me so much of what it meant to love in the chaos these past several months. And hadn't I told Finn he was family, that I would consider him as such for the sake of our child? For the sake of peace?

But where did that leave me now?

I swallowed, watched Amos's eyelids flutter in sleep, wondered again at the legacy his grandfather left for him. Not in riches and gold, but in charity and faith.

I picked up my phone again and dialed Tripp's number.

❧ 28 ❧

Tripp stood above Josie's hospital bed, drinking in the sight of her with Amos—a babe he'd already come to love as his own. He studied her, tried to look deeper. As if studying would help the words she'd spoken connect in his head.

"I'm sorry. Please say that again, my darling, because I thought you just asked me to drive seven hours to play nursemaid to your ex-boyfriend who knocked you up then fed you to the fishes."

"Tripp." The wounded look on her face made him rethink himself.

He sat on her bed, shook his head. "I'm sorry, Josie, it's just— what do you owe this guy? I mean, it stinks what happened to him, it really does. But maybe that's why normal people don't go jumping out of planes in the first place."

Okay, he was angry. No use denying it. Apparently he'd never forgive the learned professor for what he'd done to Josie.

"He doesn't have anyone, Tripp. I'd go myself if I could. I even thought of asking Bronson but he just started classes and is studying his brains out for an upcoming exam. I know I'm asking a lot. I know you have your work and all that, but there's something within me—something almost urgent—telling me he needs us. I told him I'd consider him family."

Tripp grit his teeth. She wanted to be a family with the guy now? Fine. But that didn't mean he had to get in on it.

He twirled from the bed, paced the floor toward the door and then back again. He supposed he should be grateful Josie wasn't in a position to up and drive to New York. Wasn't there something women were known to fall into—Florence Nightingale syndrome or some such hogwash? Still, it bothered him that she cared so much.

"Tripp." She held out her hand to him. She looked so vulnerable beneath the white sheets, her thick hair in a braid, the nursing tank she wore forming to her curves. He closed his eyes. *That* was certainly not where his mind needed to be. She squeezed his hand, gave him a playful smile that told him she'd caught the direction of his gaze. "Seriously. You showed me so much this past year. After rejecting your proposal, ignoring you for months, running into another man's arms. I didn't deserve any of the love you gave me. But you loved me nonetheless."

"Because I *do* love you. It wasn't hard, Josie. Well, it wasn't hard some of the time."

Those gray eyes seared his heart. "Maybe love counts more in the hard. Remember the seedling, Tripp? Dad'd be on a train to check on Finn even if he hadn't seen him in years. I'm asking a big favor, I know. I'm asking you to take his place. To do this thing because it's right. I won't hold it against you if you don't, I promise. But I have to at least ask."

He groaned. God knew he loved her, but everything about this went outside his comfort zone—trains, the big city, strange hospitals, paralyzed professors. He sniffed hard, knew he would end up doing it, no matter how hard, because he loved her.

"What do you want me to do when I get there? What do you want me to say? I mean, what do you say to a guy who's just lost everything?"

"You tell him he hasn't."

Tripp's gaze fell to Amos. Right. Finn's son. Not his.

Man, this was hard. How much easier to be hundreds of miles away from Amos's real father, to hole up in their safe little bubble in Camden and pretend he didn't exist?

But that wasn't right either. Poor guy was practically in a body cast from the sounds of it. What did God want Tripp to do?

Seek justice, love mercy, walk humbly with your God.

Tripp rubbed the back of his neck. "Okay, I'll go."

Josie squeezed his hand. "Thank you. I don't take it lightly. Really, Tripp. And I know you'll help him. I have this feeling."

He kissed her, then ran a hand over Amos's head, bending to plant a kiss on his forehead. "You better be praying for me the whole time, because I'm going to need all the heavenly help I can get."

She grinned. "I will be. And...I love you."

He moved closer again, covered her mouth with his own. When they parted, he glanced down at Amos. "I love you, too. And I can't believe how I already love this little guy here. There's nothing more I want to do than be with you both, watch over you and keep you safe forever."

"I know. That's why your going means so much to me."

"I better go pack a bag. I'll call you when I get there?"

"You better. Tripp...thank you. Really and truly."

"Don't thank me yet, Josie. It's going to take a miracle for this to go anywhere near well."

I LUGGED AMOS'S CAR SEAT UP THE STAIRS TO MY NEW apartment, Maggie following close behind. "I'm going to be skinny in no time," I grunted.

My sister shouldered my hospital bag. "You sure will. Never

mind running—carrying that guy around and going up and down these stairs will have you back in shape by Thanksgiving."

I opened the door to the apartment, a bit cowed by the thought of all that was to be done. Lizzie said she'd prepared my bed and the crib, but surely there'd be boxes to unpack, baby things to buy.

"Surprise!"

I gasped at the sight before me—Mom, Lizzie, Bronson, Amie, Aunt Pris, Esther, and even August squeezed into the tiny apartment. Blue and white balloons tied to a plush glider. Tasteful, sheer curtains hung on the windows. My bookshelf with some of Dad's beloved books. A quick glance into the two adjoining rooms showed my room with my bedspread and pillows, a bassinet on the side. And Amos's room with his crib, a sweet little animal mobile hanging, stacks of diapers beside it, a little bookshelf with classics such as *Goodnight, Moon* and *The Very Hungry Caterpillar*.

"Guys..." Tears pricked my eyelids. I looked at their expectant faces, smiles on all of them—even Aunt Pris's. "You didn't have to...oh, but I'm so very glad you did." I placed Amos's car seat on the floor, hugged each one of them. "Thank you. It's beautiful."

"Tripp stayed up all night to finish the bathroom," Bronson said. "Aunt Pris and Mom went shopping, and Lizzie and Amie set it all up."

I shook my head. "I have the best family a girl could ask for. And no matter what anyone says, Amos has a good start in life because he already knows all of you." I thought of Tripp, working to make this dream come true. Again. Staying up all night to make sure I had a place—a home—to come home to, and then taking off for a long drive to New York City. I'd call him soon. I could only hope he'd opted for the train but experience told me otherwise.

"And look." Amie took my hand and dragged me into Amos's room. She pointed at the top molding of his bookshelf where she'd painted a small mouse reading a book. "Little Mouse. Get it?"

I threw my arms around her. "It's perfect. Thank you." I pulled back from her. "I'm so glad you were the one with me when I went into labor. Are we okay, Amie?"

She kissed my cheek. "Yes. I was terrible to you, and I'm sorry. Maybe I do have some growing up to do. You know, seeing you deliver Amos, seeing the birth of a new life...it really hit me how fast things can change, how precious this life is—how precious you and all my siblings are. I don't want to waste any more time on grudges or lost loves. Even if it might be hard, I'm ready to move forward."

I hugged her again, and we joined the others, where I caught Mom unbuckling Amos from his car seat, totally disregarding the "never wake a sleeping baby" rule.

"So, I have to know. How bad was the damage to the Alcott room? I'm assuming we have to replace the rug after Amos baptized it in his birth waters."

Amie wrinkled her nose. "You're always so tactful, aren't you?"

"We've already had it professionally cleaned. Once you're settled, we have an open house to plan." Mom tucked Amos into the crook of her elbow.

"Did we already get the occupancy permit?"

"Final inspections should be next week. Trusting we'll be good to go."

I smiled down at my son in Mom's arms. "I noticed the sign near the street when we drove in. It looks fantastic." *The Orchard House Bed and Breakfast*. It was really happening. I turned to Aunt Pris. "And how are you feeling about all this?"

"That is yet to be determined. I like my new kitchen, but I'm still not sure how I feel about having strangers in my home." She shrugged. "I guess it's too late now and I'll have to make do."

Amie gestured out the window to the orchard beyond. "Are you kidding, Aunt Pris? Look at this place! The bookshop, the rooms, all the work Bronson did on the orchard. It's coming alive again."

"I get goose pimples just thinking about it!" Esther drew a giggle from the group.

After a few more minutes, Mom handed Amos to me and joined Lizzie to start supper. Aunt Pris and Esther soon followed with Bronson and Amie until only Maggie and I remained.

I lifted Amos over my shoulder, his tiny legs held curled to the rest of his body, his bottom sticking out. "Do you want to hold him?" I asked my sister, patting his back a few times.

"Really?"

"Of course."

She held out her arms and took him with the greatest of care, bouncing up and down with slight movements. She smiled at me, then gazed back at him. "He's so small."

"Right? Though he didn't feel so small making his way out, I'll tell you."

Maggie laughed, stared at Amos again. "It's crazy that I'm a mother, and yet I don't know the experience of having a baby this small. Of carrying it for nine months, feeling it move within me."

"Oh, Maggie. Those aren't the things that make you a mother." I didn't miss the tears at the corners of her eyes. "You are the world to those boys. I can only hope to be the kind of mother you are. And you *will* have your own child. I just know it."

She sniffed. "Thanks, Josie. But I feel like it's never going to happen."

"It can take time, right? Are you at least having fun trying?"

She laughed, shook her head. "The pressure kind of takes some of the fun out of it, I have to admit. And Josh's still working for Tripp after school most days. He's beat when he comes home."

"Have you talked to him, yet?"

"He seems so happy with the construction work, you know? I hate to make a big deal out of it. He thinks he's doing it for us, for our family. He talks about buying a bigger house, maybe building it himself. But all I want is him. And there's always so much to do —the kids' school and fundraisers, stuff at church, now the B&B."

"Mags, you've always been too hard on yourself. You have a lot on your plate. Maybe it's time to start saying no to some things."

She sighed, sat in the glider, Amos snuggled in her arms.

I sat cross-legged on the floor, my happiness dimming at the sudden turn of my thoughts. "I found out yesterday that Finn was in a skydiving accident. One of my old professors told me they don't know if he'll walk again."

"Josie...oh dear Lord, be with him." She dragged in a quivering breath. "Do you know how he's doing?"

"He's not answering his phone. I could have called the hospital I suppose, but I'm not sure they would tell me anything anyway."

"Life can change so fast."

"Tripp's on his way down."

She stopped rocking. "Down?"

"To New York. I asked him to go see Finn."

She leaned back on a rock. "Wow. *Wow*."

"You think that was out of line?" Maybe it'd been wrong to expect so much from Tripp. Maybe I'd taken advantage of his love, asking him to do the unreasonable. But Finn, in a hospital bed, unable to walk. How could we not do something?

"I—I don't know that it was out of line. I just don't know that it's exactly *in* line. Josie—are you still in love with Finn?"

No was the easy answer, the right answer. I'd said no to his marriage proposal after all, of course I wasn't *in* love with him. I was in love with Tripp.

But I wanted to be real and honest, here and now with my sister.

I picked at a thread of the area rug, tried to form the words in my head. "I'm not in love with him, no. But I suppose there's still a part of me that does love him. I don't know, it was more like infatuation from the beginning, but I fell out of that pretty quick after he cast me aside so easily." I looked at Amos, rubbing his mittened fingers against his face. "Still, he needs help now. He's the father of my child. That's always going to mean something."

Maggie nodded. "I think I can understand that. I've spent a lot of time evaluating Josh's feelings for his ex-wife. She's dead now, which you think would make things simpler as far as my jealousy goes, but it doesn't. She will always be the woman who birthed his children. His first love. And even though I know he doesn't wish things to be different, it's been hard to compete with, I guess. I can put myself in Tripp's shoes."

I put my head in my hands. "I only want Tripp. But that doesn't change that I want to help Finn. Do you think I made a huge mistake asking Tripp to go to him?"

For a moment, the only sound that filled the room was that of the gentle glide of Maggie's chair as she rocked my son. Finally, she spoke. "No. I think you asking shows how much you trust him, how much you care for both of them. And I think Tripp going proves he will go to the ends of the earth for you. That's the man you want to marry."

I twirled my fingers in the carpet, glad to hear her say the words I'd been thinking myself. "Sis, I think it's time to go ring shopping."

❧ 29 ❧

When Finn first woke, all was fog. Slowly, the haze gave way to a dull pain in his head and neck, one that traveled to his elbow and radiated to the rest of his body.

The steady beep of a hospital machine forced him to open his eyes. He scrambled for his last memories.

Jumping.

The wind carrying him away. Landing in a tree, the sharp jabs of the branches.

Nothing is too hard for you.

The memories jolted him awake. He was in a hospital room. He tried to turn his head to the side but a sharp, searing pain traveled up into the back of his head. He gasped, bracing himself, unwilling to do anything that might cause a repeat of the pain.

He worked his tongue around in his mouth to wet his dry lips. So dry.

The scent of roses wafted in the air, and then a cheery voice. A young Asian American woman with gleaming black hair and scrubs peered over his bed. "Oh my, you're awake. I'll be right back with the doctor, okay?"

The next minutes were a series of questions such as his name, date of birth, what day it was. Asking him to blink, wiggle his fingers and toes. The nurse gave him a drink of water. It was the sweetest thing he'd ever tasted.

"You're a lucky man." The doctor, an older man with a tuft of white fluff on top of his head moved within Finn's line of vision. "I wasn't certain of the extent of the brain damage with all that swelling, but you still have your wits about you and feeling in your feet. All very good signs."

"W—" Finn licked his lips. "What about the rest of me? I'm guessing you don't put your patients in these casts for fun."

"No, you're right. We certainly don't. You had several broken vertebrae, a herniated disk, a broken femur, broken arm, and a bad flesh wound in your side. We performed surgery on your back and it went well. I have every reason to believe the swelling has gone down but we will continue to monitor. Right now, your best bet at healing fully is immobilization, patience, and hard work."

He could heal. He'd be able to walk again, to teach again, to jump again. "How long, doctor?"

"You'll have to wear the back brace for at least three months. The casts for six weeks. We'll keep you here for another several days to monitor things before we transfer you to a rehabilitation center. You have a long road ahead of you, but considering what could have happened, I'd say someone's giving you a second chance at life."

A second chance at life.

Nothing is too hard for you.

Finn remembered the notion he'd had on his last jump—that there was more to life, that he was just on the edge of it, ready to claim it, fall into it.

Instead, he'd fallen into a tree, landing in a medical setting for the foreseeable future. He should be grateful. Why then did despair nip at his broken spirit? How would he keep sane in the weeks ahead? Weeks that included a lot of time sitting in a hospital bed, doing nothing—something he'd never been good at.

ONE OF THE GUYS WHO'D TAKEN THE RIDE OF SHAME BACK down to the airport that day came by for a brief, awkward visit on the second night Finn was awake. His colleagues at NYU sent flowers and a note—a note that told him to take as much time as he needed.

That was it.

He'd been here three blasted days and already his mood had spiraled downward. Why had God even allowed him to live at all? Was it worth it? What did it matter? He was a vegetable. Couldn't even go to the bathroom or use his hands. Couldn't walk. Couldn't do much more than listen to the television playing in the background. He'd lost his phone sometime during the rescue—probably when they'd cut him down from the tree—so he couldn't even ask the nurse to push the button on his playlist. And while the logical part of his brain told him this was temporary, the emotional side descended into depression. What was the point of living anyway?

Even Katrina, the person he'd been closest to, the person who'd been with him during the accident, hadn't come to see him. Surely, she knew where he was. At first, he'd thought that perhaps she'd shared the same fate as he, but after asking one of the nurses if anyone else was injured during the jump, he'd ruled out that option.

The reality was, nobody missed him. Nobody needed him. And isn't that what he'd wanted so badly all this time? To be independent, free? Well, here he was. Complete freedom in a virtual body cast.

He sighed, listened to the news anchor droll on about a fire in the south side of the city. His eyelids grew heavy, and he longed for the black hole of oblivion and nothingness—his only peace these days.

A knock came at his door.

He opened his eyes, silently cursing the intruder. He was downright sick of these nurses poking and prodding and disturbing his only escape of sleep. "What?"

A clearing of a throat. Manly. He only had one male nurse, and the guy'd left earlier that morning.

"That you, Bill? Hate to tell you, but if you're waiting for me to turn my head and welcome you in, you might be waiting until Christmas."

Another clear of the throat. "It's Tripp. Tripp Colton. Josie's...friend."

He groaned. The last thing he needed was for this kid to see him like this. "Come to add another black eye to my long list of woes?" The words came out harsh, ugly, bitter. But that's what happened when you were sleep-deprived and overdue for your next painkiller, wasn't it?

Tripp placed himself in Finn's line of sight. "Look, man, I'm not here to earn my Eagle Scout badge. I'm here because Josie asked me to come. She was worried about you."

"She was?" Josie. Sweet Josie. He never did deserve her. What had he been thinking treating her so poorly last winter? If she wanted the baby so bad, he should have worked with her, respected her decision, not bullied her to the point of no return.

"Yeah, she was. But I guess I've done what she asked. You seem right fine. I can drive the seven hours back home and tell her you're peachy."

Something in him loosened. "Wait. Please. I'm sorry, don't go."

Tripp stared at him a moment, walked over and looked at the flowers by the window his colleagues had sent.

"Would have been faster to take the train," Finn said.

"I don't do trains." Tripp came back into his line of view. "My parents died on one when I was a boy."

"I'm sorry."

Tripp nodded in Finn's direction. "So what's the verdict? You going to be able to walk again?"

Finn smiled. First genuine smile since he'd fallen into that tree. "You're direct. I like that, kid."

His jaw tightened. "I'm not a kid. In fact, I've acted more like an adult than you have many times over this past year."

Finn tried not to let the truth of the words loosen his own angry ones. Hadn't he acknowledged his faults? Why was it so much harder to do with this kid—this man—before him?

"How's Josie?"

"She's good. Really good."

Of course she was. He wanted that news to make him happy, really he did, but instead it served up a feeling of deep want within him. She was fine without him.

"That's good. Baby's coming soon, huh?" He should be the one to know. He shouldn't have to ask this guy.

Tripp smiled, and it was genuine. "He already came."

"H-he? He did?"

"He. Amos Arthur Martin." Tripp took out his phone and scrolled through, holding it up for Finn to see.

Something broke loose in Finn at the sight of the small face, so much like Josie's, and the dark hair, so much like his own. *His* son. *His* child. Without warning, a harsh sound bubbled up in his throat, a sob powerful and deep that released a flood of tears that shook his insides. He tried to hold them back, but they just came harder. More intense and overwhelming. As if the tears he'd shed at night all led up to this outpouring.

He had a *son*.

He closed his eyes to block out the image of Tripp standing there, shifting from foot to foot, looking nervously toward the door.

"Do you want me to...get someone?"

To help him stop crying? No. While his head knew he should

perhaps feel some sense of shame for crying like a baby in front of this man, his heart could only welcome the release. After another moment, he gathered a few deep breaths that ended on quivering exhales. "Thank you."

"He's a cute little guy, isn't he?"

"Blasted cute. He's early though, no? Is Josie okay? Is he healthy?"

"They're both wonderful. Just got home. He was born on September 18th. 1:38PM. 8lbs, 3oz."

He listened to Tripp rattle the information off as if it were engraved on the back of his hand. September 18th. The same day he'd last jumped, the time of birth almost the exact time he'd landed in that tree. Somehow, it felt like more than coincidence. It felt like fate—or maybe indeed the offer of a new beginning.

Nothing is too hard for you.

"Thank you for taking care of them," Finn pushed out.

"Hey, let's get one thing straight. I'm taking care of them because I love Josie with every breath of my being. I'm not doing it for you or anyone else or out of pity or guilt. I love Josie, and I love her son. And you better not mess with them once you're back to walking around, got it?"

His pride wanted to argue with Tripp, but a tiny voice inside him told him to relent. To humble himself and trust that this mess had a purpose. "Got it."

"Good." Tripp hung his thumbs in the pockets of his jeans. "So what do you do for fun around here? I mean, *I Spy* must get a little old after awhile, huh?"

"Funny."

"No, I'm serious. They roll you out and make you sing show tunes or anything?"

"No rolling. Just sitting here, listening to the TV most of the time."

"That rots."

He sighed. "Yup."

The sound of a chair slid over the linoleum. "Well, I have the rest of the afternoon if you want company."

"Company?"

"Yeah. I don't know. We could talk. Tell me stories about you and Amos debating at school. Josie always liked those, anyway."

Finn bit his lip, gave himself over to the urge to open up, to be vulnerable.

"If you don't mind, I'd rather hear more about my son."

❧ 30 ❧

Tripp hated to admit it, but he almost liked this version
of Finn Becker—the one stuck in a hospital bed. The
one not puffed up with his own knowledge and
wisdom, the one humbled by the image of his son, the one who
truly seemed to have Josie's best interest at heart.

He told Finn the details of Amos's birth. He told him about
the apartment above the bookshop where Josie and her baby
would live, of the orchard beyond, the work Colton Contractors
had done on the bed and breakfast. When he'd run out of things
to say, Finn took over, speaking about how he'd admired Amos,
how the Martin Thanksgiving had been the first he'd had since his
mom had passed, how he hadn't truly had one since his last with
Josie's family. He spoke of his childhood, of his abusive father.
Tripp in turn spoke of losing his own parents, of living with his
grandfather and trying to be both father and brother to August.

The guy listened, and maybe it was that rotten psychology
degree, but he even had some valuable insight that made Tripp
feel as if he'd done the right thing when it came to August. The
fact that Tripp had sat down to talk—that he and Finn couldn't
see each other's faces because Finn's neck brace forced him to

look at the ceiling—made it easier somehow, almost like talking to someone on a dark car ride or spilling your guts to a priest in a confessional.

Tripp returned the next day, an inner pulling prompting him to do so. He didn't question it. Besides, it would surely please Josie.

Tripp and Finn listened to the news together, talked away most of the day. Tripp even face-timed Josie so Finn could see Amos. Even as Tripp realized the weirdness of it all, he accepted the fact that he didn't hate the professor's guts any longer.

As the sun sank closer to the horizon, Tripp promised to come back the next morning before making the drive home. They said goodbye, and Tripp walked out of the room with a strange feeling of peace like a balm around him. Compassion had replaced hate. It was more than a small miracle.

He opened up the map app on his phone, looking for the nearest superstore, an outrageous idea forming in his head. An idea so outrageous he didn't think it could be his own.

And it likely wasn't, for it came attached with a verse. A verse he wanted to fend off and give into all at once.

Each of you should use whatever gift you have received to serve others, as faithful stewards of God's grace in its various forms.

God's grace.

He tried to rein himself in, knew his good intentions could sometime get the best of him. But then again, he was pretty certain these weren't *his* good intentions at all.

He'd have to talk to Josie about the idea first, of course. But knowing her—and the legacy her father left—Josie'd be all in on it.

WHEN TRIPP COLTON CAME INTO HIS ROOM THE NEXT DAY, Finn couldn't stop himself from smiling. Strange how he'd practically hated the guy up until two days ago. But now, he was almost like an old friend, an angel who had brought good news of his son.

Amos.

There couldn't be a more perfect name for his friend's grandchild, for Josie's son.

For *his* son.

"Morning, Professor." Tripp placed a bag on the table, then got to work fastening something on the rail of the hospital bed. Finn tried to turn, but found the neck brace doing its job. For Pete's sake, he'd never take a single bone in his body for granted again.

He glimpsed a black metal pole out of the corner of his eye, a stand on the end with a clip that Tripp adjusted to Finn's line of vision. "What's all this?"

"You'll see." Tripp opened the clip, stuck a photo in it.

Of course.

Finn's bottom lip quivered. Why was he so blasted emotional all of a sudden? "Thank you."

He couldn't think of a better motivation to get well than seeing his son every day.

"And—" Tripp held up a new smartphone. "I synced it with my phone, so you have some audio books on here. Hope you like the Bible and *Diary of a Wimpy Kid* series, because that's all I got. But you can buy more when you want."

"*Diary of a Wimpy Kid?* Really? Are you sure Josie picked you over me?"

Tripp pointed at him. "You better believe it, buddy."

"Almost feels like my birthday around here. All we need is a cake and a skimpily clad lady jumping out of it to complete my day."

"That's where you're wrong. I have something much better than satisfying your perverse desire to use women for your pleasure. I have an offer."

"An offer?"

"I talked it over with Josie last night and we'd like you to consider a rehabilitation clinic near Camden. We could visit you, even bring you some of Hannah's cookies now and then. Best of all, you'd get to know your son. And after you're out of there, if you still need some help getting around, there's an apartment on top of Grandpop's garage that no one's using. You'd be on your own, but close enough for help if you needed it. I could build a ramp easy enough." Tripp looked at the floor, as if he doubted the worth of his offer. "Just until you got on your feet, of course. Literally. Figuratively. Might be nice to be away from the city for a bit, get to know your son."

Finn blinked, fast. "Why are you doing this?"

Tripp rubbed the back of his neck. "Honestly? I really don't know. Realistically, you're a threat to everything I love most. But something within me wants to help you. If Amos were my son it would kill me to be apart from him. I can't wish that on my greatest enemy. And you know, after yesterday, I'm thinking there's some kind of hope for friendship between us. If Josie ends up accepting my proposal someday, I'll be Amos's dad, too. Why should we have to hate each other? Why couldn't he have two terrific dads—one who can teach him how to read long, boring books on topics he'll never use and another one—a cool one, who can teach him how to build things and share a good Superman comic with him once in a while?"

Finn laughed. "You're serious?"

"I'm serious."

"And Josie's okay with this?"

"She is."

Finn dragged in a quivering breath, thinking of Josie and Tripp and Amos, of the entire Martin family.

A family.

His family.

Part of him was afraid to accept such outlandish kindness. To depend on people too much. Another part couldn't bear the thought of rejecting the offer. Of being a part of something bigger than himself, of being a part of love.

"I don't want to be a bother."

Tripp shrugged. "You already are. Might as well be a bother without me driving seven hours away." He slapped Finn's leg cast with the back of his hand. "I'm just kidding, man. This feels right, you know? Like it doesn't make sense, but that's how I know God's on board."

Finn closed his eyes. It didn't make sense. And crazy enough, he had that strange feeling of anticipation and peace again, much like he'd had on his last jump. He pressed his lips together before jumping in. "Okay, on one condition."

"You're making conditions now?"

"I am."

Tripp raised his eyebrows. "I'll entertain your condition for kicks and giggles alone. Shoot."

"You let me take you skydiving after I'm all in the clear. My treat."

"Treat? I think you mean torture. No way. I like the use of my limbs, thank you very much."

"It's really quite safe—"

"Says the guy in a body cast."

"I shouldn't have jumped in that wind. Will you at least think on it?"

Tripp held up a hand, slapped it back to his thigh. "How are you in any position to call the shots here?"

"I'm not. But I'm just wondering how crazy you actually are after this entire proposition."

"Have I not proven I'm of sane mind, then?"

"Can I be honest?"

"Of course."

Finn pressed his lips together before speaking. "I hate asking for help. I like being able to handle myself, you know?"

"There's nothing shameful in needing help. I know it's sometimes hard for us tough guys, but if you can't admit you need help now, there's no hope for any of us."

Finn laughed.

"Josie and her family want to help. I do, too. I can't believe I do, but I do. Don't overthink it, just accept it, okay?"

Another trembling breath. "I screwed up a lot this year. Even asking Josie to marry me. My intentions were honorable, but my heart wasn't in it. I just wanted to do the right thing, you know? Get rid of the guilt."

Tripp didn't answer right away, and for a moment Finn wondered if he'd left, or fallen asleep. "I feel like maybe God spared you for a reason. Whether it's for a second chance, to be a father to Amos, or maybe even to teach me a thing or two, you're here when you have every reason not to be. The question is, how are you going to live now? What do you want the rest of your days to look like?"

"That's a loaded question."

"But it's a good one. And maybe you need to take a while to figure it out, you know? But would you rather figure it out alone and isolated here, or with your son and people who care about you in Camden? It's your choice."

Finn inhaled deeply, ready to take the plunge. "Then, I choose Camden. I choose my son."

"Good." Tripp gave Finn's arm a firm pat. "Josie's already made a list of rehab places and did some research on reviews. She can get the ball rolling faster if you're willing to make her your health proxy. She suggested it, not me. I'm assuming you don't have one?"

"You assumed right." He had no one.

But that wasn't true.

Not anymore.

❦ 3 1 ❧

I fluttered around the bookstore, a bundle of nervous energy as rain tapped out a steady rhythm against the large windows. Two hours at most before Amos would need feeding again. Although he was just upstairs with Lizzie and Amie, I already felt the pull of his absence, an ache in my chest at the separation.

But this needed attention now. While the role I wanted Tripp to have in my life was clear before Amos was born, it was all the more so now. Seeing Tripp press a kiss to my son's forehead in the hospital before he left for New York, talking with him over the phone, aching for him at the same time, I was beyond touched at his crazy generous idea to bring Finn home to Camden. Everything Tripp did—every act of true and genuine love he performed —made me long for him with a tenacity so powerful it almost frightened.

And while I tried to chalk it up to post-labor hormones, it was no use.

This was the man I wanted forever. No more excuses, no more pushing it off. Sure, the town might gossip about me marrying so soon after having another man's baby. It sounded terribly scandalous even to my own ears. But none of what took place the last few months made sense—selling the Martin home and opening a B&B with Aunt Pris, quitting school to run a bookshop, thinking I could be a competent single mother, and now, welcoming a needy Finn back into my town and my life—and yet I could say with confidence that I was better off for all of it. I'd been broken, consumed in myself. But all that had changed. Now, I could only think about continuing to move forward, to plan this night especially for me and Tripp.

I tucked my wet umbrella behind the bookshop desk and surveyed the simple table before me, the hot dishes simmering under metal lids. Mom insisted on making one of Tripp's favorites when I'd shared my plan—linguine and clams with her special pink sauce. She'd broiled vegetables and tossed a salad and provided some bread and sparkling cider for the occasion.

I'd bought a value pack of tea lights and placed them on the empty bookshelves of the store, their glowing reflection off the floor-to-ceiling windows, now streaked with rain, creating an illusion of vast majority and light, the dim recessed bulbs above just enough to see our dinner. A subtle classical jazz music played in the background.

I wiped my sweaty palms on my maternity dress, wished that the weight would come off as easily as it'd come on. I looked forward to using the new jogging stroller once Amos was a little older. We'd have lots of good runs together.

I straightened the platinum wedding band glowing off the candlelight on Tripp's dinner plate.

He better say yes after all of this.

And then the door opened and Tripp swept me up in his strong arms. The clean woodsy scent of his cologne mixed with that of rain and drowned me in pleasure. I sunk into it, savored the feel of his lips over my eyelids, grazing my cheek, then finally meeting my lips.

"Boy, I missed you." His mouth moved to my neck, his arms tight at my waist.

"I missed you, too. Thanks for coming. I know you must be tired from the drive."

"I wouldn't have been able to sleep without seeing you first. Although now, I probably won't be able to sleep because I've seen you." He pulled back, pushed a lock of hair from my face. "You are gorgeous. I don't know how I survived last winter not seeing you for months at a time. These last few days were torture."

"What you did down there...it was over and above anything I asked of you. When you suggested bringing Finn here, I thought you'd lost it."

"I'm losing it, all right." He didn't stop kissing my neck, moved to my collarbone. It felt wonderful, and while I wanted to give myself over to him, I had a baby upstairs who would need feeding all too soon. Not to mention the proposal I intended to make.

I pushed him lightly away. "Seriously, Tripp. I—I'm trying to talk to you. Really talk to you."

He straightened, shook his head as if to clear his thoughts. "Right, talking. I love talking."

I couldn't contain a smile. "What I mean is, some things became super clear to me while you were away. Like, I felt lost without you."

"I'm liking this kind of talking. Go on."

I slapped him on the chest, but kept my hands there, fingering the buttons of his shirt. "And like I want to be with you all the time. I want to love you how you love me. More, if that's even possible. So much more than a couple cupfuls." I inhaled a deep breath. I hadn't meant to dive into my question two minutes after his arrival, but why not? I'd never been good at holding back. "Tripp, I want you. All of you, every day. I want you to be Amos's father—step-father, whatever the right term for it is. I want you to be my husband." I turned to scoop up the ring and held it out to him. "Tripp, will you marry me?"

He eyed the ring. "You're proposing to me? Josie Martin, you've had a lot of crazy ideas in your day, but this might top them all."

I brought the ring closer to my body, lifted my chin, bracing for a fight. "Why shouldn't I propose to you? I think it's fitting after rejecting your last two attempts."

"You didn't reject me the second time. You put me off. Now, you're trying to take credit for the idea."

"I am not." I froze, shook my head. "How come we can never propose to one another without fighting?"

One corner of his mouth hitched up in a half-grin.

I blinked. "None of it matters, right? Do we want this or not?"

He stepped closer, cupped my face with his hand. "I want it more than anything else in the world. So what do you say—you want to get married?"

"Yes," I breathed, sealing it with a kiss before I could give into the temptation to point out that he'd just twisted it around so he was the one doing the asking.

I'd let it slide. This time.

And with the way he kissed me, with an urgency and passion that hinted of things to come, I'd let it slide a hundred times over.

When we finally parted, he gazed at me, the candlelight playing off his handsome features. "I love you, Josie Martin. Always and forever I've loved you, and always and forever I will love you."

"You've shown me real love my entire life, but especially these past months. I never want to know what it's like to be lost again."

He kissed me again, long and slow, kindling heat within me. "Can we get married tomorrow?" His husky voice whispered near my ear.

I laughed. "Don't you think we should get through the opening of Orchard House first?"

He groaned, kissed the top of my head, spoke a soft prayer of gratitude. His stomach gurgled at the end, and I led him to the table, lifted my sparkling cider. "To what's behind, and what's ahead. To you, Tripp Colton, for loving me at my worst."

He lifted his glass. "To you, my soon-to-be wife. You will always be the woman of my dreams."

The clinking of our glasses rang up to the rafters of the barn, a pleasant anticipation of the promises we intended to make to one another soon. I looked across at the man who would soon be my husband, thought of the secrets I'd held and how his love had pulled them from me, opening me up and pouring me out.

That truly was radical, scandalous grace.

❧ 32 ❧

Columbus Day weekend brought tourists aplenty to enjoy the long weekend and seek out the brilliant red and orange leaves against a blue sky...and the official opening of The Orchard House Bed and Breakfast. Maggie worked hard to get the word out through as many newspapers as she could—both near and far—as well as online.

The cooler weather brightened the leaf-swept grass. Cheery mums in planters splashed the porch with color, and Amie stood behind a table at the side of the driveway serving hot chocolate and Mom's cookies. Two teens Mom hired from the high school served trays of bacon-wrapped scallops, spinach phyllo rollups, and parmesan and lobster stuffed mushrooms. Maggie had posted herself at the front desk inside, and last I checked had taken a handful of reservations. In the background, the old orchard celebrated in its own holiday attire of red and burgundy, its work for the year done. And in many ways just beginning.

The Orchard House Bed and Breakfast was in business.

Among the tourists and townies were Esther's family, Liam and Rose Hornwell, and a group of bedraggled men from Dad's mission whom Mom planned to hire for lawn and maintenance work.

I shifted Amos onto my shoulder and breathed in the fruit of our creation. More than simply a new business, but a legacy and tribute to Dad.

A hand came around my waist from where I stood on the side walkway, greeting newcomers and ushering them into the house. Tripp leaned over to kiss my head. "The bookshop looks great. You even had a few customers."

I had shown one of Esther's great-granddaughters how to handle the register and the sales. The girl seemed to have a knack for it and Aunt Pris hadn't put up a fuss.

"How was Finn this morning?" Tripp ran a finger along the bottom of one of Amos's booted feet.

"Good. Amos smiled for him and the man practically melted into a puddle. He's really changed, hasn't he? I still can't believe it." Though Finn's movement was still limited, the neck brace had come off, which proved encouraging. Things would remain slow, but his spirits seemed high.

Tripp nodded, thoughtful. "You think...well, I don't want you having any regrets about us. I mean, if Finn turns over a new leaf...."

"You think I asked you to marry me because I didn't have any better options?"

A smile teased one corner of his mouth. "Let's get one thing straight—I get the credit for the proposal."

I nudged him with my shoulder. "Just so you know, I had no better options. Because there is no one better for me than you. It may have taken a while for me to get that, but now that I do, you're stuck with me for life."

His hand tightened around my waist. "That better be a promise." He pressed his mouth to mine in a kiss that weakened my knees. "I'm going to go see if there's any cookies left."

"Okay. Hurry back, though. I have something I want to give you."

He wiggled his eyebrows. "Is it a date for our wedding?"

"No, but I do want to talk about that."

He grinned. "Good, me too. I'm thinking sooner rather than later."

My heart tripped over itself, looking at him, imagining him my husband. "I think I'd say the same," I whispered.

He kissed me again, and I watched him walk away, my heart spilling over. Sooner rather than later indeed.

I turned at the sound of new voices. Three women—maybe a mother and two daughters?—getting out of their sedan. "Welcome to Orchard House!"

"Oh, it's just gorgeous." The older woman gushed and held out her hand. "My name's Marjorie."

"So nice to meet you, and thank you so much." I looked back at Aunt Pris's home, caught a glimpse of her sitting regally on the rocking chair on her porch, a satisfied grin on her face. "We've been working hard to get it ready. Go on in and take a peek if you'd like. There's hot chocolate and cookies inside and outside as well. Help yourselves."

One of the younger girls stepped forward. "We're really interested in seeing the Alcott room. We're thinking of a mother-daughter getaway and since we have some family history surrounding the Alcotts we thought this might be a perfect place."

"Really? I'd love to hear about it if you have the time."

The young woman named Nicole explained how one of her ancestors, a Johanna Suhre, had been a good friend to Louisa, how she'd gifted Louisa a book of poems discovered only months before on the property of Orchard House in Concord, Massachusetts.

"You're giving me goose bumps. That's amazing."

The other woman, whose name I learned was Amber, nodded.

"We thought so, too. We've been kind of obsessed with all things Louisa May Alcott ever since."

I laughed. "Well, you're certainly in the right place." I explained my parents' own obsession with literature, told them all my siblings' names.

"Yikes, so you were the one named after Jo, huh? Are you a writer?"

I smiled, found I no longer hated the expectation. I thought of my gift for Tripp. "You know, I think maybe I want to be. In the meantime, I'll be running the bookshop here."

Marjorie put her hand on her chest. "A bookshop, too? Girls, we may never want to leave!"

We laughed, and I led them into the house where Maggie directed them up the stairs.

"How are we doing?" I asked my older sister.

"I can't believe it, but we've already booked most of the rooms through Christmas. The press release must be doing its work because people are booking online like crazy." She squeezed my arm. "This is it! This is really going to work, Josie!"

Mom came around the corner, offering a plate of mushrooms. "Do I hear celebrating?"

"You sure do." I told her the news.

She pressed her lips together, her eyes shining against the subtle glow of the candles she'd placed throughout the windows of the house. "It's really happening. Girls, thank you. I can't tell you what this means to me. And look at this place! Full, like it was always meant to be." She threw her arms around both of us and when we parted we all blinked back tears. "Is Josh going to make it today, Maggie? He worked so hard on all this, and I don't want him to miss out on these mushrooms."

Maggie's smile tightened. "He said he'd be here."

I opened my mouth, but Maggie shook her head. Clearly, she didn't want to get into anything now. I'd respect that, though I thought they'd been doing so well.

Amos's belly gurgled, and I knew he'd need a diaper change soon. But I had a mission to complete before I left. Actually, a couple. I slipped outside and onto the porch, waved to Amie who was serving a little girl a plate of cookies. Behind her, Isaac stood in line. Amie grinned and waved back, sending warmth swirling inside of me.

Family wasn't always easy, but these were the people I could count on, the ones who loved me in the no-matter-what. I thought of Marjorie and her two daughters touring the rooms upstairs, how we could play a part in their family as well. My insides turned squishy thinking about it and a holy whisper settled over me, reassuring me of one beautiful fact.

This...*this* was the great I was made for. Maybe it wasn't the something great I'd intended to do, but it didn't make it any less important. Mom's dreams, little Amos's sweet body cradled in my arms, helping Finn, making opportunities for the needy, building a life with a man I loved. I couldn't imagine anything greater.

I searched the crowd, peace settling deep within me. "There's the old girl," I whispered to Amos as I approached Aunt Pris.

"Well, are you happy with yourself, Josephine?"

I bent to plant a kiss on her cheek. "I'm happy, Aunt Pris. And what do you think of all this?" I gestured to the crowd, the orchard off to the left, the harbor off to our right, past the library. The hum and life of the place.

She gave me a hard look, but it softened into a smile. "I think, dear girl, that I am quite happy."

I grinned and hefted Amos into my arms. "Do you want to hold him?"

"Goodness, no. I had you build that apartment upstairs in the barn for a reason. When he starts using his appendages for something other than flailing needlessly, I'll do more associating."

I shook my head. "You're one tough cookie to crack, Aunt Pris."

"And yet, you've seemed to have done some cracking this year, haven't you?"

"I suppose I have." I fumbled in my coat pocket and pulled out two sheep figurines. I held them out to her with my free hand.

She cocked her head and took the figures from me. "What's this?"

"I couldn't help but notice your bedroom décor during renovations. I saw these two downtown and thought of you." Aunt Pris's bedroom and curtains were all dressed in decorative sheep fabric. It struck me as tender that she would be so attached.

She took the figures from my hand. Two sheep in cream and black with bells around their necks, and adorable black faces.

Aunt Pris cleared her throat and blinked hard. "That's thoughtful of you, girl. Very thoughtful. Thank you."

Our gazes tangled for a moment, and I felt real peace between us. A camaraderie of sorts. "Thank *you*," I said. I hoped she realized the gravity of my gratitude.

"Hey, Aunt Pris." Tripp came up beside me.

I excused us and led my fiancé around the wide porch to the far corner where we could be alone. I handed Amos to Tripp and lifted the screen of the window, sticking my hand inside to grasp my gift.

I pulled out a thick stack of papers tied with twine.

"My gift is a reading assignment?"

I gave him a sly grin. "You might like this story."

"Pictures?"

"No."

"Flying men in red capes and dashing tights?"

"Nope."

He stroked his chin. "Characters with the first name of Captain and the last name of Underpants?"

"Definitely, definitely not."

"Then what will I like about it?"

I slid it into his hands and retrieved Amos. "It's the story of us. You told me when I first came home you'd read anything I'd written because I wrote it. This is my heart, Tripp. And now it belongs to you."

He ran his hand over the printed title of the book. *Where Grace Appears*. "Wow. Josie, I don't know what to say. I mean, of course I want to read it." He flipped to the first page, the sentence still stuck in my head.

The nature of secrets is that they long to be kept and long to be told all at the same time.

This...this was life. Seeking hope and kindness in the midst of the hard. Using our gifts to bless others. Walking in the light of love.

I snuggled into Tripp's arms with Amos, the sun spreading warmth over us.

This was our life. And it was only just beginning.

Dear Reader,

It's been such a privilege to share this story with you. Ever since I completed research for my dual timeline novel, *The Orchard House*, I wondered if I could really be done with Louisa May Alcott and her *Little Women*. This new series, it seems, is the result of that wondering.

I hope you enjoyed the Martin family—how they struggle, how they learn, how they love one another. Lord willing, our plan is to release this six-book series over the next 18 months, so no long waiting times with these!

If you enjoyed *Where Grace Appears*, I would be so very humbled and appreciative if you might leave a review on Goodreads or wherever you purchased this book (even a few words is helpful!). Reviews give novels street credibility—an immense help for this author. Thank you!

Please turn the page for a look at the next book in The Orchard House Bed and Breakfast Series, *Where Hope Begins*. Enjoy!

WHERE HOPE BEGINS

Happy endings, and even happy beginnings for that matter, were a lot of work.

I craned my neck to look past where my sister Josie walked up the makeshift aisle of the Camden Library amphitheater. She wore a simple ivory lace dress. Her face glowed as she locked eyes with her soon-to-be husband at the end of the aisle.

If only *my* husband would make an appearance, this day would be perfect.

Where was Josh? He wouldn't miss Josie and Tripp's wedding day. He wouldn't.

I bit my lip, moved my focus to my younger sister. Josie was stunning. While she hadn't lost all of her baby weight from having Amos last month, the extra pounds suited her. The sun shone through the near naked branches above, splashing off her shoulders and giving warmth to those in attendance. And Tripp stood at the end of the aisle all handsome and tall, his gaze caught up in his bride's.

The wedding was a simple affair, just Josie and Tripp before Pastor Greg surrounded by no more than fifty guests. No wedding party. No fancy reception hall. Nothing but a whole lot of family and love and a beautiful blessing of an unseasonably warm day.

I twisted in my seat again, willing my own handsome blessing to appear. This not-showing-up thing was becoming a frustrating habit.

Six-year-old Isaac squirmed beside me. "Mommy, I have to go to the bathroom."

I pressed my lips together. Ceremonies were tough for little boys to sit through, but this one had just started. I leaned down to whisper. "Are you sure? You just went before we got here."

"I *really* have to go. Bad."

I glanced at Isaac's twin, Davey, who seemed preoccupied with a loose thread on the cuff of his button-down shirt. "Okay." I leaned around the boys to get my sister Lizzie's attention. "Would you watch Davey?" I whispered.

"Sure thing, sis." Lizzie bounced Josie's seven-week-old son, Amos, gently in her arms.

My brother Bronson tapped me on the back from where he sat behind us. "You want me to take him, Maggie?"

I looked longingly at Josie walking up the aisle with unusual grace, but shook my head. Isaac was my son. Inconvenient bathroom duty was part of being a good mom. "It's okay, I got it. Thanks."

When Josie reached the birch arbor at the end of the aisle, I led Isaac toward the library. Familiar faces smiled at us as we passed up the aisle, and I returned the gesture to family and friends in attendance—most who genuinely cared for the bride and the groom, a few who came for the sake of gossip.

I scrambled over the manicured grass in my high heels, trying to keep up with Isaac and praying he wouldn't have an accident in his new dress pants. He'd always had a good bladder, but two nights ago he'd even wet the bed—something he'd never done.

We slid into the library bathroom and I tapped my foot as Isaac released his bladder for what seemed an interminably long time. When he finished, I helped him tuck in his shirt. Hmm, strange. "Are these Davey's pants? They're a bit loose on you." I checked the size on the tag.

He yawned. "I don't think so."

He was right. They weren't. "Feel better?"

"I'm real thirsty."

"I have a water bottle in my bag." If I'd learned one thing in the fourteen months I'd been a mother, it was to be prepared. Snacks and wipes and extra clothes and drinks always came in handy. I clutched Isaac's hand and pulled him back outside.

He'd fought a small stomach bug the entire week—a little nausea and dizziness. Maybe I should have taken up my mother-in-law on her offer to watch the boys today. But I'd wanted the twins here. They *belonged* here. While I wasn't certain Josh's mother always thought so, I wanted to cement that truth in the boys' heads—when I'd married Josh I'd married the twins as well. I couldn't love a child from my own womb any more than I loved these boys.

There truly was nothing better than motherhood.

Even if I *did* feel like a single mother much of time.

A wolf whistle sounded from behind, and I turned. Josh jogged toward us, his muscular torso filling out the suit he'd worn on our wedding day. My heart softened at his bright smile and off-kilter tie.

He pulled me in for a kiss, enveloping me in the scent of after-shave and Gucci cologne. For just a moment, I sank into it.

"You look gorgeous, Mags." He ruffled Isaac's hair. "Hey, little man. How'd the soccer game go this morning?"

I didn't let Isaac respond. "Where have you been?" I walked toward the courtyard amphitheater, tried not to let the sight of him all handsome and charming dissuade me from my just anger.

"I was working on something important and lost track of time. I'm so sorry, honey. I know Josie's wedding's important to you. It's important to me, too."

I opened my mouth to tell him if it was that important, he would have been here. *On time.* But before the words poured forth, I snapped my lips together, a habit I'd adopted from Mom in our growing up years.

None of my stress mattered in the end. When it came down to it, there was nothing in all the world I wanted more than this life, this husband, these two sons. I reached a hand out to Josh and the other to Isaac as I released my grudge and sneaked us back to our seats.

The wedding was simple and sweet, but not without tears, especially when the bride and groom said their vows. Pastor Greg spoke on 1 Corinthians, pulling out a point about *agape* love that I thought to incorporate into the next Bible study lesson I planned.

"This is boring," Davey whispered, oblivious that his voice was loud enough to reach the ears of all in attendance. A few giggles rippled through the group, and Josh ducked down to whisper to Davey.

I watched my husband and our son, my heart overflowing. If only Josh had been at the field today to see Davey score twice. He would have been so proud. Video clips sent via text just weren't the same.

I leaned back in my seat, taking in the lacy train of Josie's gown beside an arrangement of sunflowers and eucalyptus. She'd had quite a year, but this happy ending couldn't have been more perfect.

My gaze landed back on the flowers beside the arbor. They needed to be transported to the reception barn after the ceremony. I needed to remind Amie to get some good pictures of the Orchard House barn after we set up the flowers—we'd transformed it into a rustic yet elegant reception area. I'd put the pictures on the B&B website after creating a new page advertising our availability to host events.

We might even book some holiday parties. Josie'd say I was in over my head, but we could make good money with such events.

The bed and breakfast had to survive. Our family had risked too much for it to fail.

Besides, Christmas would be beautiful at Orchard House.

Christmas. My favorite season. Last year had brought new kinds of magic with Josh and the boys. Stockings hung in our small, cozy living room. The four of us stuffed tight into a pew of our historic church on Christmas Eve singing *Joy to the World* with the rest of my family tucked behind us. Hot chocolate and holiday cookies. The scent of pine mixed with dried oranges. The delight of the boys at finding their Elf on the Shelf, nicknamed Buddy, performing various and impossible acrobatic tricks.

I blinked to attention as the crowd clapped and I stood to join them, chastising myself as Tripp kissed Josie. How many times had I vowed to be present in the moment, to be intentional with what God put before me?

Celebratory bubbles floated through the air, and the triumphant wedding march sounded out over the harbor. Josh squeezed my hand and winked at me. I wondered if he'd been reminiscing about our special day just over a year ago—the happiest day of my life. No doubt he hadn't been ruminating about the antics of our Elf on the Shelf.

As soon as the newlyweds cleared the aisle, I scooted forward to grab up floral arrangements alongside Lizzie. Planning the wedding on such short notice meant we all pitched in. Having the reception at the bed and breakfast meant our family was in charge of both the decorating and the transporting of the decorations.

Josh untied a bold arrangement of sunflowers from a chair in the front, where my mother had sat during the ceremony. "You think we can take a quick ride together later? Maybe Lizzie or Amie could keep an eye on the kids?"

"Um...yeah, maybe." I shook my head. "Josh, I'm sorry, I can't think of anything else right now until this is all broken down. Fifty guests may be small, but we have tons of food to put out once we get back. Can we talk about a ride later?"

He clapped his hands together, as if ready to coach his high school track team. "Yeah, absolutely. Whatever you need, Mags."

I blew out a breath. "Thank you."

"Mommy, I'm thirsty."

I peered from behind a large arrangement of sunflowers, eucalyptus, and baby's breath. "You finished all the water I gave you already, honey?"

He nodded.

Josh held a hand up. "I got this." He scooped Isaac up and threw him over his shoulder. "I have a cooler full of water in the back of my truck. Let's go, kiddo."

Josh took the boys in his truck and I took the flowers in the SUV, making the short ride across the street to the Orchard House barn. I pressed the gas pedal of my Honda Pilot harder up the slight incline of the driveway of the bed and breakfast.

Merry mums embraced the walkway and porch. Hanging planters of begonias and trailing vines clung to their last weeks of life on the large winding veranda of the old Victorian. Historic turrets and gables spoke of bygone times that guests seemed to find irresistible. And off to the side and the back of the property, for acres and acres, a grand apple orchard rolled up a gradual hill, their branches naked of leaves for their upcoming winter hibernation.

I still couldn't believe we'd pulled off the renovation and the start of a successful business in such a short amount of time. Not only had Aunt Pris allowed Mom and my siblings to move into the old home, but she'd let us turn it into a thriving inn. Mom's long-held dream come true.

I parked beside the patio of the bookshop. Through the large windows, I glimpsed strings of lights alongside bookshelves. Josie still got googly-eyed over the bookshop Tripp had built. I couldn't blame her. Together, they'd breathed life into the place.

Josh and my siblings helped me set up the flowers on the

tables in the barn while Josie and Tripp took pictures at Curtis Island Overlook.

Aunt Pris's old orchard barn had been transformed into a fairytale. We'd strewn lights along the rafters and decorated the tables with Lizzie's flowers alongside centerpieces of books—both classic literature and classic comics in honor of the bride and groom's preferences.

It was rustic and romantic and done on a whim, and I couldn't think of anything more perfect for my untraditional sister.

The sun hovered over the horizon, giving way to the arrival of the bride and groom, toasting and eating, dancing and celebrating. I wiped away tears when Mom danced the mother-son dance with Tripp. Ed Colton, Tripp's grandfather, danced the father-daughter dance with Josie. At one point, Tripp took a spin on the floor with baby Amos. That's how it was in this group. Family, even if not by blood. Family, filling in the places where others fell short.

The twins fell asleep on a row of empty chairs pushed against one side of the wall and Josh pulled me close for *Wonderful Tonight*. I relaxed into the warmth of my husband's arms, the tune and words of the music swirling within me. The scent of spiced candles filled the room, strings of lights on the rafters above created romance and elegance. Even Aunt Pris and Ed Colton took a turn around the dance floor.

"I've missed you." I snuggled into Josh's embrace, the ambience of the night and the glass of champagne wrapping me in contentment.

"I've missed you, too." Josh pressed his lips to the top of my head and pulled me against the length of his body. A stir of desire started deep in my belly. It had been too long. We'd missed one another for weeks on end. I'd been so involved in the opening of the B&B and keeping up with the boys' schedules that on the rare occasions Josh was home, I collapsed into bed at night, sleep trumping any desire for intimacy.

What happened to the heat and passion of those first weeks of marriage? We hadn't been able to keep our hands off each other, had savored those long sweet moments when the boys lay sleeping and nothing but the entire night lay between us. When had that stopped? We'd only been married fourteen months. How had the passion cooled so quickly?

"You want to get out of here?" Josh whispered in my ear, a slight tease in his tone.

I giggled. "I'm not leaving my sister's reception to go have sex."

"Not sex. Though I'm not saying I'm against that." He wiggled his eyebrows. "Seriously, Mags, I have something I want you to see. Something I've been working on for months. Just a quick drive."

"Is it something you built with Tripp, because I can see it tomorrow just as well as tonight." Hopefully, I didn't sound tired of his building obsession. I wanted to be supportive, but Josh's summer job working for Colton Contractors had turned into a permanent part-time job. With school back in session, not only did he work as a history teacher and cross-country coach, he ran himself ragged on the evenings and weekends with Colton Contractors.

Maybe if he wasn't always working so much, I'd actually stand a chance at getting pregnant.

"It's not something for Colton. It's for us. Please?"

My lips inched upward at the adorable plea on his puppy dog face. "Okay." I looked around the room, spotted Amie dancing in the arms of August Colton, Tripp's younger brother. "Let me ask Amie if she'll keep an eye on the boys. We'll be back before the sendoff, right?"

"Absolutely."

I pinched Amie lightly on the arm. She lifted her blonde head off August's shoulder. "Hey, can you watch the boys for a half hour? Josh wants to show me something."

August grinned wickedly. "I'll bet he does."

Josh punched him in the arm. The two worked with one another enough at Colton Contractors to be comfortable. Clearly. "Get your mind out of the gutter, kid. The *surprise*."

August sobered up. "Oh, the *surprise*." He winked at Amie. "I'll help you watch the little guys if you want."

Amie shrugged. "Sure. They don't look like they're making much mischief right now."

I looked at the sweet faces of our boys puckered in sleep, pressed to the cloth-covered seats of chairs we'd borrowed from the church hall. "I think you'll be safe."

"Great." Josh grabbed my hand and led me out into the chill of the night towards his truck, the lights of the bed and breakfast playing with shadows on patches of green lawn and herb gardens.

I shrugged off the cold climbing my arms. "So even August knows about this?"

Josh held the door of his truck open for me and offered his hand to help me up. "I've been working on the idea since summer. August and I worked together almost every day back then, so I did mention it a time or two." He went around to the other side and started the truck.

"Since summer? Now I'm really curious."

I didn't miss his grin, and it stirred something like hope within me. Maybe all the magic hadn't been lost after all. Maybe I needed to be more understanding. Patient. Maybe here, now, could be a new beginning for us.

JOSH GRIPPED THE STEERING WHEEL TIGHT WITH HIS LEFT hand, the slight sweat of his other palm dampening the skin of his wife's fingers. He'd waited so long for this moment, had dreamed about it for months now. He hoped she liked it. He hoped she loved it.

He drove into town, past the closed shops and restaurants where the harbor shone beneath moonlight on his left. Once on Bay View Street, the denseness of the buildings gave way to sparse, tasteful inns and homes nestled within woods. Josh turned right on Limerock then left on Chestnut, his heart pounding out a steady beat against his chest. Maybe he should have waited until tomorrow morning. Better to see it all in the light. Then again, with the amount of work needing to be done, dark might be better.

"Where are we going?" A nervousness coated Maggie's voice.

"You'll see." He drove for a couple of minutes before turning right into a gravel driveway. Divots caused the truck to lurch back and forth. He pointed his headlights toward his destination. There. The moonlight helped as well. He imagined the rundown farmhouse restored to its former glory, the boys running around in the massive yard, Maggie and him sitting on the front porch to capture the amazing sunsets.

He turned to his wife, who squinted past the headlights.

"I—what is it?"

"It's a house. Our house, actually."

He studied the hazy outline of her profile in the dim light, willed her to say something.

She cleared her throat. "Our—but we have a house."

"Not *our* house. Not really." He'd purchased the small house they now lived in with his previous wife. A wife who chose a fierce addiction over him and their two sons. A wife who, by the time she'd given birth to the twins, had been a small fraction of the woman he'd married.

He thanked God every day for sending him his second chance at family and life by sending him Maggie. By saving his boys in the accident. He refused to mess any of it up again.

"Our house now is small. The yard's no bigger than a pocket handkerchief. You deserve better, Maggie. So much better."

She slid her hand up his arm. "Josh, I have everything I could possibly want. I don't need a bigger house or yard. I just need you."

"I want to do this for you, Maggie. For us. For the boys. Let me, please?"

She shook her head, her earrings glittering off the moonlight. "I just don't see how it can work financially. Despite the obvious work it needs, I'm cringing imagining the asking price."

"I already made an offer. They accepted it today."

Her hand froze on his arm. "An offer? What did you offer them—a plate of cookies? Because that's about all we have that's of any value. Even if we sold the house, we don't have enough equity in it to make a dent. Josh, what were you thinking?"

He grit his teeth. She didn't understand. She didn't believe in him. "I've been working like a madman saving, Maggie. For this. I —I thought you'd be happy."

"Honey, I'm happy with the house we have now. I'm happy when you come home in time for supper. I'm happy with just being a family with you and the boys. I don't need to live anywhere else, not now. Isn't that okay?"

On the surface, he supposed it was, but just beneath the surface, just an inch deeper, it wasn't. It wasn't at all.

He dragged in a deep breath. "When we got married, I told myself it didn't matter that we were in the same house as, you know."

"You and Trisha."

"Yeah. Me and Trisha." He rubbed the back of his neck. This topic of conversation was foreign soil for them. Maybe it shouldn't be. "I mean, it's just wood and sheetrock, right? Some plaster and paint. It shouldn't matter. But I've been struggling with it. Like something in my spirit is tied down there. I want to break free of it." He lifted a hand, let it fall on the steering wheel. "I know I sound crazy right now."

A sigh from the passenger seat. "No. No, not at all, honey."

She leaned her head back on the seat, and he could just

make out her petite profile, her pert little nose and striking lashes and lips. His wife was beautiful. Not just on the outside, but on the inside. He wondered what a child of theirs would look like. God only knew she deserved a child from her own womb. But in some ways, he felt the house he'd shared with Trisha—the house where she'd shot up numerous times and hid her hard liquor inside the back of the toilet, the house where they'd argued and loved and cried and hated —had kept that happiness from them.

More than anything, he wanted to build a future with his own hands. Provide a place of safety and shelter for his boys, for Maggie, for whatever children God had in mind for them. One where he could come home and truly rest.

He bit his lip hard, looked out the side window into the dark. Maybe he really was losing it. Where was his faith? His assurance in God to help him through his struggles with a strength not of this world?

Yet, even as he wrestled with such questions, a nagging prick of something bitter stirred within him. He tried to brush it aside. Did God really expect him to forgive his long dead wife for all she'd put them through?

Maggie inhaled a quivering breath, the only sound other than the idle of his truck engine. "Okay, then."

"Okay?"

"We buy the house."

"Wait, really?"

"Yes. If it means that much to you, then I'm behind it. But Josh, we have got to change how things are. You're never home. I feel like a single mother most of the time. I miss you. The boys miss you. I'm not sure a new house with no husband in it is the answer we're looking for."

He dove across the seat to kiss her. "Things will change, I promise Mags. I already saved a good amount. Once we sell our house, we'll be in good shape. I'll give my notice to Tripp. And with the B&B booming, you'll be getting a raise for all the great work you're doing in no time."

"Mom did say we're booked into spring already."

He tapped her chin with his knuckles. "See? Everything's going to work out. And we can redo the floor plan if you want. You can pick out kitchen cabinets and countertop, plumbing fixtures and all that jazz."

"And we're going to see you every night for supper?"

"Every night."

Her smile warmed his insides. He didn't deserve this woman— her love and understanding for not only him, but his sons. *Their* sons, he corrected himself.

He leaned closer, caught the subtle scent of the lavender shampoo she used. "I love you, Maggie Acker. With every fiber of my being. Every day I'm more and more amazed by you."

"I love you." She reached for him and he drew closer, dropped his mouth to hers, gave her bottom lip a tease of a kiss. Her arms came up to the back of his neck and they sank deep and slow into one another, needing, aching.

"We have to get back to the kids," she murmured between kisses.

"I'm not thinking this will take too long."

She laughed, kissing him harder and deeper, running her hands over his chest and neck, driving him to distraction.

From the dashboard of the truck, his phone lit up. For a second, he ignored it.

"Josh...."

From her handbag, Maggie's phone let out a loud ring. A coincidence?

He grabbed up his phone at the same time Maggie answered hers.

"Hello?"

It was Tripp. He almost didn't recognize the panic in his friend's voice. "Josh, you got to get back here. Now, man. It's

Isaac. We were having trouble waking him up. His color looked off. Then he started throwing up, a lot. He said he couldn't breathe. Hannah's calling the ambulance now."

Suddenly, nothing else mattered. Not the land they sat on, not the house he intended to build them. He had to get back to his son.

He didn't remember hanging up the phone, was only conscious of Maggie panicked in the front seat, talking on speakerphone to Amie who assured her Isaac was in fact breathing, though his heart was racing and he was struggling to talk.

Josh pushed the gas pedal harder, peeling out of the gravel driveway. He squeezed his wife's arm, wanting to comfort. "It's going to be okay, Maggie. He's going to be okay."

He hoped God didn't prove him a liar.

ACKNOWLEDGMENTS

A huge thank you to brainstorming extraordinaire, Melissa Jagears, who also doubled as my editor on this project. Melissa helped me form the concept for this series, and I'm so very grateful!

Thank you to my agent, Natasha Kern, for giving me confidence to start this series. Thank you to my critique partner, Sandra Ardoin, for handling the nitty-gritty first draft, and to beta readers Karen Sargent, Daniel Chiavaroli (hubby and construction expert), and Donna Anuszczyk (a.k.a. Mom) for helping it shine.

Thank you to Doug and Louise Goettsche, who own our favorite inn, the exquisite and charming Cornerstone Victorian Bed and Breakfast in Warrensburg, NY. Not only are Doug and Louise fabulous hosts, they were beyond generous in answering my many questions and sharing their experiences and stories with us. The Orchard House Bed and Breakfast (including Hannah's five-course breakfast) is modeled after the Cornerstone Victorian. I highly recommend a stay!

Writing would not be possible without my supportive family.

Thank you to my boys, James and Noah, and my husband Daniel for continuing to cheer my stories on. Love you so much! Lastly, thank you to the Author of life for allowing me the privilege to create in this manner. May all glory go to You.

ABOUT THE AUTHOR

Heidi Chiavaroli (pronounced shev-uh-roli...sort of like *Chevrolet* and *ravioli* mushed together!) wrote her first story in third grade, titled *I'd Cross the Desert for Milk*. Years later, she revisited writing, using her two small boys' nap times to pursue what she thought at the time was a foolish dream.

Heidi's debut novel, *Freedom's Ring*, was a Carol Award winner and a Christy Award finalist, a *Romantic Times* Top Pick and a *Booklist* Top Ten Romance Debut. Her latest dual timeline novel, *The Orchard House*, is inspired by the lesser-known events in Louisa May Alcott's life and compelled her to create The Orchard House Bed and Breakfast series. Heidi makes her home in Massachusetts with her husband and two sons. Visit her online at heidichiavaroli.com

Made in the USA
Middletown, DE
05 February 2022

59548737R00182